I0534785

AT FACE VALUE

LEE ANN SONTHEIMER MURPHY

This is a work of fiction. Names, characters, places, and incidents are products of the author's imagination or are used fictitiously and are not to be construed as real. Any resemblance to actual events, locations, organizations, or persons, living or dead, is entirely coincidental.

World Castle Publishing, LLC
Pensacola, Florida
Copyright © Lee Ann Sontheimer Murphy 2023
Hardback ISBN: 9798392579082
Paperback ISBN: 9781960076649
eBook ISBN: 9781960076656
First Edition World Castle Publishing, LLC, May 15, 2023
http://www.worldcastlepublishing.com

Licensing Notes

All rights reserved. No part of this book may be used or reproduced in any manner whatsoever without written permission, except in the case of brief quotations embodied in articles and reviews.
Cover: Karen Fuller
Editor: Karen Fuller

Chapter One

What started as a light rain became sleet and then ice. Belle wished she'd checked the forecast before she headed south from Kansas City into the Ozarks to spend Thanksgiving with the family she'd never met. Her trusty Toyota slid a little as the roads acquired a coating of ice, but she managed to correct the slide and stay on the road. The unfamiliar two-lane highway had more hills and curves than the interstate, and she still had miles to go. At some point, according to the directions she'd been given, she would leave it for an unmarked county road, then to a dirt road leading to her grandmother's house. The lines of the old song she learned in grade school, 'over the river and through the woods, to grandmother's house we go,' flitted through her head, but she shook the tune away, concentrating on driving.

Through the heavy precipitation, Belle saw a turnoff for a county road on her left, so she took it. She had nothing but the directions she had scribbled onto a sheet of paper to guide her way. The back road proved to be more treacherous than the highway as it wound tight around the hills and across an old iron bridge above a creek or small river. Her tires spun on ice as she exited the bridge, but once more, she regained control. Her hands held the steering wheel in a vise-like grip, sweating beneath the leather gloves she wore. She reduced speed to decide whether she should turn onto a tiny track, barely wide enough for a car or travel up a steep, graveled hill when her Toyota skidded.

Belle shrieked but couldn't get the car to stop or remain on the road. It traveled in a wide circle, crashed through a barbed wire fence on the right, and came to rest half in a ditch, just short of a large tree. Heart pounding, nerves rattled, Belle unfastened her seat belt and took a deep breath as she reached for her phone. When she turned it on to call for a wrecker, no service was available.

"Damn!" She slapped the dash with one hand in frustration.

Should she get out of the car or not, she wondered. Ice still fell, tinkling like glass as it coated her windshield and the car windows. Footing was probably precarious, and if she fell, there was no one to pick her up or offer a hand. The warmth of the car had already begun to fade. Belle buttoned her coat and put on the knit hat she'd tossed into the passenger seat back on her head. She tried the phone again without luck.

Great. I'm stuck in the car on some back road in an ice storm. I might freeze to death before anyone finds me.

No traffic traveled the road in the frigid weather. At first, Belle did her best to remain positive and calm. She drank the rest of the still warm coffee in her Thermos but wished she had stocked the car with the items recommended for winter travel, a blanket, a first aid kit, snacks, and extra ice scrapers. She had one scraper but doubted it would be easy to clean the windows now. Besides, with the car not running, the ice froze on contact with the glass and coated it.

Belle started the motor every half hour and let it run for five minutes. She didn't dare go longer, concerned she might run out of gas. After two hours, she was shivering and hungry. Fatigue set in, but she refused to sleep, remembering something she had heard, true or not, that people freezing to death often go to sleep but never awaken.

Just past the three-hour mark, the ice continued to fall as it grew darker. Although it was not quite evening, the heavy cloud cover brought dusk early. Belle blamed herself for not checking the weather report, her birth family for inviting her to meet them, and God for not delivering her from this mess. In a moment of panic, she thought she would scream, and if she did, Belle doubted she would be able to stop. Shivering, she fought off fatigue, and a harsh thump interrupted her pity party thoughts, and when it repeated, she sat straight up in the seat. Then she realized someone outside was pounding on the driver's side window. Belle turned the key and lowered the window. A man stood there, dressed for the weather in layers, a Carhartt coat, gloves, a heavy scarf around his neck and a black ski mask over his face. All she could tell was that he was tall and broad shouldered.

"Come with me," he said, his breath puffing through the mouth slot in the ski mask, a cloud in the frigid air. "You'll freeze to death if you don't."

Belle grabbed her purse, stuck her phone in her jeans pocket and managed to open the door, although her fingers fumbled. Maybe she should be wary, but right now, he offered the rescue she needed. As she stepped out, her foot slipped on the slick road, and she would have fallen if he hadn't swooped her up into his arms. "Hang on," he told her.

"I will, but I need my suitcase and laptop bag!"

He retrieved both from the back seat and then carried her to an older model Ford truck and deposited her on the passenger side. He returned for the bags, then climbed in beside her and pulled away, slow but steady. "I'm Nicholas Reilly. I live down this lane, so I'll take you to my house. The power's out, but I have a fireplace and plenty of wood, so you won't be cold. Soon as the storm lets up, I'll pull your car out of the ditch."

"I'm Maribel Barbier," she told him. "My last name sounds like "Barbie," but it's French and has an extra 'r' on the end. I prefer to be called Belle. Thank you – I'm glad you came by. I thought I was in some serious trouble."

"You're lucky you didn't end up in the creek, and you may not be out of the woods yet. The way you're shivering, I'm concerned you may have hypothermia, but I think once you warm up, you'll be okay."

She wondered how he could see to drive but realized his windshield, unlike hers, was clear. The truck's heater made the cab cozy, and she closed her eyes, savoring the warmth.

"Don't go to sleep – we're almost there."

The truck traveled down a long lane so narrow that tree branches hung over it, and some scratched against the vehicle as it passed. Belle forced herself to be alert and peered out as they approached a house. It loomed tall in the evening shadows, two stories high with a wide front porch and a fieldstone chimney on one end. Smoke trailed from it, and as she opened the door to step out, she caught the tangy scent of woodsmoke on the breeze.

When she tried to stand, her legs wobbled, and before she could move, Nicholas Reilly caught her and carried her into the house. Belle cuddled against his broad chest, although she tried to see her surroundings.

They entered a room with a staircase at the rear and little furniture. An open archway led into a larger room where a fire burned in the hearth. Two recliners flanked a long sofa before the fire. He placed her in one of the chairs and scooted it closer to the fireplace. Then he fetched some blankets and quilts, covering her with some of them.

"Are you wet or just cold?"

"C-c-cold," Belle replied. "I didn't get out of the car."

"Smart thinking. Do you want soup or some hot apple cider?"

"I'd love a cup of lemon tea."

"No can do, precious," he told her with a light laugh. "No caffeine yet. If you want soup, there's tomato, chicken and rice, or beef broth."

"Chicken and rice. If I had tomato, I'd have to have a grilled cheese sandwich with it."

"That may happen later."

He lit a coal lamp that stood on the mantle, then two candles. "Power's out from the storm, but the stove is propane," he told her. "So, I can heat soup and cook. If it wasn't, I could still cook over the fire if necessary. Get comfortable – when you're warm enough, shed the coat. I'll be back."

Belle sat back in the recliner. He'd shucked some of his outerwear, but he still wore the ski mask, and she wondered why. Although she knew they were warm, it made her think of armed robbers, but Nicholas didn't seem the type. By the time he returned with a lap tray bearing a mug of soup with a few crackers, she wasn't as cold.

As he placed the tray across her lap, she looked up and saw his face, revealed since he no longer wore the ski mask. She stifled a gasp as she schooled her expression to remain bland.

"Thank you," she said.

"You're welcome."

He sat down in the other chair with his own bowl, and as she ate, Belle sneaked glances in his direction, noting the burn scars that disfigured his face. His left eye pulled a little lower than his right, reminding her of the way a hound dog's eyes drooped. Ridges of scar tissue crisscrossed his face, some stark white, others still red. His face lacked the usual shape, and, in some places, it almost appeared that his flesh had melted. His chin seemed abrupt, and his lips on one side were more than a little twisted. His dark hair was cropped short, military style, and she noticed that part of the right ear was gone. The scarring continued down his neck and along his arms, although his hands, though scarred as well, were dexterous as he used the spoon to eat soup.

The poor man, she thought, *he must have suffered so much.* He must have been a handsome man and still was once you looked beyond the scars. Guessing at his age, she figured he probably served in Afghanistan. He had to be in his mid to late thirties, maybe early forties, not too distant from her own age of thirty. His scarring wasn't new – he must have been burned a decade ago, maybe more.

As if he read her thoughts, Nicholas said, "In case you're wondering, I'm a Marine who served in Afghanistan. Freedom isn't free. And now that the US pulled the troops out and the Taliban took the country back immediately, it leaves me wondering if my sacrifice even mattered, mine or any of the men and women who paid with their lives."

"That doesn't make what you gave any less," she said without thinking. "You paid the cost, no matter what happened afterward."

He nodded. "Whatever, but hey, at least I came home, and it wasn't in a body bag. No one had to play Taps over me. It's all good, so save your pity."

His tone, which earlier had been kind, became harsh, tinged with bitterness.

"I don't have any," Belle said. Her heart ached for him. "I'm just glad you brought me here, Nicholas."

"Would you have come if you'd known I was dragging you to the Beast's Lair?" he asked, voice harsh.

"Beast's Lair? What are you talking about?"

He waved one arm. "That's what I named this place. It fits, don't you think? My little niece, Teagan, loves that Beauty and The Beast story. She decided when she was about three that I must be the beast. She calls me Uncle Beast even now. I don't have the heart to tell her that there's no rose dropping its petals or magic spell that will restore me even if I find a woman who loves me, which won't happen. She's five now, almost six and still believes in fairy tales. I don't – do you?"

"Sometimes," she replied, although her mouth went dry. His sarcasm tainted each word as he spoke. What anguish he still must hold, she realized, and his scars must run more than skin deep.

Nicholas lifted his soup bowl to his lips and drank the remainder, slurping as he did. She thought he displayed poor manners on purpose to highlight the fact he was a "beast."

"I'm not surprised," he said, when he'd finished. "After all, your name is Belle, right? Oh, my niece would be delighted if she knew you were here. She would expect you to be wearing the same dress as in that Disney movie and want you to sing with the furniture or teacups."

Hot words bubbled up, but Belle decided to take the high

road and not say them. After all, no matter how messed up this guy might be, he'd brought her out of the ice storm, let her get warm and offered soup. "This is good," she told him as she spooned up the last few bites. "Did you make it?"

She knew he hadn't, but her effort to turn the conversation around worked.

"Hell, no," he said with a faint grin. "It's store brand, chicken and wild rice. You're just cold and hungry. Are you getting warm?"

"I am, thanks," she told him. She set the lap tray on the floor and folded back the covers he'd brought. Belle unbuttoned her coat and removed it along with her gloves. She walked over to the fireplace and held out her hands. "The fire is nice, especially tonight."

Nicholas nodded as he gathered up the tray and his bowl. "Do you want something else to eat?"

"I'm good for now."

"I can make that tea you wanted earlier," he told her. "And there's cookies, oatmeal raisin. They're not from the store – my sister, Suzanne, made them."

"I would love both, please," Belle answered. "Thanks."

"*De nada.*"

Despite the circumstances that put her there, it proved to be a pleasant evening. Belle sat in the chair with her feet tucked beneath her in a favorite position. She sipped the sweet lemon tea and nibbled at the cookies, basking in the warmth from the fireplace. Nicholas, whose mood had mellowed a little, sat in the other chair nearby. It would have been near perfect until she remembered that her grandmother had expected her.

"Do you have a landline phone?" she asked.

Nicholas shot her an inquiring look. "It's in the kitchen.

Why?"

"I was on the way to my grandmother's. She might be wondering what happened to me."

"Your grandmother? Are you from the area?"

She would rather not tell the story but shook her head. "No, I'm from Kansas City, well really from just north of there, St. Joe, and I've never met her. I was adopted when I was four months old. I found out who my birth parents were last year, so my grandmother invited me to come for Thanksgiving. It will be the first time I meet her or any of my father's family."

Nicholas stared at her. "Wow. That's complicated. Will your parents be there?"

Belle shook her head. "I don't know. My birth mother is deceased – my birth father is Ethel's son, but he lives in Oklahoma."

"That sucks," he sounded like he meant it. "C'mon, the kitchen is through here."

He carried the coal oil lamp through the dining room and put it on the kitchen table. The phone hung on the wall beside the back door, a classic 1960s Bell black phone with a cord stretched to twice the original length. It was a rotary dial, and after Belle got the number from her purse, she dialed it, amused at the uncommon act.

"Hel-lo."

"Ethel?" She called her grandmother by her first name at the woman's request. It would have seemed hypocritical to call her grandma or grandmother and, worse, to call her Mrs. Simpkins.

"Yes, who is this?"

"It's Maribel. I've been delayed by the weather, but I wanted you to know I will make it on Thursday."

She saw no need to tell the elderly woman that her car had slid off the road or that she'd taken refuge with Nicholas Reilly. That would complicate things, and Belle wasn't one who liked complications.

Ethel sighed with relief, audible over the phone. "That's good. I was a little worried when you hadn't arrived, but it is just Tuesday, so I thought you might have waited until the weather improved. My electric is out right now, so I won't be doing any cooking just yet, but hopefully, it will be back on by Thanksgiving Day."

"I hope so, too." As always, she was at a loss for what to say to this woman she'd never met, her unknown father's mother. "I'll see you Thursday, with any luck at all."

"I will look forward to it. Feel free to bring Nick if you want."

Wondering if the woman possessed psychic powers, she asked, "Nick?"

"Nick Reilly, of course. I have the Caller ID."

"Oh. Okay. I'll see."

Belle hung up the phone and turned around to find Nicholas behind her.

"Everything okay?"

She nodded. "Her power is out too, but yes. She invited you to come to Thanksgiving."

His eyes widened, his jaw went slack, and his mouth opened wide. "She what?"

Belle fought the urge to laugh. "She has Caller ID, so she knew where I was calling from, and she said to bring you to dinner."

Nicholas recovered his usual bland expression. "I don't do holidays, not anymore. I'll probably get a take and bake pizza or nuke a turkey TV dinner."

She shrugged. "It's your call. I just hope she's a decent cook. Doesn't your family miss you at the table?"

He turned around and pretended to check the fridge. "My family, except for Suzanne, lives in Texas, most in the little town of Rusk. My parents are there, and my brothers aren't far away, one over at Shreveport, the other in Palestine, Texas. My grandpa Reilly is still alive, living in Rusk, too. I'm not even going to list the aunts, uncles, and cousins except for Timothy. We're almost the same age, less than a year apart. In a lot of ways, he's more my brother than the ones I was born with. We stay in touch. I'm close to some of the other cousins, too. The family might miss me, but it's the old me, the one without scars and an attitude. I went there for a month after I was out of the service, but I couldn't handle the pity or the way my dad ignored me."

"Oh." His tendency to dump bombshells about his life with a few sentences disturbed her, along with his notion he was unwanted. Belle ached to reassure him that he still had worth, that he wasn't repulsive, but she didn't know how.

When he turned back to face her, she stepped forward until they stood just paces apart. In the flickering light that cast tall shadows on the wall, his features were softened, although she could still see the scars. Belle touched his cheek, her hand caressing some of the ridged scars. Nicholas' hand shot out and covered hers.

"Don't," he said. "Don't mock me."

"I'm not." She stood on her toes to be taller and leaned forward to kiss him. She meant it to be just a brush of her lips against his, but once her mouth touched his, a wild heat seized her. She let her lips linger on his, searching and seeking. Her hands rested against his chest, and for the first moments, he remained still. Then Nicholas put his arms around her and took command of the kiss. He brought his lips against hers hard and hot, taking her mouth with hunger. Her body came to attention, a sweet heat swirling through her blood. Her nipples perked, and her pussy heated. She tasted desire, and she thought he did too, until he ended it.

"Let's go get some sleep," he said. "Unless you want something more to eat."

"No, I'm tired."

They didn't undress. Belle settled into one of the recliners, and he sprawled on the couch. They both piled on the covers, and before he lay down, Nicholas poked up the fire and added more wood.

Marooned with a stranger in an unfamiliar house in a weather emergency, Belle should have been wary and on edge. Instead, she drifted to sleep as comfortable as if she slept in her own bed. The last thing she remembered was his husky whisper, "Good night."

She didn't think she answered, but she slept long and hard.

Chapter Two

Nicholas was hot, burning with heat. The desert sands radiated back the harsh sunlight, but there was more. He could smell the burning fuel, the melting rubber, and he roused. Despite incredible pain, he found his feet and stared at the Humvee, now overturned and in flames. He tried to call out the names of the others, but he couldn't. For a few minutes, he couldn't remember, and then he did, riding with three other Marines on patrol in Helmand Province, a routine task until they must have hit a roadside bomb. There were moments of chaos as the vehicle exploded, then rolled, ending up in flames. Had he crawled away or been thrown? He couldn't remember, and that bothered him, but the pain grew stronger, his face, his neck, his chest. Over it all, he could hear the roar of the fire, and he screamed.

He woke on his feet in his living room, throat dry from yelling. Nicholas caught his breath – he was panting as if he'd run a race - and oriented himself. He was home. He was stateside. The power was out due to an ice storm, which explained the lamp and the dimness. Okay, he could deal with that.

"Nicholas?" the quiet voice cut into his thoughts with the force of a bull whip. Christ Jesus, he'd forgotten that he had rescued a woman and brought her home. "Are you all right?"

She placed one tentative hand on his left shoulder, and he flinched. If it had been anyone else, he would have thrown her away from him with force. He surprised himself when instead, he reached over and put his hand over hers.

"Yeah, just a dream."

"A nightmare."

"Yeah."

"PTSD."

He realized she wasn't asking questions – she had pegged what he'd experienced.

"What do you do for a living?" he asked, curious. It wasn't every woman who could recognize PTSD. "Are you a nurse?"

She shook her head. "No, I'm a writer. I was a reporter, but newspapers have been going belly up so fast that I became a broadcast journalist for radio. I do a lot of freelance writing, too, and my grandfather spent time at the Harry Truman VA medical center in Columbia. I learned a lot while he was there. Are you okay?"

His heart continued to pound like a galloping stallion, and he had the shakes, a common after-effect of his nightmares. "I will be."

Her deep blue eyes met his, and he realized she was an attractive woman. Her hair, tossed up on her head in a messy bun secured with a clip, was auburn, and her oval face featured dainty features except for her full, lush lips. She was speaking, and he had to focus on the words, lost in her looks.

"If you want me to make some coffee, I can," Belle offered. "If you have meds, I can go get them for you. I can cook breakfast, depending on what you've got. Or, I can leave you alone until you want company, whatever you need or want."

Fuck me then, he thought, *turn me inside out and every which way but loose. That might help as much as anything.* If he said that, though, she'd probably run as fast as she could or call for help. Aloud, he answered, "I don't do meds – I was prescribed Paxil, but it made me sick, so I tossed them. Some coffee would be good if you think you can wrangle the stove, but you'll have to use bottled water. I have a well but the pump's electric. I won't go back to sleep again."

"It's morning anyway," she told him.

Nicholas thought about trailing her to the kitchen but didn't. She could find the coffee and the stovetop pot without much difficulty. There were a few gallons of water to make coffee. If she wanted to cook, he had bacon, eggs, and bread for toast if she made it old-school style in the oven. Although the electricity was out, if she opened the refrigerator quick and didn't dally, it should be fine.

He poked up the fire, added another log, and settled back in the recliner as the room warmed up. Although he never fell back asleep after a nightmare episode, Nicholas almost dozed off until Belle handed him a cup.

"I put in sugar but no cream," she said. "I didn't see any."

"I don't use it – thanks."

Nicholas tasted it and nodded. She'd brewed it strong, which was how he preferred it, and added the right amount of sugar. The coffee helped evaporate most of the lingering angst. They'd eaten light the night before, and when his stomach growled, he realized how hungry he was. He rose, prepared to find her in the kitchen, when he caught sight of his face reflected in the mirror above the mantel. He'd forgotten it was there and had been accustomed to avoiding it. Most of the mirrors in the house he'd taken down or broken in a fit of resentment. His scarred face, red in places, marred with ridges of twisted skin, his mishappen lips, and the rest of his disfigurement shocked him. For too brief of a span, Nicholas had felt normal. He'd forgotten what a freak show he'd become. Reality surged through him, dark and difficult. His emotions rose, a strange shame mixed with anger and regret.

What could she have thought? Does she think me a Beast like little Teagan does or a monster like Frankenstein?

His hunger vanished, and in rage, in fear, he lifted his fist and hit the mirror with it. The glass shattered with a tinkling sound as he roared a wordless cry of protest. The noise brought Belle dashing from the kitchen.

"What was that? Did something break?" she cried, then halted when she saw the shattered glass. She stared from the broken shards to him. His fist was crisscrossed with small cuts and had begun to bleed. "You broke it? Why?"

"I didn't like what I saw," he said and knew as he said the words how lame they were.

Belle sighed. "I thought a tree branch fell and broke a window or something. It frightened me."

Sick at heart, his stomach twisted with nausea, he said, "And I don't?"

In the gray early morning light that filtered through the windows, Nicholas watched her eyes narrow, then go wide with shock. "No," she told him. "You don't. You're hurt, though. Come with me, and let me take care of your hand. You're bleeding, and there's probably glass in the cuts."

Nicholas gazed down at his left fist and the blood oozing from a dozen small abrasions. Each one stung, and his hand hurt.

"It's all right – never mind."

She touched his arm with gentle fingers. "It's not, Nicholas. For the love of God, come to the kitchen, and I'll take care of it. I was on my way to ask if you wanted something to eat."

He shook his head back and forth, then he let her steer him through the dining room into the kitchen. She had the oven on with the door ajar so that the room was cozy. She had also lit the old candle stuck in a wine bottle for more light, although the windows without curtains let the daylight provide natural illumination. He took a seat at the small table while she dug through drawers and cupboards.

"Do you have tweezers?" she asked. "Alcohol or peroxide or antibacterial cream and some adhesive bandages?"

"Maybe in the bathroom." He inclined his head toward the one across from the walk-in pantry.

Belle found most of what she needed and retrieved her purse for the remainder. She heated some water on the stove in a saucepan, then washed away the blood, which had slowed. Then she picked a few bits of glass from his flesh and dabbed it with rubbing alcohol which burned. He grimaced and groaned. She smeared some of the cream over it, then slapped a couple of adhesive bandages on the largest cuts.

"There. Does it hurt much?"

"Naw, not really. I've had worse." Nicholas didn't know what prompted him to say that, but the words were out, and he couldn't pull them back.

"I imagine you have." Her tone was mild as she put away the first aid supplies. "Would you like another cup of coffee or maybe something to eat?"

His gut loomed empty. "Maybe. I think there's bacon and eggs in the fridge – just be quick hauling it out. If the power doesn't come back, I'll have to put it all outside or something so it doesn't go bad."

Belle topped up his cup, which was his favorite mug with a Marine Corps devil dog image on the side, one of his few possessions from his former life. Most of the time, he tried not to think about his years as a Jarhead. Until he'd been injured, he had loved the Corps, but nearly dying and 18 months of recovery had tempered that affection. Now he wished he'd stayed in college, had a different career, and still had an unblemished face. Nicolas remembered though the old nursery rhyme that if wishes were horses, beggars would ride and knew he was fucked. There wasn't going to be a do-over or a second chance. *I'm a fucking idiot for having her here, crazy. She's not going to want to stick around, and I already like her, probably too damn much. I need to get her car back on the road and wave good-bye as she drives off to meet her grandmother. I can't run with this thing. If I were still a good-looking Marine, I'd want Belle, but now that I'm a scarred, bitter son of a bitch, it's better to quit before I get in too deep to get out.*

Lost in thought, he'd failed to hear a question she asked. "What?"

"I said, how do you like your eggs? I'm going to fry them in the bacon grease unless you want something different."

"That's fine – I like mine over easy," he said, dismissing everything he'd just decided. He'd see about getting her on her way after he ate.

Nicholas sighed when she delivered a plate with three strips of crisp bacon, three perfect over easy eggs and two slices of toast she'd made in the oven smeared with butter. He inhaled with pleasure. He hadn't eaten like this in a long time and never at this table. The warm, tasty food made him sleepy, but he vowed he would stay awake. Belle chattered as they ate while she cleared the table and heated bottled water to wash the dishes. At the sink, he watched as she reacted to the scene outside.

"Wow!" she cried, gazing through the window. "Nicholas, it's beautiful outside, like a winter wonderland. Everything is coated in ice until it looks enchanted."

He'd seen it before, but he rose to peer around her. The sun shone today in a sky as brilliant blue as a robin's egg in a spring nest. As she'd noticed, every tree, limb, fence, and surface were coated with ice. It sparkled like diamonds in the sunshine, and although it was still cold, it would start to melt. The power lines drooped, weighted with the ice. The ice would melt, but it might take time for the repair crews to restore electricity.

"It's pretty," he said. "But it may take days before the power is back. Once it melts, though, maybe we can get your car back on the road and get you on your way."

As he said the words, Nicholas knew it was the right plan of action but something within balked. He liked her company and would hate to see her go, leaving him to his solitary existence.

"Oh," she said, but her tone wasn't as happy as he expected.

"It will be a while yet, I'm sure," he said. "I'm not getting out until I can be sure the roads have melted. It was treacherous last night, and I'm not taking any chances."

Her scent, a blend of sweet perfume, citrus shampoo, and pure woman, wafted into his nose as he stood behind Belle. It roused his desire, and his dick responded, growing hard and longer within his sweatpants. Nicholas ached to touch her and did, first caressing the soft skin at the nape of her neck above her ponytail with gentle fingers, then kissed her there. Her skin was cool against his coffee warmed mouth, and he shivered at the contrast. Goose bumps formed on her skin, so he thought she liked it. She turned around and gave him her mouth, her arms stretching to lock around his neck.

Her mouth took his with eagerness, her tongue straying from her mouth into his, which made his cock harder. Her lips caressed his and nibbled. Belle moved her mouth from his and went lower, kissing his throat with the same hungry nibbling. Her teeth gnawed at this neck, skirting the worst of the scars as he shuddered. No woman had shown such desire for him since he returned from the sandbox. Her fingers fumbled until they undid the buttons on his flannel shirt, then she kissed him at the top of his chest, shoving down the thermal undershirt he still wore.

"Belle," he said, groaning with want. "Maribel."

She glanced up. "Yes?"

"What are you doing?"

"Finishing that kiss from yesterday."

Nicholas almost told her to stop, but he wanted her too much.

"It takes two to get that accomplished," he said. He planted his hands on her lovely round butt and pulled her closer so she could feel how hard he'd become. As she kissed his neck and chest, he took her mouth and kissed it hard, his lips lingering on hers with heat. She tasted like breakfast, and he liked that.

As he Frenched her, she undid his shirt all the way and used her tongue to lave his nipples. Each came to attention, hard and so proud they ached. He thought he might shoot his wad before they progressed any further, especially after she kissed the scars on his chest, each one rough and ragged, with slow, sweet kisses that demonstrated she didn't find them repulsive.

He couldn't wait much longer, or he'd come, so he unzipped her jeans and lowered them. Then he lifted her long enough to heist her ass onto the kitchen table, rattling his coffee mug in the process and held her in place as he nailed her. He shoved his hard dick into her wet, waiting pussy and moaned with pleasure as it slid deep. She moved in a way that caressed his cock, and as the sensations rolled through him, the anticipation and need spiraled out of control. At the same time, he locked his lips on hers and kissed deep until it burned.

In those moments, there was nothing but his need, his want overpowering all else. Nicholas didn't think about the ice storm or his damaged body or that he'd wanted to run her off before his emotions engaged. For now, his cock ruled him, and the emotions took a back seat to the driving force that brought them together, locked in passion.

"Come," he said. "Come, Belle, let me take you all the way."

She made small sounds that encouraged him more. Her cries brought him closer to orgasm as he pumped back and forth in her body, supporting her against the hard wood of the tabletop.

Everything exploded at once in a wild rush of fever, light, and extreme pleasure so deep his body trembled and shook as if an earthquake had struck. He cried out. His voice was hoarse and harsh as she screamed, her hands gripped tight against him. She clung to his sleeves as they rode the powerful sensations, spiraling them both higher and wilder. He came, pouring his seed into her, her shrieks ringing in his ears, his own wordless outburst mingled with hers.

Afterward, his legs shook, and he thought he might drop her, so Nicholas staggered into a chair and pulled her onto his lap. He cuddled her close, his heart full, but he wasn't sure what words, if any, should be said. He hadn't experienced such a glorious release since he'd been injured, and if he were honest, never one of such magnitude. He hadn't even thought about a condom, and he knew there were none in the house.

Belle's head lay against his chest, and he stroked her hair which had come loose from the ponytail. He kissed her, his mouth gentle. She murmured to him, tiny sounds that reminded him of a kitten.

"Good follow through on the kiss," she said when she could speak.

He realized he'd ravished her and tasted regret, certain she would loathe him and want to leave, despite the ice. But she'd liked it, and that filled him with wonder, so he spoke with honesty.

"I thought so myself. That was incredible."

"Awesome."

"I didn't have a condom," he whispered, worried he'd break the mood, but she made a soft noise of mirth.

"I get birth control shots," she told him. "So it's good, Nicholas, all good."

He would take her to his bedroom for another round if it weren't so frigid upstairs. He would enjoy the luxury of sprawling out in comfort. Still, there was the sofa in the living room, so he gathered her up to carry her there when he paused.

"Somebody's coming," he said.

Belle paused. She didn't see or hear anything to indicate anyone approached. Belle unwound from his arms and stood, pulling her garments back in place as Nicholas did the same. He buttoned his shirt and ran a hand through his hair.

"How do you know?"

He shot her a look. "I pay attention. Can't you hear the car?"

She didn't, but a few minutes later, someone pounded on the front door with a powerful and urgent fist. At the same time, the wall phone began to ring.

"Shit," he said.

"I'll get the door if you'll answer the phone," he said. "It might be your grandmother – I don't get a lot of calls."

Her face remained flushed, but she nodded.

Ignoring the ringing phone, Nicholas dashed through the house.

"I'm coming, I'm coming."

He jerked open the front door to find the local sheriff on his porch. He'd met Sheriff Will Kingston several times, including during his few visits to the local VFW post. Nicholas didn't know him well, but from what he'd observed, the man was ramrod straight, an old jarhead, and tough. In his dark brown Stetson, he reminded Nicholas of a frontier lawman. His brown uniform was crisply pressed beneath his sheepskin coat, so he looked professional.

"Good morning, Nicholas," Kingston said.

"What can I do for you?"

"One of my deputies called in an abandoned car up on the road, half in a ditch, but before we got there, someone hit it," the lawman replied. "We ran the plates – it belongs to Maribel, uh, Barbier out of Kansas City. I wondered if you'd seen her. It's very cold, and I'd hate to think she's wandering around out there on foot."

He pronounced her name as Barber, and without thinking, Nicholas corrected him. "'Barbie,'" he said. "Her last name is said more like 'Barbie', and she's here. I picked her up during the ice storm."

"Was she injured?"

Nicholas shook his head. "No, just cold."

"Can I speak with her? Her car is totaled, I'm afraid. I

called a wrecker to tow it."

Fucking hell! So much for his plan to retrieve the vehicle and send her on her way. That would be the wisest, and he knew it, but after their intimacy, it wasn't what he craved. Nicholas wanted to keep her around, at least long enough to know what might happen between them. It wasn't anything like hearts and flowers, but he liked her, and she hadn't shown any indication she found him hideous and, even better, had shown no pity. Most gals either demonstrated how loathsome they found him now or showered him with pity. That he couldn't abide. Kindness, empathy, some compassion, yeah, he could handle but not pity. He struggled enough with his own.

"That really sucks," Nicholas said. "Come in, and I'll go find her. She's in the kitchen."

He led Kingston into the living room and stirred up the fire again. "Take a seat – I'll be right back."

It might not be a big deal to most people, but it was for Nicholas – it was the first time he'd invited anyone into his home that wasn't family since he lived here. First Belle, now the Sheriff. He hoped it wasn't about to become a trend because he valued his solitude. The secluded old farmhouse was truly his lair, like a wild animal's den.

When he walked into the kitchen, he found Belle on the phone. "Hey, Belle?"

She lifted one hand and held her palm toward him, shaking her head. "Yes," she said into the receiver. "He's perfectly fine. He just walked into the room if you want to talk to him. You don't, but you'll call later? Alrighty, then. Bye."

"Was that your grandmother?" He would have lifted an inquiring eyebrow if he still could. He couldn't imagine why Ethel would want to speak to him except to reinforce her Thanksgiving dinner invitation. Only a select few had his landline number – he groaned as he realized who it must have been. "Don't tell me – it was my sister, Suzanne."

Her eyes met his, and she nodded. "Yes, she called because she was worried about you in this weather."

"Bullshit," he said, then regretted it. "She phoned to make sure I hadn't blown my brains out with my trusty shotgun or put my head in a noose with some clothesline rope."

Nicholas thought the gruff question would silence Belle, but it didn't.

"Should that be a concern?"

He blew air between his lips, torn between exasperation and amusement.

"Not much these days," he replied. "When I first got out of the hospital after a year and a half, it was sometimes on the table. She still thinks I'm leaning toward suicide."

"Are you?" The woman was brave to ask.

"No, I've accepted living out my life with a face like a monster from someone's nightmare." He kept his tone calm, although he meant every word.

"Nicholas…."

"Don't go there," he warned. "You have your own crap to deal with. The local sheriff is here to see you – he's waiting in the living room."

Her smile faded. "Why? What's wrong?"

For two or three seconds, he considered making her wait to find out. Then, because he wasn't mean, he said, "He's here about your car. The bad news is someone hit it, and it's totaled. He had a wrecker tow it to get it out of the way."

"Ohhh."

Her outcry struck him hard, and his heart ached for her.

Bad news, for sure, and he didn't have the damnedest idea what he could do about it. The thing was, he wanted to do something, and he shouldn't. Getting involved would be a mistake. He'd been there, done that, and had the scars to show for it.

Chapter Three

Her lips were sore from the fierce kisses, but cradled in Nicholas' arms, she hadn't minded a bit. She had some lip balm in her purse to apply later. Belle had instigated the kiss, but she hadn't expected it to go from zero to ninety so fast. It'd been at least six months, or honestly more, since she'd had sex with anyone, but it hadn't been like this, wild, fast, furious, and fantastic. The encounter had left her bones limp and her heart pounding. The scarred man who had held her with such gentle hands had been an amazing lover, and she thought he wanted more. So did she, although Belle had never been one to do the deed with someone she hadn't even known for a full day.

If the phone hadn't rung and someone hadn't pounded on the door, she thought they would have gone for a second round. Nicholas had hurried to answer the knocking, and once she had composed her mind, Belle picked up the phone. Like Nicholas, she figured it was her grandmother calling back.

"Hello, this is Belle," she said.

There was a long pause, and she thought the caller had hung up until a woman's voice said, tempered with shock. "I'm sorry, who is this?"

Great, Nicholas must have a lady, she thought, one who would be pissed to find he had a woman under his roof. If she knew what they'd just done, she would break up with him, and that would be Belle's fault. "I'm Belle Barbier. If you're calling for Nicholas, I can go get him to the phone. Who should I tell him is calling?"

Now I sound like his personal assistant or secretary, Belle thought. *How lame is that?*

"I'm his sister, Suzanne," the woman said, very hesitant. "I just – is he okay? This ice storm is terrible."

Aside from being fucked up from PTSD, with issues about his scars, and with a cut hand, Nicholas was peachy keen. "Yes, he's good – *we're* good, although the power is out."

Suzanne sighed into the phone. "Oh, that's what I needed to know. Mine's out, too, but I was a little worried. How do you know my brother, and why are you there?"

Belle wondered how to explain. Should she claim friendship with a man who had just rocked her body and soul? "I haven't known him all that long.:

There was a long pause. "Uh-huh. Where did you meet him, since he never goes anywhere and he's, well, uh, a bit shy."

Shy? Or scarred? She didn't ask but said, "My car slid off in the ice storm, and he brought me here, got me warmed up and took care of me."

"*Nick* did?"

"Yes, he did."

"Shut the door!"

Suzanne's exclamation sounded more shocked than

pleased, so Belle attempted to reassure her. "You must be Teagan's mom, right?"

Suzanne snorted. "Yeah, I am. I can't believe he told you about her. He's, uh, sometimes sensitive about all that."

"You mean the Uncle Beast thing? And calling the place Beast's Lair? I got that, loud and clear, but yeah, he did."

"For fuck's sake," Nicholas' sister said. "I don't understand this, not at all. You're telling me that my brother, the scarred and troubled Marine, told you his most personal shit, and you're still there? He didn't run you off?

Talk about a direct question. "He didn't, and I am," Belle said. Despite the fact she'd known him less than twenty-four hours, she was already into Nicholas in a huge way, despite his very apparent issues.

Suzanne gasped. "I don't understand, not at all. Look, I don't know who the hell you are or what you want, but my brother doesn't pick up strangers from the road, bring them home and tell them about his life. He doesn't. So, I have no clue what's going on, but I don't think I like it."

The subject of their conversation strolled into the kitchen. "Hey, Belle?"

She held up her hand to silence him.

"Is that him?"

"Yes, he just walked into the room if you want to talk to him."

"I'll call back – when I can talk to him without an audience when I can make sure he's really alright."

"Sure," Belle said. She had no idea why Suzanne was so hostile, but she'd had enough.

"That was my sister, I assume?"

"It was – apparently, she was concerned about the storm

and all."

"Bullshit. She just wanted to make sure I haven't offed myself."

Before Belle could digest that, Nicholas yielded more information about his past struggles with suicide, enough that maybe she understood his bitch of a sister a little more. Then he delivered the worst news of all — her car had been struck by another vehicle, totaled, and towed.

Sheriff Will Kingston confirmed it. Nicholas joined Belle, one hand on her shoulder in silent support as she listened. She nodded at the appropriate moments, spoke the right polite phrases, and thanked the lawman when he departed. After the door shut behind him, once his footsteps had crunched out to his cruiser over the ice coated grass and he'd driven away, she broke down and cried.

Without any hesitation, Nicholas pulled her into the circle of his arms.

"Hey, what's the matter?"

"My car!" she wailed like a three-year-old who'd lost her favorite doll. "How will I get around, and how will I get home?"

"Calm down," he said. "You have insurance, right? Then you'll be able to get another car. For now, you can rent a car, or I can drive you where you need to go."

"To Kansas City?"

"If necessary, yeah."

"Why would you do that for me?"

He smiled, his misshapen lips turning up and lighting his face. "I like you," he said. "Damned if I know why because I'm not fond of people, but I like you."

Those simple words stirred something within. "Good – I like you, too."

And she did. Something about this disfigured, damaged man touched her. He'd suffered. That much was obvious, but beneath the scars, there was substance. His self-depreciation disturbed her, and she saw it for what it was – a way to cover deep anguish. Nicholas had named his home "The Beast's Lair," but it wasn't funny. He saw himself as a freak or monster, but he wasn't. Between his bitter commentary and sarcastic moments, Belle saw flashes of the man behind it all. The Nicholas who rescued her, the man who fixed her soup, who held her now as she cried, he wasn't an ogre or a brute. His sister's comments provided more insight into the man.

He still had his arms around her, and she leaned against him, savoring his solid warmth. Nicholas bent and locked his lips on hers, his mouth hot and demanding. He kissed Belle like he was a starving man, and she was a meal being served at the table.

"Would you like to see the upstairs?" he asked, withdrawing from the kiss, which confused her. "It'll be cold, but I don't think we'll freeze."

"Absolutely," she said. "Let's explore."

In the dark, she'd seen little of the house except for the living room and kitchen. Now, because daylight illuminated the entry way and stairs, Belle saw more. It was a rambling farmhouse that dated to the early 1900s, she guessed, more than enough space for one man, perfect for retreating from the world at large.

Nicholas took her hand and led her up the stairs, which had a landing and turned halfway up. She paused at the landing to gaze out the window and saw the house sat at the end of a long lane. The road where she'd slid wasn't even visible from here. It sat in a three-sided valley. The rugged hills ranged around the structure like an embrace, open on the front, which faced a long field that stretched down to the river. A forest surrounded the place, and with the ice over everything, it resembled an enchanted castle far more than a lair.

If she still were a journalist, she could write an amazing story about the battle-scarred veteran who lived like a recluse, whose niece called him 'Uncle Beast.' She could still write a freelance feature, she realized, but never without Nicholas' approval.

"What are you looking at?"

"This lovely little valley," she told him. "It makes an awesome setting for the house."

He shrugged. "I guess so. It's been here more than a hundred years and was built as a farmhouse for the original family. They were supposed to have been pioneers and replaced a cabin back by the spring with the house in the 1880s."

"There's a spring?"

Nicholas shook his head. "Yeah, there is, at the back of the house, where the hills come together like a woman's crotch. There's a spring box to collect the water – I'll show it to you when it warms up."

Upstairs, a single hallway led from the front to the back. A large bedroom with multiple windows filled the front of the house. The hallway led toward the rear with four more bedrooms, two on each side. To her surprise, there was no upstairs bathroom, and she commented on it to Nicholas.

He laughed. "This place was built before indoor plumbing was a thing. I'm lucky they added one downstairs, off the kitchen, with both a tub and a shower. I doubt you noticed, but they added electricity, too, probably in the late 1940s. That's why the fuse box is on the side of the house, on the front porch."

She lived in Kansas City now, but she'd been raised in the

smaller city north of the metropolitan area where the Pony Express began and outlaw Jesse James met his end. Her grandmother had lived on a farm, a place she'd loved to visit as a child, so the old farmhouse charmed her. She could enjoy living here very much.

"If you're from Texas, how'd you find this place, and why did you move to Missouri?"

Nicholas shrugged. "Suzanne was here – her husband came from the area, and I decided I didn't want to live where everyone knew me, which they do back in Rusk. I'd rather not be the object of public pity every time I go to town or hear about my glory days back in high school as the state champion quarterback or the ROTC ball king or senior flirt. Plus, I liked the place – it's got character and good bones."

So do you, Belle thought but didn't say so because he'd argue. "Which room is yours?"

The huge front bedroom was all but empty, so it had to be one of the smaller rooms. Three of the four rooms had a bed, a chest, and a dresser, but none had any personal touches that would indicate it belonged to Nicholas. The fourth room had a desk with a laptop. The windows overlooked the surrounding forest.

"This is where I sleep when it's not colder than a witch's tit," he said, rubbing his hands together. "It's freezing up here – let's go back downstairs before we get frostbite."

Belle noted the room, stark with an antique iron double bed made up with a faded blue chenille bedspread, a battered chest of drawers and a dresser that lacked the mirror. There was a single wooden chair, a desk, and a closed closet. No pictures or memorabilia hung on the wall. It could have been a guest room, she thought, or a room left by a previous owner. If this was his lair, it was a lonely one.

In the living room, she huddled close to the hearth to get warm after Nicholas added a log to the blaze. With the power still off, there wasn't much to do, and it was too soon to cook another meal. Her skin tingled at the idea of another impromptu sexual encounter, but Belle tried to ignore it. She wasn't one to sleep with a guy on the first date, and this hardly qualified as a date. She chalked it up to a combination of weather and boredom –plus attraction.

Despite his scars and his bitter attitude, she found Nicholas attractive in a way that went far more than skin deep. He intrigued her, not just the man he'd become now but the man, the Marine he must have been before.

He made a small groan, and she noticed he sat hunched forward with his right hand splayed flat over his belly.

"Does your stomach hurt?" she asked.

Nicholas glanced up and nodded. "Yeah, my belly's griping me. It's not a big deal. It happens."

He winced and rubbed his abdomen back and forth.

"Is it my cooking?"

He managed to grin. "God, no. It's just part of the damn PTSD – I never know when I might get slammed with a gut ache or headache. It's not just nightmares and flashbacks."

"Is there something I can do?" she asked. "I could make you some tea if you have any or some medicine."

"I'll be okay, but thanks. It'll pass before long."

"Are you sure?" She wondered if he'd been to a doctor.

"Yeah, the VA docs said it's just part of the whole fucking mess. Stress triggers it, or so they said."

"Are you stressed?"

Nicholas glared at her. "Let's see, there's a power outage due to a major winter ice storm, the sheriff's been here already today, and my sister called. Not to mention a lone wolf like me has a lovely lady underfoot that I couldn't keep my hands off, plus all my usual hang-ups and looking like Freddy Krueger's twin. Why the hell would you think I might be stressed?"

Belle should have known, and now she felt like an idiot. Maybe her presence contributed to his stress, but she might be able to help relieve some of it. "Come lay down on the couch," she told him. "On your stomach, if it won't make it worse and take off your shirt."

Frowning with suspicion, Nicholas did what she requested. He pillowed his head in his hands, and although he didn't appear very comfortable, Belle sat down on the floor beside the couch. She reached into her purse, took out a small bottle of her favorite Jergens hand lotion and squirted some into her palm. Then she began to rub it into his back, her hands moving across his skin, massaging first his shoulders, which were hard and tight. She noted that he had less scarring on his back than on his face, neck, or chest. Belle massaged his flesh, working it the way she would knead bread dough until he exhaled a long breath.

"That actually feels good," he said, sounding surprised. "Don't quit."

"I'm not," she told him, rubbing with force and working the lotion into his skin at the same time. His taut muscles eased under her touch after twenty or thirty minutes. "Tell me if you get too cold."

"I'd freeze before I'd bitch about this," he murmured. "Feels fucking amazing."

"How's your stomach?"

"It's settled. Now I'm getting hungry, but I don't want to move."

"Then don't."

He sounded drowsy. Her goal was to put him to sleep. Although she'd slept during the cold night, she doubted he had much. He'd been on guard, stoking the fire and watching over her. Belle had a suspicion he probably suffered from insomnia too.

After she'd massaged for so long that her hands cramped and hurt, Nicholas slept, his breathing regular, and an occasional snore escaped his mouth. She covered him up, took care of the fire, and headed for the kitchen. It was already past lunch time so she thought she'd see what might be on hand for supper.

His cupboards proved to be almost as bare as Mother Hubbard's. She found assorted canned tamales, ravioli, spaghetti rings and soup. Belle found a few cans of chicken breast and a few more of tuna. There were a couple of envelopes of seasoned noodles and sauce. Without many options, she decided to make a bastardized chicken and noodles with a can of chicken and a package of noodles with sauce. As a decent cook who preferred to make things from scratch, she hated to use packaged foods, but it would work. Although she searched for flour, baking powder and milk, Nicholas lacked all three or she would have made biscuits as well.

When Nicholas awoke, it was late enough that dusk had gathered, and shadows loomed large in the old high-ceilinged house. Belle had lit the lamps again, or it would be dark. On the stove, fueled by propane, the quick version of chicken and noodles simmered. When he began to stir, she picked up the flannel shirt he'd discarded and prepared to hand it to him. Once he fully awakened, he rolled over and sat up with speed.

"Hey," she said before he leapt to his feet. "Here's your shirt."

He paused and ran a hand over his face. "Did I fall asleep?"

"Yes, hours ago. Are you still hungry?"

Nicholas blinked and cocked his head as he considered the question. "Yeah, I am. Did the power come back on?"

"Not yet, but I made something that resembles chicken and noodles."

"Okay," he said, sounding still sleepy. "Thanks for that back rub. It put me out."

"No problem. I was glad to do it."

He reached for the shirt but hadn't put it on yet. Belle admired his chest. Despite the prominent scarring, which was not just burns but the puckered site of at least one gunshot wound, it was flat and muscular. She placed her hand in the center of his belly, where he'd rubbed his aching stomach hours earlier. "Do you feel better?"

Nicholas placed his hand over hers, wearing a slight grin. "Yeah, I do. Thanks for asking. You manage to ask like you care, not with pity. I can't stand the "poor Nicholas" approach."

"I do care." Her voice was soft, but she meant it. He raised his head to gaze into her eyes and then nodded.

"I believe you. I'm fucked if I know why you do, though. Let's go see what you fixed to eat."

The dish was a long way from the best chicken and noodles she'd ever made. At home, in normal circumstances, she would have made chicken broth from meaty thighs and drums, then peeled the meat from the bones to use. The broth would have simmered with carrots, onions, and a few seasonings, including sage. The noodles would be homemade, using her great-great grandmother's pioneer recipe, just flour, an egg or two, and water, blended, rolled out flat to dry and cut thin.

"It's edible," she said after she tasted the concoction.

"It's not bad," Nicholas said. He thought it was pretty

damn good.

"Someday, I'll make you the homemade version. It's so much better," she told him, then wondered why she'd say such a thing. Once he delivered her to her grandmother's house, Belle wasn't sure if she'd see him again. She wanted to, sure, but there were no guarantees. She half-expected that he'd frown or say something pithy, but he nodded.

"I'd like that. I seldom get any home cooking. I'm surprised a reporter or journalist or whatever you are likes to cook. You said you're on the radio now?"

Belle had said that, but she hadn't told him the entire truth. After a long sigh, she did.

"Well, I was. The station made some budget cuts and eliminated several staff positions, including mine. You know, the old last hired, first fired rule. I figured I'd wait until after New Year's to get serious about finding a new job. I can do some freelancing in the meantime. And I love to cook. My grandma – well, the one I was raised with – taught me how."

She watched his face as her announcement made sense. He didn't say a word for a full minute, then he said, "So, you don't really have to be back in Kansas City on a deadline?"

"No, not really."

"So, no hurry?"

"None."

Nicholas ate a few spoons of chicken and noodles. "That's interesting."

Her heart kicked up the beat from steady to rock and roll. "Is it? Why?"

"Then you could stay in the area awhile, past Thanksgiving if you wanted."

She could, but she wondered where – stay with Ethel,

remain here, rent an extended stay hotel room or what. "Yeah, I suppose I could."

He nodded. "Okay. Well, then we'll see what happens, I guess."

Belle smiled. She'd never been much of a risk taker, instead someone who just rolled with what happened. She liked to plan, to know what she was doing that day when she rose in the morning, and to carry out the day as planned. Now, she would have to play it by ear and for the first time in her life, she thought that might prove intriguing and possibly more.

"*Cie la vie,*" she said, then added her favorite get-down-and-party sentiment. "Let the good times roll."

Nicholas grinned, catching the Louisiana references as she figured he would. The first, in French, meant 'that's life.' He liked the way Belle used both sayings to make a point – take life as it comes but always let those good times roll.

She shivered, but it had to be from the cold, not from his smile.

Chapter Four

The food she served was plain and basic, but it tasted better than most of what he ate from cans or the freezer. Nicholas had expected to be ready to send her on her way long before now, but he realized he didn't want to, not yet. She evoked feelings he'd thought lost forever, and she saw him in a way most people didn't. Belle didn't look away from him or make stupid little pronouncements like 'you must have been good-looking' or 'did you ever think about plastic surgery.' She'd tended the cuts from his outburst with gentleness and without judgement. When his gut kicked up, she'd helped without hovering or fussing or offering some over the counter medication. Sex with her, although unexpected, had been the best he'd ever known, and he craved more. Her hands on his back had been soothing and caring. Yeah, he wanted her to stay around, and he wanted to know her more. Maybe it would all still blow up faster than the Humvee had, but he needed to pursue the possibilities.

When the phone rang, he tensed. The instrument had rung

more in the last two days than in a month.

"I can get it," Belle said. "Maybe it's Ethel."

He shook his head. "My house, my phone – I'll answer it. Hello?"

"Nick, oh, hey, it's me," his sister said. "I thought I'd touch base with you, and Teagan bugged me to call. I talked to your, uh, new friend earlier. How's it going?"

Nicholas rolled his eyes, glad Suzanne couldn't see his reaction. "All is well, sister. No power yet, but we're staying warm, and Belle keeps me fed. Are you all right over there? Is Marshall home or on the road?"

Her husband was an over the road trucker, gone as much as he was present.

"Marsh is on a run to California, but we're coping. He won't be back until Saturday."

"He'll miss Thanksgiving."

"It wouldn't be the first time. Hey, Thanksgiving is why I called."

Jesus, help him. She was about to invite him for a meal. Although he loved his sister, she would hover and fuss. He adored his niece, but sometimes the 'Uncle Beast' nickname got old, and he'd rather not sit through another showing of the cartoon movie that remained Teagan's favorite.

"I have plans," he said. "I'm going over to Ethel Simpkins's with Belle on Thursday. She's Belle's grandmother."

Belle's eyes widened, and she grinned at him with a thumbs-up.

Suzanne gasped. "I didn't know Ethel had another granddaughter. I knew Mindy, but she lives in Alabama now, and this woman, this Belle, didn't tell me that. You're going to Ethel's on Thursday?"

"She invited me," he said. "And even though Belle's her granddaughter, they've never met. Belle was adopted as a baby. We'll be there, so we'll see you."

"Awesome. Teagan will be thrilled." He could tell his sister wasn't. "Besides, I really want to meet this woman, this Belle."

"Try not to scare her off, sis."

"I won't."

When he hung up, Belle came over and brushed a swift kiss across his mouth.

"I'm glad you're coming to Ethel's. I've been a little worried about it since I don't know her. From what I heard, your sister and niece are coming too?"

He nodded, lips tingling from the kiss. "Apparently, Ethel invited them. They're neighbors.

"I need to call Ethel and tell her we'll both be there," Belle said. "

"Go ahead," he said, with a nod at the phone. "I'll clean up."

She rewarded him with a smile and dialed. Nicholas picked up the dishes and put water to heat on the stove. His water stock was dwindling, and he'd have to face the supermarket soon. He eavesdropped without shame as Belle made her call and started the dishes.

"Ethel, it's Belle. I wanted to let you know that both Nicholas and I will come to dinner on Thanksgiving."

He wished he could hear both sides of the conversation but had to guess Ethel's part.

"I'm glad your electricity is back on – that makes it easier. Yes, Suzanne called and told Nicholas they'd be there too. I don't know if I'll make it over to meet you before – there's no power here yet, and my car was towed. No, no, it's all good. If we come over before, I'll call first. Yes, I'll be looking forward to it. Oh, my dad's there now? Okay. Thanks for letting me know. Thanks, Ethel."

Belle hung up and tried to take over washing the dishes. He shook her head. "I told you, I'll do them."

"Then I'll dry."

"If that's what you want, sure."

Although he hadn't showered in more than two days, and neither had she, Belle smelled good to him. A hint of her floral fragrance, lavender, he thought, lingered, and he leaned closer.

As he did, the kitchen light overhead flared to life, faded, and then returned. The refrigerator began to hum, and throughout the house, electricity banished shadows.

"The electricity's on," Belle exclaimed.

He grinned. Now he could shower and sleep in his own bed – preferably with Belle beside him. The heat kicked on, and the air coming through the ductwork smelled of dust and heat, normal after being off. He blew out the candles and the lamp, then headed to the living room to do the same. Nicholas banked the fire to allow it to die down on its own.

"It's so bright," Belle said, trailing him. "It's amazing."

She busied herself, folding the blankets and quilts that they had used. She halted and turned to him, a look of dismay on her face.

"Does this, the power's back, mean you're taking me over to Ethel's?"

"Only if you want me to," he said. Her expression lightened, so he added, "You can stay here, Belle. I'm not going to run you off. What do you think?"

Belle covered three feet in seconds and hugged him. "I'd

rather stay for now. I'm sure Ethel is a wonderful person, but I don't know her, and she said on the phone that my birth father is there now. I'm not quite ready to meet him yet."

Nicholas struggled to make sense of her story. "You were adopted as an infant, right?"

She nodded. "I was four months old."

"But you didn't know who your birth parents were until recently?"

"I didn't even know I was adopted until last year," she replied. Her voice quivered, so he guessed it had to have been a huge emotional blow. "My parents, the ones who raised me, died in the summer, not this year but last, on the lake. There was a boat collision. My mother went into the water and couldn't swim, so my dad tried to save her, but they both drowned. It wasn't until their attorney read the will that I found out."

Nicholas ached with compassion. First, the only parents she'd ever known died at the same time in a tragic mishap, then she learned she had been adopted. The double shocks had to hit hard, he thought, and there must have been a sense of anger and betrayal mingled with grief.

"That had to suck," he said. "And been difficult."

Her brief laugh was bitter as unsweetened cocoa. "It was, beyond anything, yeah. They left a letter in their safety deposit box along with a will, telling how they adopted me and included my birth family's information. I spent months just trying to wrap my head around it, then I wrote to Ethel. She wrote back, and we got in touch. I might not have, but I don't have any family otherwise."

"No siblings?"

Belle shook her head. "I was raised as an only child – I always said I was a *lonely* child. I had one grandmother, and that's it. She passed away ten years ago."

He had a huge family, parents who still lived in Rusk, Texas, one brother in Shreveport, Louisiana and Suzanne. Teagan wasn't his only niece. There were two more, as well as several nephews. He'd been raised with four loving grandparents, including his Reilly grandpa, who was still living, and a dozen or so aunts and uncles. He had more cousins than he could count. And the best one, Timothy.

"Oh," he said. It sounded stupid, but he didn't know what else to say. "Do you know why they gave you up for adoption?"

"All I know is that it was my birth mother's family who arranged it after she died when I was a baby. I hope I find out more from Ethel and eventually from my father."

"If you want to go meet her before Thanksgiving, I'd be happy to drive you over."

"I'll think about it," she said. "I'd rather do something else right now, though."

"What's that?"

"This," she said and kissed him, to his astonishment. Oh, sweet Jesus, her mouth was hot against his, and it wasn't a gentle kiss. She devoured his lips with hers, hungry and needy, seeking a response. Nicholas kissed her back, and as her hands slid under his shirt to caress his chest. Her fingers found his nipples and tweaked them. At her touch, each hardened in a way that made his dick harder too. Her lips captured his, and she let her tongue stray into his mouth, delivering a French kiss that made his senses go wild. About the time he figured he couldn't take any more of her mouth on his, she switched tactics and lowered her mouth to his throat, where she kissed, sucked, and nibbled. Her teeth were sharp as she gnawed, delivering love bites until he thought he'd come in his pants. Her eager fingers managed to strip away the outer flannel shirt he wore unbuttoned and pull the t-shirt over his head with swift motions.

He knew she liked him, that was mutual, and he had been certain she enjoyed their brief, wild sex, but this demonstrated she wanted him. Desire burned like liquid fire in his veins as Belle got creative with her mouth, lowering it down his chest, lingering to suckle his already tender nipples. Her lips delivered sweet little butterfly kisses everywhere, where he had scars, where he didn't. She dropped to his belly button and then just above his crotch.

"Let's go upstairs," he stammered. "Let's do this right."

"And slow," Belle said.

Nicholas kissed her on the mouth, using a lot of tongue, to demonstrate he was all in. They made it through the entryway and up the stairs with frequent pauses for more kisses. Along the way, he managed to strip away her blouse and undo her jeans. Her bra came off in his hands with little effort, and he dropped it, aiming for the banister but missed. It fell to the floor below, but neither cared. He almost took her on the landing, but she'd asked for slow, and he intended to give her that.

By the time they hit his bedroom, they had shed their garments and were naked. Her body was perfect in his eyes, her ivory skin smooth, her curves generous, and her breasts fit for his hands. He paused to kiss her, his lips devouring hers and his tongue deep as it could go into her mouth. Nicholas ran his hands over her body, delighting in it, fired by the small moans she made in response to his touch.

He backed her to the bed, and without bothering to pull down the covers, he laid her on her back. Nicholas hovered above her and rubbed her mound with one hand. Her pussy was hot and already wet. He fingered her, then put a finger deep into her box to touch her clit. She writhed beneath him, emitting shrill, happy shrieks. Encouraged by the response, he did what he hadn't since he was in service and used his tongue. She came up off the bed with a jerk, and with the taste of her on his lips, he entered her, his dick hard and ready.

Nicholas used it like a sword, a weapon to sink deep into her, entering slowly so that each thrust he made yielded ultimate satisfaction for both. She clenched her legs around him and drove him even deeper until he thought he'd penetrated the very core of her being.

She screamed, and in between, she talked to him, "You're fucking me to death, oh, Nicholas, you're fucking me to death. Don't stop, oh, don't stop."

He couldn't have if he'd wanted. Every cell, each atom, every nerve ending in his body reacted at full alert. The passion built in him like a brewing storm, gathering strength and power. Beneath him, Belle clawed at him with both hands, begging him to take her all the way.

When Nicholas thought he'd burst or die if he didn't yield, he allowed the orgasm to hit, a wave of the most intense, incredible pleasure he'd ever known. Since his injuries, his only sexual outlet had been his fist, and he'd come to believe he'd lost the ability for a full sensation. Now, carried on the tide, momentarily blind, his mind empty of all but sensual thoughts, he realized how mistaken he'd been.

"Belle," he moaned. "Belle, beautiful, Belle, ride with me to the stars."

Whatever sounds she made were lost in the roaring of his hot blood, but when they hit that pinnacle together, bodies intertwined, their tiny world exploded in fever, in heat so hot it burned like desert sun, in pleasure so intense it was almost pain and physical delight. They shuddered as one, trembled until the wave faded, and he lay still on her, his seed trickling from his dick. He realized he hadn't bothered to find a condom, but before he could worry, she whispered, "It's okay. I'm on the pill."

Beyond speech, he nodded and rolled to lay beside her, then took her into his arms and held her close. She fit into the circle of his arms, and when she put her head against his chest, Nicholas thought his heart might burst with emotion.

Although he'd slept after her magic fingered massage and although insomnia kept him awake most nights, Nicholas let the post-sex contentment wrap him in a comfortable cocoon. He relaxed, and his breathing slowed to an easy rhythm. Until Belle, he hadn't made love to a woman since his injuries. Nicholas had been a handsome man and enjoyed sex. After suffering injuries that almost cost his life and left him scarred, he figured no woman would want to make love with a monster, so he didn't even try. He'd almost forgotten what it was like to kiss and be kissed or to share intimacy. She touched him without repulsion or pity, and that was a marvel.

Drowsy, sated, and happy in a way he hadn't been for a very long time, his last thought before he drifted into sleep was that he didn't love her, not yet, but that he could.

That loomed huge, and rather than explore it now, Nicholas slept.

Chapter Five

If she'd been a sentimental person, Belle would have visited her grandmother for the first time before Thanksgiving Day, but she didn't. If it had been only Ethel, she probably would have gone, but the knowledge that her birth father, Peter Simpkins, was present caused her to procrastinate. Although curious about the man, she wasn't sure what to say to him when they met. A hundred or more questions rose in her mind, but asking them without going through the polite pleasantries would probably be rude.

Her emotions were jumbled enough after making love with Nicholas. The first time, in the kitchen, might have been something she could write off as a quickie, but it wasn't. There was more between them. Last night, she'd slept in his arms all night, then woke to find him gone. He'd been downstairs with coffee brewed, and he'd already showered. She offered to make breakfast, but he insisted he'd take her out, then they could shop for a few groceries and other necessities together.

Since Nicholas had seemed reclusive, she was surprised. "Are you sure?" she asked him. "Where will we get a meal?"

"There's a diner in town," he told her. "And it's conveniently right next to a small supermarket. The food's good, too. I've been there a few times. The owner's son was a Marine, too, so I don't feel so out of place."

The roads proved to be mostly clear, and the sun shone as they trekked into town, first over a series of paved country roads, then via a two-lane highway that funneled into the small town. The road hugged the curve of the rugged Ozark hills as they passed cattle in the fields, some munching on giant round bales of hay, dairy farms, chicken houses, and fallow fields that, in the summer, he told her would be fertile with corn, soybeans, and hay. She liked the rural scenes and noted they were very different than the countryside where her grandparents had once farmed. That had been flat and open, unlike these rocky, rugged hills.

The small town with a strange Native American name – Neosho – was also the county seat. Before they drove to the café, Nicholas gave her a quick tour of the downtown square where a courthouse claimed the center space. He drove by a small but pretty park with a spring flowing beneath a series of small bridges, then onto the business strip where fast food outlets sat side by side with tire shops, a chain pharmacy, two banks, and the local high school.

At the diner, they sat in a separate room, away from most of the other diners. Nicholas sat with his back to the restaurant, which had a lot of military décor that focused on the owner's late son. They enjoyed biscuits and gravy, eggs, sausage, and hashbrowns with strong coffee and easy conversation, then headed for the grocery store across the parking lot.

He'd worn a hoodie, and he'd kept the hood up as they dined. Belle noticed he seemed edgy, drumming his fingers on the tabletop but said nothing. At the store, he stayed in the truck. On the day before Thanksgiving, the restaurant had been almost empty, but the store bustled with last moment shoppers. Belle noticed, and so did Nicholas.

"The diner was enough for now," he told her. "I'll wait for you here."

"Okay," she said. "I'll go in, get the filling for pies for tomorrow. Any request?"

"I actually like cake more than I do pie."

"What flavor?"

"Chocolate," he said without hesitation.

"I'll get the ingredients to make a cake from scratch," she told him. "It'll be better than those mixes."

Back at his house, Belle baked and prepared the pork chops he'd requested for supper. She also did the baking, filling the house with delicious aromas. Afterward, they retired to his bedroom and slept spooned together, although they didn't make love. Her emotions were engaged with this troubled man, and she had no idea where they might go from here. For now, she focused on the holiday.

Thanksgiving dawned clear and very cold. Ethel had told them she planned to serve dinner, a traditional meal with roast turkey, baked ham, dressing, sweet potatoes, green bean casserole, sweet corn, biscuits and hot rolls, and gravy around one. At eleven, they loaded up the desserts she'd baked and traveled the short distance to her grandmother's house.

"It's really over the river and through the woods," Belle commented as she peered at the scenery from his truck.

Her shoulders were tight with nerves, and she struggled

with a headache.

"I suppose so," Nicholas said. His fingers drummed the steering wheel in a staccato rhythm, so she figured he had some anxiety as well. He pointed to a small house with blue shutters. "That's where my sister lives."

Belle almost bolted when they pulled into the yard, and she saw six vehicles parked. She'd hoped to arrive first, but apparently, they were last. She climbed down from the truck and started for the front door, but Nicholas stopped her. "We'll go around back."

He carried the box with the pies and cake, as he led her to the rear and a sliding glass door. Belle followed him inside and stopped. Delicious aromas filled the air from the kitchen to her left but straight ahead, the room seemed filled with people. She counted at least a dozen before she stopped. A white-haired lady approached and opened her arms for a hug.

"Welcome, Maribel," she said. "I'm Ethel. Let me introduce you, then I need to get back to the food."

Nicholas put the desserts on a bar that divided the kitchen from the living room and took a seat near a woman and child. Belle tried to pay attention as Ethel named off those present, but the only ones who stood out were her biological father and Nicholas' sister.

Ethel retreated into the kitchen, where some of the other women were busy with cooking tasks. Belle hesitated, then headed for Nicholas when he held out his hand. She took it, and he said, "Belle, this is my sister, Suzanne and my niece, Teagan. Go ahead, grab a seat."

His sister stared at her with hostility. "I'm pleased to meet you."

"Same," Belle replied, although his sister seemed anything

but delighted.

Belle sank into a swivel rocker next to the loveseat where Nicholas sat beside his sister. Ill at ease, she glanced around the room, uncertain of what to say or do. He took her hand and held it with silent support.

The little girl, who had dark hair the same shade as Nicholas did, rose from where she sat cross-legged on the floor. She wore a sulky expression and then frowned as she headed over to stand in front of her uncle. Teagan pushed up the yellow Disney t-shirt she wore, baring her stomach, and then clutched it with both hands. "My tummy really hurts," she whined.

Suzanne sighed. "I'm sorry, Nick. She's been having stomachaches ever since she started kindergarten in August. I took her to the doctor, and he said it's psychosomatic. Now she gets one every time we do anything out of the ordinary."

Teagan pushed at her belly and moaned.

"Psychosomatic doesn't mean it doesn't hurt," Nicholas said. "Come here, Teagan."

She moved closer, still clutching at her stomach.

"Did you know I get tummy aches, too?" he asked. "Sometimes bad ones."

The girl shook her head. "Well, I do," he told her and pointed to the middle of his abdomen. "Right around here."

"Does your tummy hurt right now?"

"No," he said. He opened his arms and pulled her onto his lap. She cuddled against his shoulder, and he put one hand on her tummy. "Let me hold you till it feels better, okay?"

"Okay, Uncle Beast," she said, her voice very soft.

"Nicholas, I can take her home," his sister said.

"No need. She'll feel better soon."

Belle watched as he rubbed the child's tummy with

his large hand with gentle motions. He talked to her, too, so low she couldn't make out most of what he said, but the child calmed. Then he sang to her in a soft voice until Teagan's eyes closed. Nicholas cuddled her close. As he soothed the little girl's stomachache with compassion, Belle realized she loved him. She'd never seen anyone, especially a man, demonstrate such caring. Her childhood tummy aches were always dismissed as her fault for gobbling too many cookies or too much candy or stuffing her stomach. At best, they packed her off to bed after a dose of the pink medicine she'd come to hate, but sometimes, no one offered any sympathy at all.

I love him, she thought and wondered what she'd do about it.

By the time Ethel called them all to the table, Teagan had recovered and bounced about like any five-year-old. Belle, seated next to Nicholas, held his hand during the blessing and leaned over to swipe his cheek with a brief kiss. He smiled but asked, "What's that for?"

"You have a good heart, Nicholas Reilly," she told him.

Over the holiday meal, she tried to get acquainted with her family, but it was chaotic. Peter Simpkins tried to include her in every conversation, but it was awkward for both of them. In addition to her grandmother, father and stepmother, there were two aunts and their husbands, an uncle, and his wife, two teenage cousins, and a single mom who turned out to be her half-sister. For someone who'd recently learned she had family, it was intense, and for Nicholas, who hated to be stared at, it had to be overwhelming. Belle snuck glances at him during the meal, and he seemed agitated, although he interacted with her and his sister, who sat across from him. When members of her extended birth family spoke to him, he replied, and she noticed he kept his usual snark to a minimum. Most often, he teased his niece, who appeared to adore her uncle. He ate but with slow precision, never overloading his plate, sampling a little of almost everything. She noticed he did take a thick slab of the cake she'd baked, which brought a smile.

Belle joined the other women in clearing the table and cleaning up. After the meal, Ethel brought out a stack of photo albums and called her to the table. Belle almost groaned. The headache that had threatened all day had become a full-blown reality. At this point, she longed to escape, and she thought Nicholas could use a break. He appeared a little pale, and when she looked closely, fine beads of perspiration dotted his forehead. His shoulders were tight and tense.

"Are you okay?" she whispered.

He waggled his left hand. "So, so. Have you had enough family time for one day?"

To him, she could and would be honest. "God, yes."

Nicholas laughed. "Let's go home."

Relieved he was on the same page, she asked, "Do you mean it?"

"You bet. I was ready to go an hour ago."

He announced they were leaving, and although there was a chorus begging Belle to stay, Nicholas stood firm. "We can come back when it's less hectic," he told them. "Or you can come over to my place. Just call and let us know. Ethel has the number."

Belle hugged Ethel and her dad. "I'd love to see the pictures another time," she told her grandmother, who nodded.

She knew her now, at least a little. The others were still strangers, for now.

Suzanne followed them out, Teagan in tow. "Nick, is everything all right?"

Nicholas paused for a hug and then kissed his sister's cheek. "It's fine. I'm okay. This is all a lot for Belle, that's all. If you and the kid want to come over for a bit, you're welcome."

Belle agreed. "Yes, you are. I'm glad we got to meet, and I'd love to get better acquainted."

"We'll come over tomorrow if that's okay unless you're planning to hit the Black Friday sales. If you are, you could come with." It sounded more like a challenge than an invitation.

"Never," Belle said. Even if she'd wanted to, she suspected Nicholas wouldn't want to be part of the crowds and chaos.

"We'll see you tomorrow, then," he told Suzanne.

Teagan hugged his legs. "Bye, Uncle Beast."

He picked her up and held her high for a moment. "Goodbye, kid. Take care of your tummy."

In the truck, Belle scooted next to Nicholas, her hand resting on his thigh while her shoulder rested against his. He laid his hand on top of hers for a moment, then rested his head on the steering wheel and released a huge sigh.

"Was it that bad?" she asked.

Nicholas raised his head. "No, it wasn't, not really. It's just more than I'm used to. Being around large groups of people makes me anxious. I start feeling like I can't get enough air, and even if no one's talking about me, I get paranoid, thinking that they are. Then I get antsy and want to bolt."

Belle put her hand on his back, concerned. "Are you okay? What do you need?"

"Just space," he said. "Some quiet alone time."

That stung a little, but she could understand. "If you want, I can stay here awhile. Ethel's already told me I'm welcome or you can drop me at your place if you want to go somewhere by yourself. Or I'll keep out of your way. It's a big house."

Nicholas turned to her. "No, I don't mind your company, not at all, Belle. I'd rather you be with me than not. I'm better with you. I couldn't have done this today if you weren't here, not even with Suzanne and Teagan."

Warmth radiated through her chest. "I'm glad. You were very good with your niece."

His light grey eyes darkened. "It's because I understand. Sometimes my sister is too hard on the kid. I don't know what the hell got into her, though. She could have been friendlier."

She totally could have been, but Belle said instead, "She seems like a good mom, though."

"She is, most of the time. Do you mind taking a drive?"

"No, it's fine. Where are we going?"

"I need some open water," he told her. "It's one thing that eases my soul when I'm troubled. If we go now, we can get there before it gets dark."

Unfamiliar with the area, Belle asked, "Didn't we cross the water to come to Ethel?"

"We did," he said. "And in a pinch, there are public access spots that work. But today, I'd like a little more, so we're heading for Grand Falls. If it wasn't as late, I'd go to Grand Lake – it's in Oklahoma."

"Is it a waterfall?"

"Yeah, it is," he said. "Largest in the state. I just stumbled across it one day."

As they traveled to the western side of the county, traffic was light, and at the falls, there were only a few other visitors. They parked along the narrow row and crossed to the rocky banks.

"What river is it?" she asked.

"Shoal Creek," Nicholas replied. "I've read the earliest

pioneers called it Shoal River, but now everyone says creek. It's the same stream we crossed on the way to your grandmother's today. The headwaters are in the eastern part of the county, and from here, it flows into the Spring River, which goes into Grand Lake. It widens as it travels west."

"It's beautiful," Belle said, walking across the rocks toward the water below the falls. Between the farm and here, her headache had faded away.

Nicholas caught her arm. "Be careful, babe. The rocks are usually slick and treacherous. I wouldn't want you to fall or turn an ankle."

Neither would she, so she halted. He grasped her hand, his fingers firm in hers, and she held on tight after her feet skidded on the rocks. Water covered most of them, almost to where they stood. It was a lovely scene, she thought, tranquil with the water pooling below the falls before it meandered downstream. The falls were majestic and she enjoyed the quiet sound of the river as it flowed over the rocks, like a soft voice singing a lullaby.

Beside her, Nicholas relaxed his shoulders and his grip on her hand eased. He still held it but without intense desperation. Since the river and falls sat below hills to the west, the late afternoon shadows lengthened. Shadows fell, and she realized it would be dark here sooner than elsewhere. Despite the chill in the air and the temperature that dropped as dusk descended, Belle liked the place. It provided tranquility, balm for her soul as well as for his.

She chanced a look at his expression and found it calm, as placid as she had ever seen on his face. Thankful that he could claim a measure of peace for a few minutes made her wish he could find and keep it every day, everywhere.

"It's almost dark," he said, after a long yet comfortable

silence. "We should go while we can still see. Are you ready to go home?"

Home. It conjured up the image of his old farmhouse, and it fit, for now. She linked her arm through his and said, "I'd like nothing better."

"Then let's go."

He wrapped an arm around her shoulders, and in tandem, they walked back to his truck in the twilight. Despite the strangeness of having spent it with family she'd never known before, and although the gathering had caused Nicholas more than a little anxiety, it had been a good Thanksgiving, Belle thought, the best she'd since her adopted grandmother died.

She almost said so, then didn't, uncertain if he felt the same, just as she kept back her epiphany that she loved him. *I've known him less than a week,* she thought, *but I'm sure. But I don't want to scare him or upset him.*

Maribel kept it in her heart and waited. There would be a time to share it, and she hoped it would be soon.

Chapter Six

The moments spent beside the falls, watching the water cascade down and flow into the stream, eased his troubled spirits and leached away his anxiety. Water had always been important to Nicholas, from the Neches River in Cherokee County, Texas, back home to Toledo Bend, where the once wild Sabine River between Texas and Louisiana had become a lake. The ocean had always been a favorite destination. Even in Afghanistan, the rivers and lakes could bring a measure of peace to his soul, despite the chaos around him. Since moving to Missouri, he'd discovered Grand Falls and a few other places. The Grand Lake o' the Cherokees down in Oklahoma within an easy drive called to him. Nicholas had discovered a place at the Twin Bridges State Park where he could settle onto a favorite rock on the bluffs overlooking the Neosho River. Regardless of snakes in season or the danger he might misstep and fall, he went often. He'd camped there twice, keeping solitary and venturing out in the early hours of the morning or in the late evening. If there had been time, he'd headed for that spot today.

Instead, after too many hours spent with a large number of people, most of which he didn't know, he came to the falls and brought Belle with him. That he wanted her beside him surprised him. He'd become a loner, someone who sought solitude, but he realized he was better with her. Something about her quiet acceptance, calm support, and the way she made love as if he were unscarred and whole touched Nicholas deep within. He wasn't damaged goods to her, and he wasn't a freak. As much as his sister and her young daughter loved him, there were times when he saw the pain in their eyes as they gazed at his ruined features and his many scars. Teagan loved him with her whole heart, but the fact she called him 'Uncle Beast' spoke volumes to him. Many times, he'd wanted to correct her, to ask her to say, 'Uncle Nick,' but he didn't.

On the way home, Belle said little, but she sat close beside him, her hand resting on his thigh.

"You're quiet," he commented when they were almost home.

"I'm just thinking," she said. Although in the dim cab, he couldn't see her face, he heard the smile in her voice. "It was a good day, overall. I like my newfound family, but I'm not familiar with them yet."

"I enjoyed most of it," he told her. "Yeah, I got a little anxious, but at this point, it's just part of the territory. You know, it's the first time I've participated in Thanksgiving since I got back."

"You didn't eat dinner or go anywhere?"

"No, I told you before that I'd get a pizza or nuke a frozen dinner. That's what I've done. It was just another day."

"I thought maybe you usually went to your sister's or

down to Texas."

"Uh-uh. So, this was a big thing to me, and I'm glad you asked me to go."

It was progress, something he'd never thought he would make.

"I'm glad – I couldn't have gone without you," she said.

"I didn't do anything except be there."

"And that's just what I needed," she said. "Just your presence and support."

At his house, they'd failed to leave any lights on, inside or out, so they fumbled through the dark to enter. His left eye might sag, but he retained cat-like night vision, so it wasn't a problem. Belle, however, stumbled twice until he wrapped his arm around her waist and steered her to the front door. Once inside, he flipped the nearest switch and the entryway filled with light. For the first time, Nicholas wondered what Belle thought about the old farmhouse. It needed a lot of work, and he'd been making repairs at his own pace. There'd never been any reason to hurry. Some days he did a lot, then he might do nothing for a week. Did she find it rustic, he thought, or quaint or a falling down wreck? It mattered, which surprised him because nothing had for a long time.

Belle mattered, he realized. Nicholas meant what he told her before they drove away from her grandmother's farm after the holiday meal – he was better with her. She made him forget for a few moments that he was scarred and damaged, both inside and out. Through her eyes, he caught glimpses of the man within the skin, the old Nicholas he had all but buried and forgotten.

Although it was warm enough in the house, he stirred up the fire and added a couple of logs. As they caught, he savored the aroma of the woodsmoke. Nicholas found it ironic that although he suffered third-degree burns over 45 percent of his body, mostly his face, head, neck, and chest, he still enjoyed a good fire. The contained flames soothed, but other fires caused instant angst. A trash fire, whether or not it was in a barrel, made his heart race. A few times, he'd drive past controlled burns in fields or woods, then freaked out. Twice, he'd suffered a flashback. He'd had chest pains, hyperventilated, and thought he'd die. Another time he'd come across a car wreck where one of the vehicles had caught fire.

Nicholas shuddered as he remembered. Belle, en route to the kitchen, paused and put her hand on his shoulder. "Are you cold?"

"A little," he said, although he wasn't and forced a grin.

If she saw through his efforts, she didn't call him out on it. "Are you hungry? Ethel sent home tons of leftovers if you want to eat."

He wasn't, not really. "I might eat a sandwich later or a piece of that cake you made if you brought any back, but I'm not really hungry. I've eaten more the last few days than I usually do in a week."

"When you want something, tell me, and I'll fix it. I'm not ready to eat, either." Belle said, settling down on the sofa beside him. She curled against him and leaned her head against his shoulder. "It's not that late, but it feels like it should be midnight."

Nicholas laughed. "It's not even eight o'clock."

"What would you be doing if I wasn't here?"

The question surprised him, but he scrambled to answer. "I'd probably be nibbling on cold pizza," he said. "I'd be reading – I read a lot – or watching a movie. Maybe listening to music. What about you?"

He expected she enjoyed the bright lights of Kansas City

by day and night. Long ago, he'd gone to a football game at Arrowhead Stadium, then ended up in an Irish pub. He'd stayed a couple of days, discovering KC style barbecue, Cosentino's Markets, the Nelson Art Gallery, and Crown Center. Once, he driven Suzanne and Teagan up to see the lights at the Plaza.

"Unless I was on assignment or had an on-air shift, I'd be home in my pajamas," she said. "I would probably be lounging around, watching chick flicks, or reading. I like romances and romantic suspense. I would probably pop some corn or maybe indulge in some ice cream. Sometimes I enjoyed a long soak in the tub. I went out more before my parents died – I've been hunkered down since last summer because of that. Sometimes I cook, trying out different recipes, just for me."

"I figured you'd be out on the town or at a Chiefs or Royals game," he said. "Or at some trendy upscale eatery on a date or shopping till you drop at Crown Center or the Plaza."

"I'm more of a Winstead's or Five Guys kind of girl," Belle told him. "I'd rather eat a good burger than a steak or some chef-inspired dish with pine nuts and goat cheese. I don't date much. I got tired of all the same old lines and self-centered men."

She didn't date often? That surprises me, Nicholas thought. "No boyfriend?"

She shook her head. "No."

"Then why do you…oh, nevermind."

"Why I'm on Depo-Provera? Just in case."

So, there was no one else in her life now. He let that thought lay and said, "You'd like What-A-Burger down home. It's the best, and you can get a burger anytime, even at breakfast."

"Thanks to Patrick Mahomes, they've opened a few in KC," she said. "I was planning to try it. I don't guess they have one around here?"

"They do in Arkansas, about an hour or so from here," Nicholas said. "Maybe we'll run down one day, and you can try a burger."

The second the words left his mouth, he regretted saying them. Once, he would have enjoyed the day trip, but now, he hated to be seen, and he couldn't eat a hamburger in a ski mask without drawing curious stares.

"I'd like that," Belle replied. "I really would. And, if you run me up to KC, I'll take you to Winstead's. Then we'll compare."

Nicholas wanted it, he realized. And, he had promised he'd take her wherever she needed to go, including Kansas City. "Maybe," he told her and doubted she would realize how amazing it was that he even considered the possibility.

"If you're not tied up, I'm going to have to head for Kansas City before too long," Belle said. "I only brought clothes for a long weekend. I didn't expect to slide off the road and lose my car."

His heart stumbled. "You want to go home?"

He wanted her to stay. They'd talked about it, and he thought she was planning to be around. If she went – when she left – Nicholas had a feeling he'd be lonelier than he'd been now that he had enjoyed a taste of companionship.

Belle sat up and turned to him. "I don't, Nicholas," she said. "Not unless I've worn out my welcome. But I do need more clothes and a few other things. If you don't want to drive me, I suppose I can go shopping, but I've been hanging on to what money I have until I get another job."

A burst of happiness bubbled up within Nicholas. "No, I can drive up anytime you'd like. It's not like I'm doing anything else. You can stay as long as you want, Belle. Suzanne and Teagan are coming over tomorrow, but we can go this weekend or next week, whatever works."

"Do you have to be anywhere?" she asked. "I haven't even asked if you work – "

"I don't," he replied before she completed the question. "I get disability money from the VA, and it's enough for my simple needs. I bought this place with the money I'd saved when I was in the Marines, so it's paid for. There's no problem with missing work, and I don't have any doctor's appointments till early December. And that's in Arkansas, so we could hit Whataburger if you wanted to go with me."

Belle settled back down and curled up beside him. "I will, then."

The idea he wouldn't go to a routine appointment solo filled him with a warm glow. Throughout his medical ordeal, Nicholas had endured it alone. From being evacuated out of the sandbox to the Brook Army Medical Center burn unit in San Antonio, he was solitary. His family was allowed brief visits before and after fifteen surgeries in the first year, but he spent much of his time alone. His recovery, if it could be called that, took more than two years. He'd been shot three times on the day he was burned, and he'd had three additional procedures to address those wounds. He spent a month in Rusk, but his mother hovered, his father avoided, and most people pitied him, so he headed for Missouri, where Suzanne had settled with Marsh. He still traveled on his own to any VA or doctor appointments.

Her simple statement made him emotional. "Thank you," Nicholas told her. "No one ever has."

"You go to your medical appointments alone?" She sounded surprised. "What happens if they do a procedure? Or, what if you get less than positive news?"

Nicholas shrugged. "On the first, I wait until they clear me to drive, or I spend the night in the hospital. It's happened. If it's bad news, I just suck it up. None of it's going to be worse than the time I saw my ugly mug for the first time and realized it was gonna stay this way forever."

Belle folded her right hand and laid it across his cheek. He tensed at her touch, expecting her to tell him bullshit, the way most well-meaning people did, saying, "Oh, come on, it's not that bad," but instead, in a soft voice, she told him, "It's just a face – it's not you."

Her sincere tone blew him away. Nick laid his hand over hers, searching for words to express how she made him feel, to explain how she enriched his life in ways he hadn't dreamed possible.

"You're right," he said after a long pause. "God damn it, you're right."

Why, he wondered how no one ever pointed that out to him during his months in various hospitals or in therapy. He mulled her words over again – it's a face, it's not you. His scarred, ruined face was that and no more – he lived inside of it. The simple concept blew him away and hit him at gut level. Nicholas kept repeating *it's just a face* through his mind. From the first day that the bandages came off and the medical staff thought he was ready to see the damage, he'd hated the way he looked. He seldom looked in a mirror because when he did, he cringed, and he'd broken more than a few, the most recent a few days ago. Nick wore hats and hoods as often as possible, and when it was cold enough, the ski mask that concealed his features. If he thought he could have gotten by with it, he'd worn a bag over his head with slits for his eyes, something like John Merrick, dubbed "The Elephant Man," had worn. The bag attached to a cap had covered the poor man's deformity. Nicholas had watched the movie more than once, with a combination of compassion and horror.

Belle cuddled closer to him. "Of course, I'm right," she told him. "Did you really think that the way you look defines you, that it shows the Nicholas inside, the person you are?"

He had and still did, although what she said encouraged him to change his mind about it. A few words wouldn't undo a decade or more of self-depreciation and stress, but it gave him a start. "Sometimes," he replied. "Wasn't the first thing you noticed about me the scars, that gruesome Phantom of the Opera vibe?"

She shook her head. "No, you were wearing that stupid ski mask," she said. "I thought more likely you'd been involved in an armed robbery, but your eyes were what I noticed first."

"The way the left one is puckered, probably."

Belle smacked his shoulder. "No, I noticed they were gray, and you had compassion in them."

Nicholas snorted. "Yeah, right."

"Well, you did come to my rescue," she stated. "That indicates some level of caring, don't you think? You could have left me there to freeze."

"I wouldn't do that, not to anyone."

"That's the point," Belle told him. "You saved me, brought me to your home, and made me soup. You went with me to meet the family I didn't know. I watched you take care of your little niece with kindness, understanding and compassion. You have a good heart, and you're a good man, Nicholas Reilly. So maybe you're not handsome anymore, but...."

First, he wondered how she knew he'd once been considered good-looking and hot. Then, Nicholas knew he couldn't hear another word – what she said was too intense and evoked emotions he wasn't ready to deal with. He pulled her onto his lap and silenced her with a kiss. Conflicted, he wanted to believe what she said was so, but the words also made him angry. He ground his mouth against hers without remorse or any gentleness, taking her lips by force. Nicholas expected her to protest, to pull back from him. Then he would be vindicated that maybe she did find him ugly and a freak after all. Belle didn't, though. The deeper and harder he kissed, the more she clung to him, her arms around his neck tight, giving back as good as he gave.

He wanted her – *needed* her both physically and emotionally, and he acted from a gut response to her words, which were a revelation. Somewhere deep inside, as he prepared to ravish her, willing or not, Nicholas knew he cared for this woman more than he thought he'd ever cared for any female. He didn't want her to leave. He longed to keep her in his life, and sometime, he knew he'd have to explore that thought, but for now, he sought release.

Belle's lips were locked on his, and when she darted her tongue into his mouth, he shivered as his cock grew hard. He French kissed her back. At the same time, he worked the buttons on her blouse, then removed it. Nicholas fumbled a little but managed to unfasten her bra and free her breasts. They were glorious, he thought, just the right size and her cotton candy pink nipples were hard. He caressed each tit, then massaged the erect nipples, which made her moan with want.

He took his mouth from hers and lowered it to suckle one of her nipples. The sounds she made fueled his desire, and he paused to shuck off his shirt, then his jeans. Earlier, he'd planned to make love to her upstairs, in his bed, but Nicholas couldn't wait. He had to take her now or die from want. His stiff dick ached, and when she managed to remove her jeans and the panties beneath them, he thought for a moment he'd come now. He forced himself to wait, very aware that his cock might have other plans.

Her hands traveled over his nude body, pausing to caress the scars and touching him where he yearned for it most, his chest, his back, and his cock. Belle delivered light kisses on his throat and then used her teeth to mark him with love bites. Then she lay back on the sofa, as naked as he, with a smile on her face.

"Take me," she told him.

He didn't need any further invitation as he parted her legs and fit his dick into her warm, ready space. Belle moaned as he filled her, and somehow, as he found his way home within, his urgency shifted into gentleness. Nicholas slowed down and took time to savor every moment, each frisson of delight, all the pleasure. As he worked his way in and out, each time delighting in the sensation, he let his hands roam free, stroking, squeezing, and fondling. From her moans, she liked it as much as he did.

As he built toward release, Nicholas enjoyed the tension and kept it going so he'd have the maximum orgasm. He wanted the same for her. Belle writhed beneath him, her hands clawing at the couch. "Please," she cried. "Nicholas, let's come. I'm dying here."

If every fiber of his body wasn't straining, searching for that ultimate moment, he might have laughed. Instead, he put his mind to the task and finally let his body guide them to that final high.

He came in a wild rush of sensation and heat, her cries ringing in his ears as he thrust into her for the final time. His body sang with intense pleasure and powerful release. Several waves of glorious delight cascaded through him before he was spent. After he cuddled her against him, still half-joined and savored the feel of her skin against his. They both fit on the couch, but it was tight, and his last thought before he drifted asleep was fear they might fall onto the floor.

Sated, his body radiating contentment, he didn't care if they did.

Nicholas woke far into the night, a little chilled since the fire had died down to ash, but he was loath to move, so he managed to drag some quilts he kept close over them both and went back to sleep with Belle in his arms.

Chapter Seven

Belle woke, and in the first moments, she had no idea where she was, but she was aware Nicholas cradled her close and that they'd share what she ranked as the best sex ever. As she roused, she realized they were on the couch. She wanted coffee but couldn't move, so she nibbled at his ear lobe with her teeth and brushed his lips with her mouth.

"Nicholas," she whispered, then raised her volume. "Hey, Nicholas."

He came awake in an instant, his gray eyes alert and fixed on her.

If she hadn't remembered what they had shared on awakening, she thought he did because his cock stirred against her.

"Hey," he said.

She stroked his face with the one hand she could free, loving the look in his eyes and barely noticing his scars. Yesterday, watching him at her grandmother's holiday dinner, Belle had realized she loved him. That thought returned, stronger than ever. *I love him – and I'm in love with him,* she thought. Her life in KC seemed distant, and she wanted to stay right here, with this man and in his arms.

"You're amazing," she told him. "That was awesome."

He grinned; the twisted side of his mouth raised too.

"I thought it wasn't half bad," he drawled, and she could hear the East Texas in his voice.

Belle laughed. "Well, I'm hungry – how about you?"

"Starved."

She collected her scattered garments and put them on. "After breakfast, I'll shower, but for now, I'll wear yesterday's clothes. Do you want real breakfast or leftovers?"

"Sausage and eggs," he said. "With some of that chocolate cake you made on the side."

"That works," she told him. "Coffee, first."

"Hell, yeah."

Belle headed for the kitchen, buttoning her blouse as she walked through the dining room. She put the coffee on first, then dug in the fridge to find the sausage and some eggs. After she patted the bulk sausage into patties and put them in a skillet, the phone rang.

"Who's calling this early?" Nicholas asked as he entered the kitchen. "That damn phone almost never rings – or it didn't until you got here."

If it wasn't for his light tone, she might have thought he was complaining, but she thought he liked it.

"It's probably your sister," Belle told him. "Didn't she say she was coming over with Teagan?"

He nodded. "Yeah, but I'm surprised it's this early. It's not barely six, and when she can, Suzanne likes to sleep late."

"It might be Ethel too."

"I thought you gave her your cell number."

"I did, but she has this one, too."

"Go ahead and answer it," he told her. "I gotta take a leak."

"Good morning," she sang into the phone, her mood upbeat after the fantastic night with Nicholas.

Instead of Suzanne or Ethel's anticipated voice, a man chuckled, then said, "Is Saint around?"

The question confused her, and she wondered Saint Who.

"I'm sorry," she said. "I'm afraid you might have the wrong number."

"Naw, I'm sure I don't," the man said with that same drawl she'd noticed in Nicholas' voice. "Is Nicholas around?"

Nicholas, she thought, Saint Nicholas. "Yes, just a moment."

He came back into the kitchen, headed for the coffee pot but halted when he saw her standing, the receiver extended toward him.

"Who is it?"

"Someone asking for Saint."

He grinned and took the phone. "Hey, what's up? I'm actually pretty good, better than I've been in a long while. How about you?"

Although she couldn't hear both sides of the conversation, Belle could tell from the way Nicholas talked that he knew the caller well and had some affection for him. She tried not to eavesdrop as she poured two cups of coffee. Belle added a little sugar to his and more to her cup, then handed his to him.

"Thanks, babe," he said as he took the first sip. He had stretched the cord from the wall phone far enough to sit at the table. "No, we had Thanksgiving with a lady I know, an older woman who lives nearby. Suzanne was there, too, with Teagan. How was the family feast?"

Belle finished the sausage and added eggs to the skillet, frying them in the remaining grease. She couldn't help but hear his end of the conversation and deduced he spoke with a relative.

"No, I'd rather have been here," Nicholas told the caller. "It's awkward down home. No one ever knows what to say or whether or not they should look at me. Belle answered the phone. Yeah, yeah, yeah. I think you'll like her but hands off if you meet her. Christmas? I don't know. What? Well, tell Grampa I said maybe, okay? And, no, I still don't have a cell phone."

Nicholas talked as she finished cooking and cut the cake he'd requested. When she placed the plate before him, he gave her a thumbs-up. "I gotta go, man. Breakfast is ready. Yeah, I'll call you soon and let you know about Christmas, all right. If I don't come for Christmas, tell Gramps I'll come for his birthday in March. Take care. You know I love you."

Since she hadn't sat down, she took the phone and hung it up for him.

"One of your brothers?" she guessed.

He shook his head. "No, my cousin Timothy, the one about the same age as me. I'm closer to him than I am to Nathaniel or Jordan. He served in the Marine Corps, too, and got wounded but not scarred. He was in the sandbox at the same time I was, so we got to meet up a couple of times."

"Why does he call you Saint?"

"It's an old joke from when we were kids, based on my name, Saint Nicholas, Saint Nick like Santa Claus. He used to say I should have an inside edge with Santa since I have the same name," he replied. "Apparently, the family had dinner yesterday at Grampa's house, and some of them asked about me and wished

I was there even though I haven't had Thanksgiving with them in years."

Not since he got injured, she thought.

"Why don't you?"

His expression darkened. "I told you. It's the same old, same old, poor Nicholas attitude. Most of them either stare at me like I'm a freak or don't know what to say to me. Grampa and Timothy are the only ones who treated me the same way they always did. Well, some of the other cousins do, too, at least a little. My dad had nothing to say to me when I did go home after I recovered and left the Corps. He managed to have a lot of errands to run and places to be so he could avoid me."

Too aware of his emotional baggage, she didn't touch his remarks but asked, "How old is your grandfather?"

"He'll be ninety in March. I'd like to see him, some of the others, and Mom. I think there's a party being planned – I might go down for that if you'll go with me for moral support."

Belle would walk to Texas for him if he asked, but she didn't say that. Pleased he thought she'd still be part of his life in a few months, she said, "Sure, I will if you want if I won't be in the way."

"You'd never be in the way, not to me," he said. "And I mean it, Belle. I'll likely go if you will."

"Mark the calendar," she told him, swallowing hard around a knot of unshed tears in her throat. His family probably cared more than he thought, and she suspected he needed his family more than he'd admit. "I'll go. What day in March?

"The 17th, St. Patrick's Day."

The phone rang again, and this time, he answered it.

"Of course, we're up," he said. "What time are you coming over? Oh hell, sure, bring the kid if you want."

"Suzanne?"

"Yeah. She's going to drop Teagan off so she can hit a few Black Friday sales, and she'll be here in about a half hour."

Belle glanced down at her rumpled clothes. "I need to go shower, then."

"Me, too, but you can go first. I'll straighten up the living room and build a new fire."

"Okay, let me go find some clean clothes."

After she gathered a fresh pair of jeans and a Chiefs sweatshirt, Belle headed for the bathroom, where she scrubbed away any lingering aroma of sex. She washed her hair and wrapped it in a towel, then emerged to find a fire blazing in the hearth. While Nicholas cleaned up, she dried her hair and then pulled it back with a clip. She had just finished when Suzanne entered without knocking, Teagan in tow.

"Good morning," she called as she came through the dining room. "Thanks for watching her."

"Never a problem," Nicholas said as the little girl approached for a hug. "Are you sleepy, sweetheart? You look tired."

"She had another stomachache in the night," Suzanne said. "It kept us both up a long time."

"Do you feel better now?" he asked the child, who nodded. "That's good. Did you have breakfast? I actually have fresh milk for a change and cereal."

"She hasn't eaten yet," Suzanne replied. "I brought some coloring books and crayons, a couple of books and her dolly. Belle, you're welcome to join me if you want. I'm heading to Joplin to hit the sales."

"Thanks, I'll pass this time."

Teagan ate a bowl of cereal and a slice of cake, washed

down with more milk. While Belle washed dishes and puttered around the kitchen, Nicholas colored with his niece. One of the coloring books featured Beauty and the Beast, and when he started to color her gown a bright red, Teagan stopped him. "It's yellow, Uncle Beast," she told him. "You know that from the movie."

"I was a Marine, not a fashionista," he answered without heat. "I'm more familiar with desert camo than ball gowns, kid."

Teagan giggled. "Belle doesn't wear red. Her other dress is a blue jumper with a white top."

Then the little girl glanced up at Belle and asked, "Do you have a blue or yellow dress?"

Belle almost dropped her coffee cup. She did have a yellow chiffon formal gown she'd worn as a bridesmaid, then to a few evening events. "I have one that's as yellow as gold."

"Or Mountain Dew," Nicholas added. She noted the teasing light in his eyes and smiled.

"Good," Teagan cried. "You can wear it to dance with Uncle Beast."

Nicholas met Belle's eyes and asked, "Do you dance?"

"I've never tried, not ballroom style."

"Neither have I," he said with a chuckle. "I'd probably step on your feet."

"I might step on yours, but we could try sometime."

"Maybe."

Teagan grinned. "And then when she falls in love with you, you'll be good looking again and live happily ever after."

The enthusiasm in her voice rang loud, but Belle cringed. She watched as the lighthearted expression faded from Nicholas' face. He put down the crayon he held and shoved his chair away from the table, then stomped outside without a word. Teagan stared after him, then looked at Belle.

"Is Uncle Beast mad at me?" she asked in a quavering voice. "I didn't mean to make him mad."

Belle drew a deep breath. "I don't think he's angry, Teagan, but I think his feelings are hurt."

The little girl's lip drooped, and she appeared to be on the verge of tears. "Why?"

"Oh, honey," Belle said. She wasn't used to being around small children and didn't know what to say, but something had to be said. "Nicholas isn't ever going to look the way he did before he got hurt. Do you even remember him then?"

Teagan shook her head as her eyes brimmed full of tears. "Uh-uh, but I saw the old pictures. Mommy has some where he looked pretty."

Oh, good Lord, no wonder he's upset. "He's not ugly now, sweetie, just scarred from being hurt in a war. But he's the same person under the skin, and he loves you a lot."

A stray tear trickled down her cheek. "I wuv him too. He's my Uncle Beast."

Belle reached out and wiped the tear away. "Do you want to know a secret, Teagan?"

The girl nodded.

"I love your uncle very much."

"Even if he's never gonna be handsome?"

"I love him the way he is," Belle said. She accepted him at face value, not expecting or needing anything more. "I know 'Beauty And The Beast' is your favorite, but it's just a fairy tale, a story. It's a good story, but it's not real."

Teagan began crying, the tears pouring down her face, her body shaking with sobs.

"I know," she cried. "But I want Uncle Beast to be good

looking again. That's why I like it so much."

The child's simple words ripped Belle's heart. The innocence of a child's heart and a belief in the impossible would fade, probably today. She opened her arms, and the girl scrambled into them, weeping on Belle's shoulder as sobs wracked her little body. Belle didn't have words, so she held Teagan tight until the tears began to slack.

"Do you think he hates me now?" Teagan asked in a rough whisper.

"No way," Belle said. "He loves you, kiddo."

"Should I go tell him I'm sorry?"

Belle could only imagine how raw Nicholas' emotions must be, and she shook her head. "Maybe in a little bit, but not now. But you know what I think he'd like a lot?"

"What?"

"If maybe you called him Uncle Nicholas."

Teagan gazed at her and then nodded. "Okay, I can do it. Mommy calls him Nick, though, not Nicholas. I can try. But sometimes I might forget."

Nick. To Belle, he was and would always be Nicholas.

"That's fine. Let's go wash your face and maybe see if there's any cartoons on. Or, you could watch your movie."

She knew that among his collection of DVDs, Nicholas had a copy of the Disney film.

"Uh-uh," Teagan said. "I'd rather watch something else, maybe."

Once she'd washed her face with Belle's help, the child settled down to watch older cartoons on Boomerang. She'd calmed down, although Belle had no idea if her words had had any impact on the girl.

"I'm going to finish cleaning up the kitchen," she told her.

Teagan nodded, so Belle left the room.

She had already washed the dishes, and there was nothing more to do. She needed to find Nicholas, she thought, and make sure he was all right.

Belle pulled on an old flannel shirt hanging near the back door and walked outside. At first, she didn't see him, but then she caught a glimpse of his shirt through the trees. With her heart pounding, she walked toward him. He sat in a vintage metal lawn chair on the edge of the woods, head in his hands.

When she reached him, she put her hands on his shoulders. "Hey."

He glanced up, his face ravaged. He'd wept, too, she saw.

"Is she okay?" he asked.

"Teagan's fine. She's watching old cartoons right now."

He huffed a ragged sigh. "I probably shouldn't have run away like that."

"You had every reason."

"I just – well, hell, I don't know how to say it."

"Nicholas, I understand. But like I said, it's just a face and Teagan's only a little girl. She thought fairy tales could come true."

"They can't." His voice was harsh.

"Maybe not like in the stories, but we can still find some happiness in life."

His brief laugh was bitter, not cheerful. "I wish."

"Nicholas, it's true."

He shook his head.

"Maybe I should go back to the house," she told him. "You probably don't want company."

Nicholas reached back and caught her hand in his. "No, don't go."

Then he pulled her forward and onto his lap. He didn't kiss or caress but held her tight. Belle pressed her face against his neck and savored the feel of him. She wanted to tell him what she'd told his niece, that she loved him, but it wasn't the right moment.

After what seemed a long time but was closer to five minutes, he sighed and shuddered.

"What's wrong?"

"Headache," he said. "A bad one."

"And you're freezing, so let's go back to the house. You can get warm and take something for your headache, then maybe lay down or something," she told him as she scooted off his lap. This time, she held her hand out to him, and after a moment, he took it.

"Okay," he said. "Sure, let's go back inside."

Holding hands, they walked back to the old house. In the kitchen, she found some ibuprofen and dosed him. He asked for more coffee, and she poured him a cup. From the living room, Belle could hear Popeye declaring, 'I yam what I yam' and thought Nicholas should adopt the motto.

"Would you feel better if you stretched out on the couch?" she asked.

"Naw," he said. "Probably not, especially with that racket."

He didn't sound mad, though, just sad and resigned.

She stood behind his chair at the table and massaged his neck, then his shoulders. They were rock hard with tension. Her hands worked their magic, and he began to relax. He made small grunts and groans, then finally sighed.

"That helped some," he told her. "I don't want to lay down, but I think I'll go kick back in the recliner for a bit."

He stood, and she faced him, her hand cupping his cheek. "Sure. Can I get anything else for you?"

"You're here," he said. "That's plenty."

Chapter Eight

He'd run out of the house like a chicken-hearted coward, and that shamed him. He'd been a Marine, for Christ's sake, but he'd let the innocent words of a baby girl send him into retreat. Nicholas headed for the woods and considered pounding a tree to release some of the emotion but didn't. It would hurt, and Belle would fuss, he thought, probably rub some salve or some shit on his bruised hands. Nicholas wanted her attention, but at the same time, he didn't. He didn't want her babying or feeling sorry for him. Pity ate at his soul like battery acid at the best of times. From Belle, it would destroy him.

Nicholas retreated to a lawn chair he'd salvaged from the old barn when he bought the place. It sat on the edge of the woods in a pretty spot, one that overlooked a spring that still bubbled up from the ground. Once, it had provided water for the original inhabitants of the house. Before that, he figured Native Americans drank from it too.

He found some measure of comfort in the woods, always

had. The Ozark hardwood forest had a few cedars, unlike the piney woods with tall evergreens stretching toward the sky in his native East Texas, but he liked it just as well. As he breathed in the cold morning air, he calmed, although, after a few minutes, he shivered. He hadn't bothered to grab a jacket on his dash out the door.

Teagan's words had wounded him, and he realized he shouldn't have let them. Out of her fascination with the story, she'd spoken what she must believe – that if Belle loved him the way the other Belle came to love the hairy, ugly beast, then he would be transformed back into a handsome man. Teagan likely believed it, and Nicholas wished it was true. He knew better, though, remembering an adage Grampa Reilly was fond of sharing – wish in one hand and shit in the other and see which hand gets full first. The shit always wins, the old man would say. In Nicholas' world, it certainly had.

It wasn't just the kid's notion he could be good-looking again. The idea that Belle might fall in love with him appealed. He wanted it so much he could almost taste it, something sweet like cotton candy in his mouth. The possibility that she couldn't find it in her heart to love a scarred, bitter, fucked up Marine terrified him, but Nicholas expected that would be the reality. He'd run as much because of that fear as anything else. His feelings for her were strong, and he suspected he loved her, even if it would never be returned.

Guilt gnawed at him for his response to Teagan. He loved that kid and wouldn't hurt her, but he probably had. He imagined her crying at the kitchen table, tossing crayons in a tantrum, or suffering another tummy ache. If she did, the fault lay at his doorstep, and he knew it. Although he thought he'd already shed all the tears he had in him, he had cried a little, ashamed at his action, dismayed he'd probably upset his niece and Belle.

The old demons that whispered to him about ending his life had been absent for a long time, but now, they were back, their voices so low they were almost non-existent, but not quite. If it hadn't been for Belle in his life, Nicholas might have listened to them. Instead, he tuned them out, mumbling hymns he thought he'd forgotten long ago.

A dull ache in the center of his forehead spread and intensified until his head pounded so much he thought it might split open. Nicholas likened the pain to a winch wrapped tight about his head as it became rigid. He put his head down in his hands and sat, hoping the pain would pass.

At first, he had half-expected Belle to follow him, but when she didn't, he figured she wouldn't. Under normal circumstances, he stayed tuned to his surroundings and didn't miss anything, but Nicholas didn't realize she'd come until her hands touched his shoulders.

"Is she okay?"

He released a slow breath when he heard Teagan was watching cartoons, then pulled Belle onto his lap. He folded his arms around her and cuddled her against his chest, enjoying her warmth and the fresh scent of her shampoo. Holding her anchored him and brought him from the darkest depths of his emotions. The pain in his head grew, and he shivered from the cold.

"What's wrong?"

Nicholas would have ignored anyone else, but he admitted to having a bad headache. Belle took his hand, and together they walked back to the house. He downed some ibuprofen and drank coffee. From the living room, he could hear the distinctive music of Popeye The Sailor Man. The shriller notes cut through his head like a well-honed blade, and when Belle suggested the couch, he shook his head. He failed to realize just how tense he'd become or how tight his muscles were until she began massaging his neck and shoulders. Her hands were a gift from heaven, he thought, as she kneaded and rubbed his rock-hard muscles until they eased. As he relaxed, the pain receded to a tolerable level.

Nicholas stood to head for his worn recliner, and Belle put her hand against his cheek. The small, tender motion affected him, and he covered her hand with his own.

"Can I get you anything else?" Belle asked.

"You're here," he replied. That topped anything else she might bring him or a gesture she could make. "You're here, and that's plenty."

He eased into the chair and kicked the footrest back. Belle curled up on the corner of the adjacent couch, and he took her hand in his. Just as he was about to close his eyes, Teagan abandoned her cartoons to approach him. She wore a sad expression. Her bottom lip jutted out, and he thought there were tears in her eyes.

"I'm sorry, Uncle Nick," she told him in a voice just above a whisper.

"So am I, baby girl." He patted his lap, and she climbed into it, sucking her thumb, an old habit he'd thought she had outgrown. Teagan stretched her legs out across his lap and leaned against his right shoulder. "What did you just call me?"

"Uncle Nick."

"Why?"

"'Cause you're not really a beast."

He thought he'd heard wrong at first, but when he accepted what she had said, his heavy heart lightened. Tears leaked from his eyes with an odd combination of joy and release. Nicholas snuggled his niece close as they watched a few more cartoons before he drifted to sleep.

He didn't wake when Teagan eased out of his lap, but he roused at the sound of his sister's voice.

"Nick's not sick or anything, is he?"

"No, he had a headache earlier, but he's fine, just sleeping."

His sister's tone was concerned. "He doesn't usually sleep in the daytime, so I wondered. And what happened while I was shopping?"

Nicholas feigned sleep, eavesdropping. Her perception didn't surprise him – Suzanne had always had the knack, but he waited to see how Belle would respond.

"We fed Teagan breakfast, she and Nicholas colored, then she watched old cartoons," Belle told his sister.

From her mild tone, he could almost believe there had been nothing else, but Suzanne wasn't accepting it.

"You said Nick had a headache."

He opened his eyes a slit so he could see his sister's fierce expression and watched as Belle nodded.

"I did. It's part of his PTSD."

"I know that – how do you know that?"

"He told me."

"It happens more often when he's stressed out, so what happened? Did you have a fight?"

He'd listened long enough and prepared to sit up to explain when Teagan turned off the television and approached her mother. "It was me," the little girl said. "I upset Uncle Nicholas."

He opened his eyes, but no one noticed, focused on the dramatic conversation.

Suzanne crossed her arms and glared. "Whoa, missy. *Uncle Nicholas?* You've never called him that, not since you watched that movie. And what could you do that would make your uncle mad?"

It was time to speak up.

"I wasn't mad, Suze," Nicholas said as he put down the footrest and stood up. "We were coloring in one of her Beauty and the Beast coloring books, and she said something about how I'd be good-looking again someday. It's a sore spot for me, and you damn well know it."

"He ran outside," Teagan added. "But Belle helped me see he's not a beast and that calling him that might hurt his feelings."

His sister stared at them, then sat down hard on the couch. Her angry expression faded, and she shook her head. "Oh, Nick. I'm sorry for jumping to conclusions, but…."

"You worry," he interrupted. "I know. But you tiptoe around the reality that I'm scarred. That's not going to change. I'm starting to deal with it, and that's because Belle sees me, not the scars, not the ugly mug, but the person underneath it. I'm trying to see myself through her eyes. It's not easy, but for fuck's sake, I'm trying."

Belle came to his side and reached for his hand. Her silent support meant much to him. In front of his sister and niece, not caring what either might think, he pulled her into his arms and kissed her, slow and sweet. When she put her arms around his neck and returned the kiss, he thought he might explode with joy. He caught a glimpse of his sister's expression and laughed inwardly at the shock reflected there.

"Do you feel better?" Belle asked, after the kiss.

"Yeah, headache's gone," he told her. "And I'm hungry. Did I nap through lunch?"

She shrugged. "We haven't eaten yet. I can go fix something. I know there's leftovers."

Nicholas didn't care much for leftovers and parted his lips to say so when Teagan pulled at his shirt. "Uncle Nick, I'm hungry too."

"How about a turkey sandwich?" Belle asked. "Or grilled cheese?"

"I want a hamburger," the child said. "Can we go to McDonald's, Uncle Nick?"

He hadn't set foot inside a fast-food restaurant since he got out of the hospital. Sometimes, he used the drive-through. Suzanne was aware, and she said, "Tea, you like grilled cheese."

"But I want a burger."

"Honey, I don't think your uncle wants to go all the way to town...."

"It's a good idea," Nicholas said, surprising himself. "Kid, does it have to be Mickey D's?"

Teagan possessed some of the same stubbornness he did and nodded. "I want a Happy Meal."

"Then let's go get one," he said. He put on a coat and picked up his keys. "It'll be crowded if we all ride in the truck. Suzanne, do you want to meet us there?"

"I can, I guess," his sister replied. "But it's gonna be a hassle, going through the drive-through in two cars. And where will we eat? Did you want to bring the food back here or go to the park or what?"

"I'm planning to eat inside the place," Nicholas said. Belle beamed at him, and his sister's mouth dropped open.

"You want to sit at a table and all that?"

"Well, yeah, I do." He would do it for the kid. She deserved that and more after his performance earlier. And he wanted to do it for Belle, to demonstrate he was listening. Sure, he'd wear a hood and sit in the least busy area, but Nicholas was determined to try it.

Belle, with purse in hand, kissed his cheek. "Way to go."

"Are you sure about this?" Suzanne asked.

"One hundred percent, yeah."

"All right."

"Can I ride with you, Uncle Nicholas?"

"If it's okay with your mom."

His sister nodded. "Meet you there."

At the restaurant, Nicholas lifted his niece down from the truck. He and Belle held Teagan's hands as they walked inside, where Suzanne waited. They gathered around one of the self-ordering kiosks, something new to Nicholas since he hadn't come inside in years. Once their order was in, he picked up a number and headed for a table. Belle slid in beside him, and the others sat across the table.

His chest hurt from stress, and he sweated beneath his coat. Being in public made him tense, and he fought against the notion everyone stared at him. He drew a deep breath and glanced around. Nicholas saw diners of all ages, sipping coffee, drinking through straws, eating a burger, or munching fries. He didn't see anyone focused on him. No one seemed to notice, and his tension eased a little. Belle laid her hand on his knee. "Relax."

"I'm tryin'," he muttered.

"You did okay at that café the other day."

"I sat facing away from everyone else."

"No one's looking now."

"So far."

Maybe this hadn't been a great idea after all, he thought. Teagan chattered, all smiles as she glanced around the place. Nicholas sighed, trying to find calm in his emotional disturbance. A server delivered two trays to the table. The teenager announced,

"Here you go," as she picked up the number. "Can I bring you anything else?"

"We're good, thanks," Belle said.

The employee nodded and caught sight of Nicholas' face within the hood. Although she didn't say a word, her expression changed, and he caught it. The desire to run rose, and he swung one leg out of the seat, ready to go.

"Don't," Belle said, her voice almost a whisper. "You got this, Nicholas."

"I thought so, but no, I don't."

"You do. You can. I'm here. Your sister and Teagan are here. Breathe."

He drew a long breath, held and released it, then took another. His heart pounded like a drum in a marching band, and a wave of dizziness made his head swirl. When Belle offered her hand, he grabbed it as a lifeline. His sister put down her sandwich, and her eyes widened.

"Nick, what's wrong?"

He reached for his soda and then stopped. His hands trembled too much to pick it up. "Nothing," he told her through clenched teeth.

His surroundings overwhelmed him. The food aromas seemed to surround him in a heavy cloud. Sounds that included kids laughing, adults talking, and traffic sounds from the busy road outside amplified so much that his ears rang. His stomach clenched tighter than a fist.

"Nicholas," Belle said, and he focused on her voice. As he did, the other noise receded to a bearable level. "You're safe. I'm here. We're all here. Think of somewhere where you're happy. Think about that waterfall we went to last night. Breathe deep and close your eyes. Imagine that tinkling, rushing sound of the water. Remember how the rocks looked under the stars."

She kept talking, and he listened, shivering with a sudden chill. Nicholas centered his thoughts, remembering the falls. He envisioned the ocean stretching out calm and blue. Then he thought about the pine forests back home in East Texas until he could almost smell the fresh, sharp evergreen scent. As he began to calm, his symptoms eased one by one until he sat in the crowded restaurant and opened his eyes.

Belle remained beside him and offered him a smile. "You're back."

Nicholas released a long sigh. "I guess I am."

The panic attack had seemed to last hours, but it must have been minutes. Across the table, his sister gave him a thumbs-up, but Teagan didn't seem aware of his episode. She played with the toy from her meal as she finished her fries. As if she felt his gaze, she looked up with a grin.

"Can I have a sundae, Uncle Nick?"

He didn't have to force a smile. "Sure, kid. Just let me finish lunch, and then I'll go get you one, okay?"

She nodded. Belle leaned in close. "Are you going to be able to eat?"

"I think so," he said, taking a bite of the burger. It wasn't hot, but it wasn't cold either. The beef paired with cheese tasted good in his mouth. His belly had eased, and the food went down well. He ate part of the burger, half the fries and sipped at his soda. When he'd eaten all he could manage, he pulled out his wallet and started for the counter.

"I can go order her sundae if you want," Belle told him.

Nicholas shook his head. "I'll do it."

"Then I'll go with you, keep you company."

He figured he had to do it, or he might never be able to

do something as simple as order food face-to-face again. On the way there, his hood slipped down, revealing his face. He started to freak out, then didn't. He ordered two hot fudge sundaes, a butterscotch sundae, and a chocolate shake for himself. If the employee at the counter noticed his ruined face, he didn't react, and as he carried the tray back to the table, Nicholas felt as if he'd climbed a mountain to the top. The victory, small to anyone else, was huge for him.

After they finished dessert, Suzanne announced she planned to take Teagan home.

"She's tired, and I need to clean the house before Marshall gets home tomorrow," she said. "Plus, I promised Teagan we'd put up the tree, although we won't decorate it until Daddy gets home."

"Come help us, Uncle Nick," Teagan said, wrapping her arms around his legs.

He picked her up the way he used to when she was a toddler and whirled her around. "Not this time, kid," he told her. "That's something you and your mom can handle. Let me know when it's decorated, though, and I'll come see it."

"And Belle?"

"And me," she said.

Suzanne retrieved her daughter and hugged Nicholas. "Thanks," she said.

"For what?"

"Watching Tea, buying lunch, all of it."

"*De nada,*"

He wrapped an arm around Belle, and they walked out to his truck. Once they'd climbed into the cab, she turned to him, "What would you like to do now?"

Nicholas longed to sleep for a hundred years, deep and

without dreams. He yearned to dangle his feet at the end of a pier overlooking the ocean so he could gaze out over the seemingly endless water and sky. Though impossible, he'd like to turn back time so he wouldn't be injured and burned. He ached to trade his solitary life for a wife and family, a thought he hadn't entertained in years. Since none of those seemed within his reach, he told her the truth.

"I'm ready to go home," he said. "I'm tired, and I've had enough town for now."

"Sounds good," Belle replied. "Unless you want leftovers, we need to stop at a store somewhere. What would you like for supper?"

No one had asked him that question for so long Nicholas almost didn't answer.

"Meatloaf," he said. "Homemade meatloaf with brown gravy, real mashed 'taters, corn, and biscuits. That's my favorite meal."

Or it had been, he thought. Growing up, it was what he requested on birthdays. If he stayed over with his Reilly grandparents, that's what Granny fixed. Last time he had it, his mom made it when he came home after the hospital, but he hadn't enjoyed it much. He'd been too self-conscious and in a dark place. Food hadn't held any interest, and when he ate, nothing tasted the way it should.

She smiled. "I do an awesome meatloaf. Do we need to stop at that supermarket near the diner?"

Nicholas started the truck and shook his head. "I know a small market with better meat. You can get whatever you need there."

He waited for her in the truck while she went into the store, marveling that she wanted to cook a meal for him. Sure, she'd thrown together passable chicken and noodles using cans and packages, but if she could make good meatloaf, Belle would be a keeper.

But he knew she already had a place in his heart.

Chapter Nine

As soon as they reached his house, Nicholas settled into his recliner and fell asleep, drained from the day in town. Belle tossed a cover over him and stirred up the fire enough to add a log. It had turned sharply cold, and the room was chilly. She unpacked the groceries he'd carried inside and made a meatloaf using a recipe in her head. As she worked breadcrumbs, eggs, and a variety of seasoning into the meat, Belle realized what had been niggling at her brain all day – she needed to file an insurance claim on her car.

Between meeting her birth family, Nicholas, Thanksgiving, and the day's events, she hadn't yet and sighed. At some point, as much as she loved playing house with Nicholas, she had to find another vehicle and decide whether to return to Kansas City. Belle knew she didn't want to go back. There wasn't much there, just a handful of fair-weather friends and no family. Her tiny apartment, one of many within a huge older building near the Power and Light District, had been a place to eat, sleep and exist more than it had ever been a home. This old rambling farmhouse could use a few homey touches, but she liked it and wanted to stay. That depended on Nicholas, though, on if he wanted her to remain and if they had a future.

Her suitcase was upstairs in Nicholas' bedroom, and so was her laptop bag. Resolved to bring it down later, Belle finished the meatloaf, molding it into a long, rounded shape. Then she made biscuits with flour, shortening, baking powder, milk, and salt. She could have bought a box of baking mix, but she'd decided to go old school and make the biscuits from scratch. Once they were mixed, kneaded, and cut out using a glass since she couldn't locate a biscuit cutter. Belle placed them on a baking sheet and began peeling potatoes. As the afternoon passed, the kitchen filled with delightful aromas, and by the time the biscuits were in the oven and the shoe peg corn heating on the stove, Nicholas woke.

"Smells good," he said as he entered. "I'm hungry. When do we eat?"

Since he'd left most of his lunch, Belle imagined he was starving.

"About fifteen minutes," she said, gauging when the biscuits would be done. The meatloaf sat on a platter, ready to slice and gravy from a packaged mix bubbled in the pan. "And I need to mash the potatoes."

"Awesome," he said. "Is there any coffee made?"

"I can make some."

"Thanks."

He sat at the table while she did the final preparations. She brought a platter with the sliced meatloaf, a full gravy boat, a pan of mashed potatoes, a bowl of corn and a plate with the biscuits along with the butter and sat down. Nicholas stretched out his right hand, and she took it, then surprised her when he bowed his head.

"Bless us, o Lord, and these Thy gifts, which we are about to receive from the bounty of Christ our Lord, amen."

Belle spoke the familiar words with him, then said, "I didn't know you're Catholic."

His misshapen lips twisted into a grin. "Well, you didn't ask. With a name like Reilly, what else did you think I'd be?"

"I didn't really think about it, one way or another."

"Since you know the blessing, I'm guessing you are, too."

She shrugged. "I am. I haven't been going to church much lately. To be honest, I've been more than a little pissed off at God since my parents drowned."

"Understandable. I was angry when I got hurt and angrier when I realized I would look like this for the rest of my life."

"Are you still mad?"

He shook his head. "Sometimes, but not as often. I do go to Mass on occasion, although I sit in the back and hope no one really notices me. I haven't been for a few months, though."

"I'd go with you if you wanted."

Nicholas nodded his head a little and said, "Maybe. Let's eat."

She wondered if he would freak out in church the way he had in McDonald's but doubted it. It was a different place, one where she'd always found a sense of peace and calm. *After all, it's called a sanctuary for a reason.*

Because he did, Belle focused on the food. While he ate with an obvious appetite, she tasted it as the cook, deciding she'd done well with the meatloaf. Mashed potatoes and biscuits were easy. She'd been baking homemade biscuits since she was ten, and the corn was frozen. Nicholas cleaned his plate and then sighed.

"Granny Reilly always made the best meatloaf," he said. "But yours tops hers, Belle. It was fantastic. Thank you."

A warm glow centered in her chest at the compliment. "You're welcome," she said. "I have a few talents, writing, photography, and cooking. Beyond that, I'm not good at much."

"I don't agree," Nicholas replied. "You're good with me, and that's one hell of a skill. Most people aren't."

"It's not hard."

His laugh had a bitter note. "It must be. I don't know why you bother, but I'm glad you do."

Belle had no answer for that, not one that wouldn't sound facetious, so she reached for his hand instead. He took it. His palm was warm and smooth against hers despite the scarring on the back of each hand. Then he bent down and kissed her hand. The simple gesture touched her. She'd only known him a few days, but it seemed as if she'd always known him.

"Let me clear the kitchen," she told Nicholas. "Then we can find something to do."

She hoped they would make love. Belle adored the way he caressed her, his hands both sure and demanding. His touch kindled a fire hotter than she'd ever known, and his urgency fired hers. No matter how hungrily he took her, tenderness remained, and she savored that.

He nodded. "I'll stoke the fire."

Belle hung the dish towel to dry on the oven handle and squirted a dollop of hand lotion into her hands, then rubbed them together. As she headed toward the living room, she heard the first twang of an off-key guitar string and paused to listen. She'd seen an old guitar propped in the corner, but it had been dust-covered, and she hadn't thought any more about it.

Nicholas sat on the couch, the guitar across his lap, his left-hand chording on the frets while he strummed with the right. His head was cocked as he tuned the strings, then as she took a seat in one of the recliners, he began to sing a simple song, "I'm A Fishing Man."

At first, his voice was hesitant, and the chords were slow, but as he sang, Nicholas became more confident, and he sang the tune well. It wasn't a song Belle knew, but she liked the easy rhythm and the lyrics. Although she knew he was aware she'd joined him, he segued into another song, "That Gosh Darned Wheel," and then into a Western ballad, "The Streets of Dodge." After that, he paused, took a long drink from the coffee cup he'd carried along and smiled at her.

"I'm out of practice," he told her. "It's been a long time."

"You sounded amazing to me. I didn't know any of those songs, though. Are they yours?"

Nicholas laughed. "I wish – I used to write a few songs, but not for a long time. No, those are all songs Johnny Horton recorded. Most people know him for "Battle of New Orleans" or "North To Alaska," but I like the less famous songs. Some were just done as demos."

Belle nodded. She remembered a few Horton songs. "He died young, didn't he? A long time ago?"

"He did, in his thirties, but he grew up in Rusk, the same as I did. His parents and at least one of his sisters are buried there," he answered. "I always felt a bit of kinship with him, and I've always loved his music."

"I have eclectic music tastes," she told him. "I like almost everything."

"That's good," Nicholas replied. "I can sing some other songs if you want. In the sandbox, a lot of the jarheads were more into heavy rock and made fun of my preference for old-school country, but I didn't care. I like what I like."

"I didn't realize you played guitar."

His laugh had a bitter note. "I haven't for a long time. At first, I wasn't sure my fingers had the dexterity to play, but apparently, they do."

"I would say they do. You sound pretty good."

"I doubt I'll be on the stage at the Ryman any time soon or getting a Grammy, but thanks. Do you play or sing?"

Belle did, but not for anyone to hear. "I play very basic piano," she admitted. "I love to sing along to music but not in front of anyone."

"Why not?"

She shrugged. "I'm too afraid they'll think I sound bad, I guess."

"You'll have to sing along and see."

"I don't know the words to any of the songs you sang."

"Is that so?" The twinkle in his eyes indicated he was teasing. "Well, I want to sing you one more of Johnny's songs, then I'll play something else, maybe a song you will know. I've been thinking about this one for quite a while now, and the refrain matters to me. I don't think it's what Claude King had in mind when he wrote it for Horton, but you're the first person I've met who does."

"Does what? And who's Claude King? That sounds familiar."

"If you know any of his music, you probably know "Wolverton Mountain," he said and sang a few lines.

"I do," she said. "My grandpa used to sing that old tune."

"King and Horton were good friends," he said. "Take a listen and see if you know why I like this one so much."

Belle settled down on the floor near his feet and listened. At first, the song seemed like just another upbeat rockabilly tune from the 1950s, with mostly G and C chords with an occasional F, then she caught it the second time she heard the refrain. Tears formed, but she struggled not to shed them, afraid Nicholas might take them as a mark of pity, which they weren't.

"'I can be like a tiger or as meek as a lamb,'" she quoted when he finished, his eyes intent on her face. "'If you want to get along with me, you'll take me like I am.'"

Nicholas nodded. "And you do, babe. You take me like I am. I can't tell you what that means to me. I don't think anyone has, not really, since, well, since everything happened. Thinking about this song is what inspired me to pick up the damn guitar tonight."

"I'm glad it did," she said, her voice husky with unshed tears. "I don't remember this song at all, though."

"It wasn't ever issued on a record, just on a special boxed set that came out a few years back with songs from Horton's early years," he said. "Some of his best work, I think, is there, in the demos and never released music."

He laid the guitar down on the couch beside him. "I'm still fucked up. I probably always will be, a little, but with you, it's better. You bring some light into the darkness of my life. You don't look away from me – you look right at me. You see me, girl, and that cuts some ice. It makes one helluva difference."

The tears she'd held back flowed down her cheeks, and when he saw them, Nicholas stood.

"Don't," he said, his tone hoarse. "I don't know that I'm worth your tears. And if you're crying because you're sorry for me...."

"I'm not. Nicholas, I'm crying because your words, oh,

God, they move me."

He pulled her into his arms and kissed her, hot, hard and fast. His mouth fastened onto hers with such heat Belle nearly melted. Her hands clung to his shirt as a wave of dizzy, potent desire swept through her. Although he was more than a little rough, his kiss was cherished and caressed even as it kindled a fever that threatened to consume them both.

His fingers, which had moved with skill over the frets and strings of the guitar, touched her with the same finesse, playing a very different music across her skin. Her body sang an answer as he stroked her, then lifted her off her feet into his arms. Nicholas continued kissing her as he carried her through the house and up the stairs into his bedroom. Belle's arms locked around his neck, and once he set her down, he removed her top and bra with one fluid motion that bared her breasts. His mouth strayed from hers to kiss her throat, then sank down to her breasts.

Tit for tat, she stripped off his shirt, and if it bothered him that it revealed his scars, he didn't show it. Belle stroked his chest, both the undamaged areas and the scars, then dropped to her knees to give him head. His cock jutted out from his curly hairs, already hard as bone. She took it into her mouth as he gave her space and sucked. His legs trembled as she did, and he moaned. At the exact right moment, she removed her mouth and rose from a crouch. Nicholas pushed her back onto the bed and thrust his dick into her. She was ready, her hot box pulsing and aching for release as he filled her tight. Luscious sensations rolled out in waves over her in a tide that began between her legs.

He moved within her, thrusting and riding her with no little skill. Belle clenched tight to use her body to caress his rigid stick. As he took her, Nicholas managed to deliver a few fast kisses on her mouth, her tits, and her belly. He laved her nipples with his tongue as if they were twin ice cream cones, and he savored the flavor.

Belle's hands clutched him, and her fingers raked the smooth skin of his back. When he was close enough, she used her teeth to nibble at him. She teased his lips when he kissed her, the intimate taste of him in her mouth fueling her desire.

The thrill became urgent, and the need intense until she moaned beneath him, holding his body tight against hers with her legs, needing release. When it came, it was an explosion, a blast that detonated them both into a wild, crazy spiral of delight. Every bit of her body sang with delight, and she reveled in the delectable moment, mind empty of all else but this moment and the man who brought her home.

They cuddled, Belle with a deep bliss she savored until they both fell asleep. At some point, one of them managed to pull the covers over their nude bodies, and she woke, her skin warm against his. Sunshine filtered through the half-open curtains, and the sound of dripping water had her sit up straight. It was either raining or the ice was melting. Either way, temperatures must be warmer.

Nicholas pulled her down with one arm. God, but he was strong, she thought, recalling how he'd carried her up the stairs last night. "Lay back down, woman. Let's sleep a little longer."

"I hardly ever sleep late." Belle had always been an early riser. "Don't Marines get up early to reveille?"

"They do, but too damn early, and in case you haven't noticed, I'm not a Marine anymore. There have been days I don't drag out of bed until noon. I'm tired for some reason, Belle."

She laughed, the sound muffled against him as he cradled her close. "All right, you win, no trumpets."

"It's not like we have anything to do or anywhere to go,"

he mumbled in a drowsy voice.

It wasn't long until he snored, soft and low, but Belle lay awake. She needed to file the insurance claim on her car, and she'd planned to do that today. Sometime soon, she should make the trip back to the KC area to get more of her belongings. She had to decide if she would stay in southern Missouri. If she did, she had to be sure Nicholas wanted her in his life. No point in paying rent on her tiny apartment or letting the utility bills automatically come out of the bank. If she remained here, she could get to know Ethel, her grandmother, better and see where this fast, crazy relationship with Nicholas might lead.

I want to stay. I love him. I don't want to leave, but I know it's crazy. I've known him not quite a week, and he's got issues, a ton of them. But I have little to go back to and so much to stay here for.

Her decision was made. She planned to stay and see what happened, whatever that might be. Belle dozed on and off for a few more hours, then untangled from Nicholas and headed downstairs. She retrieved the last clean pair of panties from her suitcase and started a load in his washer after she showered. Then, hair pulled back into a ponytail, she settled in at the dining room table with her laptop. By the time Nicholas came down, she'd filed the insurance claim on her car, called her landlord to give notice, and talked to Ethel on the phone. Her grandmother had invited them both over to Sunday dinner, and Belle accepted. This time, it would be just Ethel, no pack of family to deal with.

Nicholas came down around three, wearing a pair of wash faded and well-stretched gray sweatpants and a t-shirt. He moved with stealth. She never heard his footsteps and didn't realize he was there until he kissed the back of her neck.

"I wondered where you were."

"Right here, taking care of business."

"I thought you might have taken off."

His casual tone didn't fool her – he'd been worried. Having made up her mind, she decided to go for broke. "Not me. Nicholas, did you mean it when you said I could stay as long as I want?"

"Yeah." His lips stilled in mid-kiss, and he stepped back. "I don't say things unless I mean them, Belle. Why?"

It was now or never. "I thought I'd stay."

When he said nothing, she thought maybe she'd made the wrong choice after all. Nicholas moved so that he stood across the table. The expression on his scarred face was hard to read, but his eyes were bright. "I'd like that. How long were you thinking?"

"I called to give notice on my apartment earlier," she told him, turning toward Nicholas. "I thought I'd stay, well, as long as you'll have me."

The once stalwart Marine stood straight as if at attention. He said nothing for a few very long moments, and if she hadn't seen the way he clenched the back of the chair with his hands so hard his fingers turned white, Belle might have thought he had no reaction. When he spoke, his voice trembled just a little.

"I'm glad. I'll do my damnedest not to run you off. Is there coffee? I could use some."

"In the kitchen."

She followed him out and watched him pour a cup, then reach into the cupboard for a bottle of Jack Daniels. He added a generous splash to his cup. Belle bit her lip but said nothing – until now, she'd never seen him drink any alcohol.

"It's long past noon," he said as if he read her thoughts. "Don't worry, Belle, I'm not planning to get drunk, and I seldom drink. I slept hard, and I could use the kick to get started. Not changing your mind, are you?"

"No." She wasn't and wouldn't, but she now realized that maybe this would be a much greater adjustment than she anticipated and that perhaps she didn't know Nicholas quite as well as she thought.

She loved him, though, and she hoped that would be enough.

Chapter Ten

A long time ago, he'd wanted a lot of things. In high school, he had wanted a decent car, something sporty that would go fast, be the envy of his peers and attract girls. Nicholas had worked long and hard at a local tire shop until he had saved enough to buy a 1968 vintage GTO. The two-door model had been a deep olive green and had run with speed. He had joked he could keep up with roadrunners in it, and he had, more than once, outrun the cops. Then he wanted to serve his country, so he joined the Marines. He planned a career where he would succeed and prosper. Later, he'd just wanted to survive – and had but at a greater cost than he could have ever imagined. Once, he'd wanted to find a woman who would share his heart and life, who would give him children, and who he would grow old with, fussing, fighting, fucking, and loving. Once upon a time, he'd hoped to be, if not wealthy, at least financially comfortable. But, when his luck ran out, and he got both burned and shot in an ambush in Helmand Province, Nicholas hadn't wanted much of anything. Oh, he'd wished his face wasn't scarred and horrible, but there was no changing it, so he stopped wanting and started surviving.

It had been easier to know what he didn't want. When he couldn't stand the pity and emotional stew his family provided, he left Rusk, a place where he had planned to live out his life and came to Missouri. Nicholas hadn't really chosen the Show-Me State. He relocated because his sister was there. When he bought his place, the one he'd called "Beast's Lair," he liked it well enough, but if he hadn't got it, there were two or three others he had considered. Any of them would have served as well. He wore what he had or what basics were simple to obtain. He ate what food was available and didn't really have much preference. That he'd told Belle he liked cake over pie or requested meatloaf had been major milestones, but he hadn't marked them as such until she said she planned to stay.

Nicholas had wanted that more than he'd yearned for anything in years, but he'd been afraid to admit it. He wasn't used to wishing for things because he had no expectation of receiving any. When he first found Belle's car slid off in a ditch, he'd cussed, but he had checked to see if anyone was inside. He brought her home out of duty. He still had a heart under his disfigurement and wasn't going to let anyone freeze to death. If she'd been ugly, old, or a man, he would've done the same.

When it turned out that she was pretty, he figured she would reject him the way almost every woman had done since Afghanistan. She didn't, though, and seemed to see him, the man under the scarring and the PTSD and beyond all the bullshit. Belle treated him as if there wasn't anything different about him, so much that he forgot, for brief snatches, that there was.

He thought desire had died in him, but this woman revived it, and he'd taken her more than once. She'd gloried in it and gave back as much as he took, if not more.

Nicholas wanted her to stay, and she said she was. His emotions were a bubbling stew that included joy, but it was also seasoned with more than a little fear. That's why he dumped a little bourbon into his coffee. Booze had been his crutch in the early days after he got out of the hospital, but he'd weaned himself from it. He didn't want to be dependent on anything, but today he required momentary aid. He needed Belle, and that scared the holy hell out of him. She was staying, but if she ever left, the devastation would probably kill him.

The worried glance she sent his way when he added some Jack to his cup prompted him to explain. Although she said nothing, he noticed that when he drank a second cup of coffee with nothing but sugar, her shoulders relaxed, and she offered him a smile. The small jolt of whiskey had steadied his nerves enough to ask, "Do we need to plan a trip north?"

Belle sipped coffee. "We do. I don't know when you want to go."

"Tomorrow?"

She laughed. "Ethel called and invited us both to Sunday dinner, so I said we'd come. There won't be any other guests this time, and she said she's having turkey and noodles."

"Okay. What's the weather look like for Monday?"

"Sunny and warmer, like today."

"We can go then if that's fine with you."

She fiddled with her empty mug as she scribbled what appeared to be a list. Something about the way she dabbled made him curious.

"What is it?"

Her look was all innocence. "What?"

"You're fretting about something, so tell me."

Belle sighed. "It's just I want to be sure you're ready for this trip, that it won't be too much of an aggravation."

He loved her for considering it but hated that she did. "I made it through eating at Mickey D's."

Her smile widened. "Yes, you did. And Thanksgiving with the masses."

"And it's not like we're planning to go to malls or Arrowhead Stadium or someplace with a bunch of people, is it?"

"No, just mostly my apartment so I can pack and figure out what to do with the stuff I won't take. We'll probably eat out – I did promise you Winstead's."

"You did, and I'm up for it, Belle. You helped me at McDonald's. You'll be there if I need it, right?"

"Of course."

"Then I'm as ready as I'll be. I can't promise I might not freak out a little, but I'm game to go, Belle. I need to quit holing up like a bear in my cave."

Nicholas hadn't realized how much he'd been hibernating from the world until she came. He did, now, and if he didn't change, he would spend his life alone. He didn't want that – if he hadn't figured it out before, he knew now.

True to her word, Ethel had no other guests. She served homemade turkey and noodles along with bread she'd baked and a banana cream pie. Nicholas left both his ski mask and hooded jacket at home. Like her granddaughter, Ethel didn't appear to be repulsed by his appearance. When she heard Belle planned to relocate, her delight had been obvious.

"Oh, my word! That's wonderful. I can get to know you," the old woman said. "It near broke my heart when you were adopted, but there wasn't a thing I could do about it. Your mama's people insisted it was for the best. I would've taken you if I could, but your grandpa was so sick at the time. He had cancer, you know."

Nicholas didn't, and it seemed neither did Belle. He didn't need to know the back story, but he felt Belle did. He had heavy baggage and knew it, but he suspected his lady had a bit of her own to manage.

That evening, Belle packed her smallest bag for the trip and asked Nicholas if he wanted to put his things in with hers.

"There's room," she said.

"How long are you planning to stay?"

"Probably one night, two at the most."

He dug a change of underwear, a clean pair of jeans and two t-shirts out from his dresser and handed them over. "I need to let my sister know we'll be gone, or she'll flip out."

"Will she really?"

"She'd probably call the sheriff for a well-being check," Nicholas replied. He was serious and added, "She's done it before, Belle."

Belle nodded, so he made the call.

Teagan answered the phone, squealing with delight when she heard his voice.

"Uncle Nicholas, we put up the tree!" she exclaimed. "And the lights and the ornaments and hung our stockings up. And there's already a few presents too."

"That's awesome, kiddo."

"Come over and see it!"

"Will do, but first I need to make a short trip with Belle, then we'll come. Is your mama handy?"

"Hi, Nick." His sister sounded happy. "What's up?"

"I'm taking Belle up to Kansas City to get more of her stuff," he said. "We're heading out early tomorrow, and we'll be back by Wednesday at the latest. I figured I'd better let you know before you call out a SWAT team or something."

"I wouldn't." They both knew she might. "So, she's going to stay awhile, then?"

"She's coming back to stay for good."

Suzanne should have known what that meant to him, but she didn't act thrilled.

"Are you happy about it?"

"Very."

"Just don't move too fast, you hear? You barely know this woman."

He laughed out loud, a deep old-fashioned belly laugh. He'd known Belle for less than a week, but he knew she belonged in his life. He wanted her there, and he'd do whatever it took to keep her with him. If anyone else, like Timothy, did the same, Nicholas would probably have tried to talk him out of it, but this was his life, and for once, he didn't question it. Fast? They were already at warp speed. "I won't."

"Nick?"

"Yeah?"

"Are you going to be fine to go to KC?"

"Suzanne, I will be. I managed to take y'all to McDonald's, didn't I?"

"Yes, but you had a few rough moments...."

"And Belle was there to keep me grounded. Did Marshall get back?"

"Yes, he did." Judging from the relief in her voice, Suzanne welcomed the subject change as much as he did. "We got the tree up and decorated. He'll be here most of the week, doesn't leave until Friday."

"Good."

"Stay in touch, will you? Then I won't worry so much. I wish you'd get a cell phone."

"I don't need one. You have Belle's number, don't you?"

"She gave it to me, yes."

"I'll use it to call – and hey, take care of the brat."

They left before daybreak on Monday and arrived at her apartment long before noon. The trip took around two and a half hours, but they hit the outskirts of the urban area early enough to deal with rush hour traffic. En route, they'd stopped long enough to pick up a couple of sausage biscuits and coffee. Nicholas would have driven through, but the line was long, so Belle dashed into the restaurant and returned with a bag. They ate in the parking lot and made one pit stop before they hit Kansas City.

He navigated the traffic skillfully, but several near misses had his chest tight and his anxiety level rising. Belle, who'd lived here most of her adult life, wasn't bothered by the traffic and offered to drive. Nicholas declined, but by the time they took the exit off I-35, he wished he'd let her take the wheel. His guts were in knots, and he had a headache of massive proportion. Belle had made the journey sitting beside him, one hand resting on his thigh.

"We're almost there," she told him. "It's just a few blocks."

He grunted, unwilling to let her know how much the travel stress affected him, but once there, they managed her one bag and entered the apartment. His pounding heart slowed, and he took a long, deep breath. To his left, a very small kitchen contained a small gas stove, a sink and a fridge lined against one wall with cabinets above. The door opened into a sizeable living room with a table and chairs for two, a sofa against one wall, one recliner and a television sitting on an older coffee table. Windows overlooked other buildings, with the KC Skyline visible in the distance. To the right of the entrance, a door led to a small bedroom which opened into a bathroom. Out of habit, Nicholas marked the exit in his mind and traced the path to go outside.

"Basic," Belle said. "I know it's small, but it's been home."

Nicholas nodded. He'd stayed in much tinier places, and he liked the simplicity. The room offered a sense of home but lacked what he considered frills. He sat down in the recliner and kicked his feet back, closing his eyes to get grounded. Once, he would have enjoyed the view, but now he missed the sweep of woods, fields, and the creek that surrounded his place in the Ozarks. There was an old saying that a man's home is his castle, but for Nick, it was his sanctuary.

"It's not bad," he said, feeling like he needed to say something. "How much of this stuff needs to go back?"

"I don't know yet, but I'll figure it out." Belle sank to the floor beside his chair. Her fingers ran the length of his left arm, then wrapped around his hand. "What do you need? Don't tell me you're fine because I can see you're not."

"I'm okay."

"Okay is not really fine, so don't bullshit me. Does your head hurt?"

He hadn't fooled her, not at all, but her concern was a balm for his soul. "Yeah, I have a bitchin' headache, and my guts are griping."

"Would you be better if you lay down? The bedroom's right there."

"Maybe, maybe not." He craved another massage and wanted her hands to rub his back and shoulders. "Give me a few, okay?"

Nicholas knew he'd probably feel better if he drank a

cold soda and maybe had something to eat, but he would wait. He shut his eyes again, and he might have dozed until a loud noise penetrated his consciousness, and he jumped to his feet, almost turning the recliner over. He was about to dive behind it, momentarily uncertain of his surroundings, when it dawned on him that it was music. It was a ringtone.

"It's my phone," Belle said. "It's just my phone."

He set the chair right. "I know that – now. I'm sorry."

God knows he was. He wanted to build a relationship with this woman, and here he'd freaked out in her apartment, came close to toppling a piece of furniture and acted like he was starring in a freak show. Look up the word 'weak' in the dictionary, and his picture should be there, he thought.

"No reason to be. I'll change the ringtone to something a little quieter, less raucous."

Her calm voice eased him a little. "You don't need to – it won't change how messed up I am."

Belle shrugged. "I don't really like it, anyway. Do you want some coffee?"

"You made some?"

"I have a Keurig, and I can make you a cup if you want."

"All right, sure. Who was on the phone anyway?"

"Your sister, but I didn't answer it. You can call her back in a bit if you want."

Great, just freaking awesome. Suzanne would probably be upset and concerned. He would have explanations to make, and if he wasn't careful, she'd discern the truth – that he'd had a few bad moments.

The dark roast coffee laced with more sugar than he usually took helped. So did Belle's low-key response. If she had hovered or peppered him with questions, he would have resented it. Instead, she brought him coffee and remained close but not smothering. He took the acetaminophen she provided, and when she offered him an oatmeal raisin cookie, Nicholas took it. He ate it slowly, enjoying the taste.

"There's more if you want another."

Mouth full of cookie, he shook his head. "What's for lunch?"

"The choices are limited since I haven't been here – canned soup or we can order something in."

His stomach had eased, so soup sounded like a plan, but he still asked, "What happened to Winstead's?"

Belle smiled. "We can go if you really want, but I thought maybe you'd like to stay in this evening. I'm tired."

They ate a late lunch of chicken noodle soup with crackers that were barely stale. Before they had finished, her phone rang, and this time, prepared, Nicholas didn't jump.

"It's your sister," she said and handed him the device.

"Hello."

"I guess you got up there," Suzanne said. "I was getting anxious. Everything all right? How's KC?"

"It's good – and we're good, sis. How's life down south?" He adopted a casual tone, and to his surprise, he didn't have to fake it much.

"Same old, same old, although with Marshall here, it's better. Teagan's at school, and we did a little Christmas shopping this morning."

"You must be almost finished."

Suzanne laughed. "Not really, but I'm getting there. Are you sure you're okay? You sound a little weird."

Her radar tracked him closer than a weather system, and he sighed. "I'm fine."

Nicholas rose and walked to the far end of the living room with the phone. He gazed out over the skyline, over other tall buildings, and described the view to his sister. Then he heard someone tapping at the apartment door, so he remained in place, unwilling to display his grisly face to a stranger.

"Someone's here," he told her, then. "I gotta go – I'll call later, if not tonight, tomorrow for sure."

Strangers made him wary, so he remained with his back to the room but with every sense on high alert and eavesdropped without any remorse. The gruff male voice put him on edge, but the man sounded older, mature, and most likely no risk for Belle.

His tone inquired but didn't demand, and he didn't raise his voice at all. Listening to Belle's response, Nicholas could discern this was someone she knew but didn't like. There was a guarded note in her voice, so he paid attention.

After a few moments, he turned to see the speaker and saw an older man, probably mid to late sixties, maybe seventies, with a pot belly. He wore suspenders over a plain white T-shirt and baggy pants that had seen plenty of wear. Reading glasses hovered at the end of his nose, and his mostly bald head sported tufts of gray around the edges. In a quick assessment, Nicholas judged him to be unarmed, and although possibly unsavory, he posed no immediate threat.

In case he could be mistaken, however, he walked across the living room to stand beside Belle. He heard the man exhale a harsh breath, and when the man said, "Damn, Miss Barbier, who do you have here, the fucking Elephant Man, or is it Quasimodo?"

If the man had been even a decade younger and if Nicholas hadn't built up a thick skin when it came to careless words, he would have punched him. His fingers curled into a tight fist, and he wanted to, very much. Instead, he drew deep on inner reserves he barely knew he still possessed and said, "Gunnery Sergeant Nicholas Reilly, United States Marine Corps."

He spit out the words with some bitter venom, but he didn't expect the man to push back his t-shirt sleeve to display a devil dog tattoo.

"Marine Corporal Borgmann, long retired jarhead."

They exchanged a glance, then Nicholas held out his hand to shake and the moment that could have become volatile passed.

Chapter Eleven

Although he hadn't said so, it was apparent to Belle that Nicholas was ill at ease. Whether it was Kansas City, the trip, the fact he was out of his element or the PTSD kicking up, she wondered if they should have come. She did need to get her belongings and move out of the apartment. Belle hadn't changed her mind about moving in with Nicholas, but she realized it might be more complicated than she had expected. Somehow, she had thought it would be easier, despite his many issues and his appearance. *I thought it would be because I wanted it to be,* she realized now.

She'd grown up about fifty miles up the interstate in St. Joseph, an old river town with a tough reputation and a frontier history. It had the feel of a larger city, although the population hovered about 75,000, and it wasn't. Statewide, it fell somewhere around the 8th largest, and she'd lived in KC so long that her hometown seemed smaller now. Until now, she would have sworn that she had adapted well to metropolitan life, that noise and traffic didn't bother her in the least and that she admired a skyline view made up of buildings and freeways.

Belle realized she missed the quiet at Nicholas' place, the one he'd dubbed 'Beast's Lair.' The old rambling house had begun to feel like home to her. She enjoyed the soft sound of the wind as it rattled against the windows and blew through the bare tree branches. The hills that cradled the place had a certain majestic beauty, and so did the creek that traveled through the edge of the property. The short drive to her grandmother's house was picturesque, and she looked forward to getting to know her. Until now, she could have sworn she'd become a city girl, but since arriving in the Ozarks, she'd been reminded of her grandmother's farm, a place she'd adored while growing up.

She knew Nicholas suffered from PTSD, and none of it, even his reaction to the cell phone ringing, upset her. Belle wanted to make things easier for him, though, and he'd enjoyed the cookie and coffee. His conversation with his sister appeared to go well, but when someone knocked at the door, she tensed. First, she had no idea who it could be, and second, she didn't know how Nicholas would react – or how whoever was there would react to him.

Belle opened the door to find her landlord, Mr. Borgmann, there. The mature man unsettled her. He never seemed friendly at all, and he had a crusty manner that she didn't like. He was abrupt and bordered on rude. His interest in her personal affairs had always been more than she liked, and today was no different.

"You're here. That's good," he said as he barged through the door to stand in her apartment. "When do you plan to be moved out? I hope soon – I got a chance to rent the place, but I can't show it while your junk is still here. I suppose you found someplace you think is cheaper or better, probably newer."

"I'll be out tomorrow or the next day at the latest," she

told him. "I believe my rent is paid, though, through the end of the month."

He grunted. "That's in two days."

She hadn't paid a lot of attention to the calendar, but a quick glance at the one she'd hung in January confirmed it. "I'll be out by then."

"Are you going to clean the place? 'Cause if you want the deposit back, it's gonna have to sparkle."

"I will if I have time. I don't really care about the deposit."

Borgmann wheezed what she took to be a laugh. "Just as well, then. You plan on taking all this furniture?"

Belle hadn't decided, but she made up her mind. "Probably not. I won't need any of it where I'm moving."

"Going to some furnished dump, are you? Well, good luck with that. I could buy this stuff off you, give you a hundred bucks maybe."

The furniture in question consisted of the sofa, recliner, coffee table, recliner, table and two chairs. It was worth more than that, but she didn't need it or want it. She'd keep the television and her stereo. In the bedroom, a bed frame with a mattress and a chest of drawers could go south with her. Maybe Nicholas could use it for a guest room.

"How about a hundred and fifty?" she asked, some latent bargaining skill emerging.

Before the landlord could answer, Nicholas joined her, his presence at her side protective.

"Damn, Miss Barbier, who do you have here, the fucking Elephant Man, or is it Quasimodo?"

Belle tensed, but Nicholas handled it well. Borgmann's bluster vanished, and he shoved up his grimy t-shirt sleeve to display a tattoo she recognized as relating to the Marines. It surprised her that he'd been in the service, but she suspected he'd never seen combat.

The two men shook hands, but Nicholas didn't relax.

"I'd say two hundred at least for the furnishings," he told the older guy. "Maybe even two fifty."

His light grey eyes burned like burnished steel as he spoke.

"All right, all right," the landlord muttered. "Leave the junk here."

"Where's the money?"

With a huge sigh, Borgmann dug into his pocket and pulled out a wad, then peeled off two century notes and handed them to Nicholas.

"It'll be here," Nicholas said. "You can get the furniture once we're gone."

Any hint of camaraderie had gone, and with a nod, Borgmann turned on his heel and exited.

"Lock the damn door," Nicholas said with a small laugh. "Hell, if you weren't leaving, I'd say fumigate the place."

She giggled, delighted.

"I didn't know he'd been a Marine."

"He may have been, but he's a pog, a Fobbit," he told her, and when she looked perplexed, added, "Someone who never saw real combat, more than that, a screw-up. Do you have boxes or what? Let's pack."

"I ordered some totes," she said. "They'll be here in an hour or so. I figured three would be enough – all I need to pack are kitchen things, my clothes and stuff, and everything else miscellaneous. I do want to take the stereo, though. And maybe the bedroom stuff, the bed and chest."

"There's plenty of room in the truck."

Once the totes arrived, with Nicholas in charge, they

packed with extreme efficiency. They started in the kitchen, with her few pots and pans on the bottom, her utensils next, her sparse dishes, three dish towels and two potholders.

"This is all you had?"

She nodded. "Yeah, a few plastic plates, cups, mostly ones I got from take-out or something, and a little bit of silverware. I never needed anything else, not really."

"You have one decent skillet, two saucepans and a bigger pot plus two cookie sheets and the coffee maker? And that's all?"

"Except for the food."

She had another can of soup, one of tamales, and some Splenda packets. There was half a box of coffee pods, a nearly empty butter container in the fridge, salt and pepper, a half-used bottle of barbecue sauce and mustard. Her freezer was empty except for ice cubes, and the few items in the fridge could be tossed. She wrapped her knick-knacks in the kitchen towels, a miniature Eiffel Tower, a Pony Express statue replica and two ceramic angels she'd picked up at a flea market. Nicholas took down her two posters and rolled them neatly, securing each with a rubber band, then added two pictures from the wall.

"Don't close it yet. There's still some space," he said.

Belle had more clothing than kitchen accessories. She divided them into two piles, one to keep and the other to donate. She'd long intended to sort her garments, and this was a good chance. The keepers filled a tote with space for some bath towels and other items from the bathroom. She tossed most of her heels into the donation stack, keeping a few pairs, one for dressy occasions. Belle kept the rest for every day. What didn't fit into the tote tucked easily into her suitcase.

Her CDs, DVDs, and books went into the last tote, along with anything else miscellaneous, including spare blankets, extra sheets, and such. For now, she left the bed fully made since they'd sleep in it tonight. Come morning, she would toss the bedding into her laundry bag and call it good.

It was almost seven by the time they finished. They'd worked in tandem with light conversation but nothing important or hard. Still, Belle enjoyed the time spent together. Sometimes she shared a little story about one of her possessions, and once in a while, he asked a question. When everything that could be packed had been, he looked around.

"I could load the truck and save time in the morning."

She shook her head. "No, someone would steal it all long before tomorrow."

"Makes sense," he said. "What's for supper?"

Belle laughed. "Anything you want that we can order in."

"No Winstead's?" he asked.

"Maybe another time," Belle replied. "What would you like?"

When he had no preference, she ordered fried chicken from Church's. When it arrived, they dined on two of the plastic plates she'd decided not to take, eating the crisp fried chicken paired with mac and cheese and slaw.

"They have Church's back home," he told her as he devoured his second piece of chicken.

"So, it was a good choice?"

"Very."

When they finished, he stretched. "We probably should turn in before long to get an early start tomorrow. I should shower, but I'll wait till morning."

Tired from the trip, Belle should agree, but she wanted something more.

When Nicholas stood, she rose and stood as close as she

could to him. "Love me, Nicholas," she told him. "I want a sweet memory to be my last of this apartment."

A grin teased the corners of his misshapen lips. "Were you happy here, Belle?"

She shrugged. "Yes and no. It's mostly been a place to go at the end of the day, somewhere to sleep and eat a little. I wasn't unhappy, if that makes any difference."

"It does," he replied. "I want you to be happy in my lair."

Belle noticed he'd dropped the word "beast" from it and was glad.

"I will be," she told him. "Just make me happy now."

She stood on tiptoe to reach his mouth and kissed him. She let her lips linger on his with a slow heat that leapt between them and threatened to combust. Nicholas locked his arms around her, held her tight against his chest and kissed her back. Belle yielded to desire, and within moments, they had stripped naked. He didn't carry her to the bedroom this time but took her on the couch in with swift, savage passion. Nicholas rocked her, his stick weaving in and out in a rhythm as old as the earth, as timeless as the stars. Neither took their time but came together with a glorious delight that left them breathless, collapsed on the couch together.

In the morning, they rose before daybreak and dressed. Belle longed for coffee, but everything was packed, and it was too early to have any of the food delivery services bring breakfast.

"Is there a convenience store close?" Nicholas asked. "I could go grab some coffee."

"We'll get some down the road." She figured he'd wear the ski mask, and the staff would think he came to rob them, and it could go bad fast. "Let's get your truck loaded."

He had already taken apart her bed, and everything else

was packed or stacked by the door. Belle reached for one of the totes, and he shook his head. "I'll carry it all down. That's too heavy for you, babe. You can bring the bags and small boxes."

"I can...."

Nicholas stilled her protest with his mouth. Then, with her in his arms, he looked straight into her eyes and said, "Are you totally sure about this? Once the truck's loaded and we go, it's done."

Belle's chest tightened, and her stomach felt like she'd swallowed ice. "I'm certain unless you have cold feet, Nicholas."

If he rejected her now and called this off, it would hurt.

"No," he told her. "I want this more than I've wanted anything in a long time. I've known you a week today, but it seems like I've always known you. Somehow, we've packed more into seven days than some people do in a year. But I need to know you're sure that you're not going to change your mind when we get home and run away to Ethel's. I think that might kill me, Belle."

"I'm as sure as I am that the sun rises in the east and sets in the west," she told him, swallowing tears of relief. "I don't have any doubts at all."

He stared down at her and sighed. "Good, because I don't either. Let's get out of here."

She touched his cheek and started to tell him she loved him but stopped short. He hadn't said it, but then neither had she. Maybe he did, maybe he didn't, but Nicholas needed her, and that, she thought, was a beginning.

Rush hour traffic had begun to pick up as they wound their way out of downtown to head south, but at least most of the traffic was incoming, and they were outgoing. Neither said much until they'd cleared the metro area, then they stopped at the first café they found. Belle cradled the heavy cup in her hands as she sipped coffee, saying little.

She told the truth when she said she had no doubts. She didn't. She wanted this too, no matter how crazy it might seem, but Belle had questions. They were together, sleeping together, and soon to live together. For some women, that would be enough, maybe, but she wondered about the future. *I love him, but what's ahead? He's got issues, a lot of them, but I'm up to handle them and to support him.* They had now, but she wanted forever.

"Belle, you're awfully quiet," Nicholas said.

She gave him a smile. "I'm just thinking," she said. "And I'm hungry."

"So am I."

They sat in a corner booth, Nicholas with his back to the restaurant. No one had paid much attention when they entered, and she hoped that wouldn't change. Lost in thought, she'd almost forgotten what courage it took for him to sit in a café, drinking coffee, ordering bacon and eggs. She reached across the table and grasped his hand.

"Your hand is like ice," she said.

He shrugged. "I'm a little cold."

"Is that all?"

"I'm a little antsy, too," he said. "Not used to that big city traffic, but I'm all right, Belle."

She nodded. Over breakfast, she watched him, but he ate with relish. He drank three cups of coffee and sat in a relaxed position. They chatted, and when he sang the refrain with the jukebox, her worries eased.

He offered her his hand when they left the booth, and she took it. After he paid for breakfast, they walked hand in hand to his truck and then headed south for home.

Chapter Twelve

He hadn't slept much, but then he seldom did. In her unfamiliar apartment, Nicholas had been on alert and kept watch, so he was tired, but he said nothing about it. Beside him, Belle snuggled close and talked, which helped to pass the time. He half-listened, reveling in the soft, sweet sound of her voice but paying little attention. Between that and the hum of the tires against the pavement, he became drowsy. After he'd drifted across lanes once and veered off toward the shoulder twice, Nicholas realized he needed a break, or he'd fall asleep at the wheel. That could be dangerous and lead to an accident.

"Hey, Belle, do you want to drive a while?"

"What's the matter?"

"Nothing, but I'm getting sleepy."

"I can drive."

He pulled off onto the next farm road, and they switched places. Nicholas scrubbed his eyes with both hands as he settled into the passenger seat. "It's bigger than your little Toyota," he warned. "It will handle differently, especially loaded down. There's a fair cross wind today, too, so don't let it...."

"Nicholas," she interrupted.

"What?"

"Don't treat me like I don't know what I'm doing. I have a driver's license and everything. Plus, I drove down here last week alone."

He shook his head and laughed. "Busted. All right, I'll try not to tell you how to drive."

"Will it make you nervous, me driving?"

"Probably, but I'll manage."

He could, he thought, he *would*. Nicholas preferred to be in control, and that was lifelong, not just part of his PTSD.

"Just trust me," she said and laughed.

He didn't, but he realized he did, and that was a huge step for him. "I trust you, Belle," he told her, and there was no laughter in his voice. "You're one of a very few people that I do, my sister, Timothy, my mom and my grandpa."

Those were the handful he trusted, without a doubt. To some extent, he could rely on other relatives and a few friends he'd served with, but she made the short list.

"I'm honored. Now shut your eyes and get some sleep."

Now that his attention wasn't focused on the road, Nicholas wasn't as sleepy. Still, he closed his eyes and tried to chill. Belle put on the stereo and began singing softly to most of the songs on his well-worn country classics CD. As she sang about sixteen tons then segued into trailers for sale or rent, he dozed, then he slept.

Nicholas didn't rouse until they were almost to Carthage, around twenty miles from his house. He adjusted his position in the seat and squinted at the brilliant sun.

"What time is it?"

"Almost eleven thirty."

"I didn't think I'd sleep that long."

"You needed it."

"Probably so."

"Do you want to stop for lunch before we get back?"

He considered the question. After a big breakfast, he wasn't hungry and told her so.

"I'm not either, but there's not much at the house to eat," she replied. "If we don't pull in somewhere to grab a bite, I need to stop at the store."

A large discount store or supermarket was the last place he wanted to be. Nicholas figured if he named a dish, Belle would be up to preparing it, but she had to be as tired as he was.

"The store can wait," he told her. "There's a place in Carthage that has the best lemon chicken I've ever put in my mouth. Why don't we get some as take-out, then we can warm it up when we get home when we're ready to eat?"

"That sounds like a great idea."

They ended up with lemon chicken, some rice, a few crab rangoons and egg rolls. At the last minute, he added some broccoli beef to the order. The food smelled heavenly, and as they left town, he offered to drive.

The farmhouse was cold, so he built a fire and turned on the heat. Belle stowed the take-out in the fridge as he began unloading the truck. For now, weary to the bone, he stacked most of it in the area between the front door and the stairs, leaving enough room to walk around the pile. Belle took her suitcase and bag upstairs, then dug into the clothing tote for a few things.

As much as Nicholas had longed to be home once there, he found himself edgy. Rather than flop down on the couch or settle in his recliner, he prowled the house like a hunter seeking prey. His muscles were tense and hard. His nerves were rattled, and he had to concentrate on keeping from jumping at every shadow or sound. His stomach was unsettled, and he suspected a bellyache was in his immediate future. On his third pass through the living room, Belle glanced up from where she was curled into a corner of the couch reading.

"What's wrong?"

"Nothing," he snapped, then stopped. Biting her head off wasn't going to help. It would just hurt her feelings or make her mad. "I don't know – everything."

The fire in the hearth crackled, and his heart rate increased. Nicholas stared into the flames, and although it was a tame fire, under control, in a contained space, for a moment, he saw the flames that consumed the Humvee, the fire that left the scars he now wore. His breath caught, and he took fast, shallow breaths. He wasn't so far gone that he didn't realize he was about to hyperventilate.

"Don't you feel well?" she asked, and he honed in on her voice.

"I don't," he said. "But I'm also really restless, antsy. I can't settle down, and now the fire…it reminds me."

Panic threatened to overtake him, and he fought it. Flashback images from that terrible day in Helmand Province played in his head. One minute, they were riding patrol, listening to rock and roll, joking, and someone was smoking a joint. The next, they careened over, and the world exploded in flames. As if it was happening now, heat seared his chest, his face, and he flinched. Nicholas backed away from the fire, hands shaking. All he wanted to do was retreat from the memories and to forget.

"Nicholas," Belle said his name, and he caught it like a

lifeline.

"Come, sit down, please."

He wasn't sure his legs would work, but he took the few steps to the couch and sat. He craved her touch but feared it. What he might do in response terrified him. He might lash out or hit her, and that was the last thing he wanted to do. Nicholas buried his face in both hands, shuddering.

"Focus on something here now," she told him. He vaguely remembered the therapy concept, although he'd ignored it and never used it. "Don't think about the fire. Just tell me things that you see or hear or feel that are good things."

"Your voice," he whispered. "The sound of it grounds me."

"That's good. Tell me more."

"I'm home, this couch is old, but I like it. It's comfortable," he said, grasping at straws of reality. "I can hear the wind against the windows, powerful and fresh and clean. I can smell your perfume. It's lavender, right? It's sweet. This old flannel shirt is soft. I think I can still smell the lemon chicken, and I know it will be tasty."

Belle stroked his back, and he savored her touch. "I love the way you touch me, the way your hand feels," he said, voice soft but clear. "I like this old house, the space it has, and it's my lair, the beast's lair. I like retreating here and hiding out, but it's better with you."

He slowly named off a few more things as he cataloged his surroundings, but the effort brought him back to the present. "And you, Belle," he said at last. "You're here, and that is the best thing."

Fifteen minutes had passed, or maybe thirty. Nicholas wasn't sure, but his nerves eased as a powerful fatigue crept over him. He craved sleep and told her so, although his belly was cramped hard as if there were snakes within to coil and curl and strike. It hurt so much he doubted he could sleep. "My belly's about to kill me."

She coaxed him to lie down on the couch. Her small hands reached up beneath his shirt and rubbed his back, her fingers moving over both skin and scars. He thought she talked to him, too, but he didn't listen at first, just let the sound of her voice soothe him.

He became drowsy and realized she was singing to him, her voice a low alto. He half recognized the song. He thought it was called "The Ferryman," an Irish song, but the refrain spoke to his heart, "if you ever loved me, Molly, love me now."

He had to tell her how he felt, how much she mattered to him, so he said, voice muffled and quiet, "Belle?"

"Yeah?"

"I love you."

The song halted, and then she said, "Nicholas, I love you too."

"If you ever loved me, love me now."

"I do, honey, I do. Hush and relax."

She picked up the song again, then followed it with others, but by then, he had drifted into a somnolent state, then he slept.

When he woke, it was dark outside, but she'd turned on a lamp in the corner. It cast tall shadows against the walls, but they didn't bother him now. Nicholas had turned onto his side, and a soft blanket covered him. A pillow had been tucked beneath his head. A deep contentment had replaced his anxiety, and he savored it. From the kitchen, the aroma of coffee wafted, and he craved some. A quiet clatter came from the same direction, and he sat up, the blanket falling to the floor.

"Hey, Belle?"

She came into the room with a smile.

"Better?"

"Much," he said. He'd become calm while he rested, and his stomach had settled down. "How long did I sleep?"

She sat down beside him. "Hours, it's almost ten. Are you hungry?"

"I am, but I can't believe I slept so long."

"You needed it."

He had promised his sister he'd call to let her know they were home. By now, she must be frantic. "I'd better call Suzanne."

"I did, around five. I told her you were worn out and sleeping. She was good with that."

That amazed him, but he'd take it.

"I'll warm up the lemon chicken if you want to eat," Belle said. "And I made coffee."

At the kitchen table, Nicholas savored a cup, then began to eat. The food tasted very good, but he paused to look at Belle. "I meant what I said, you know."

Her smile was as enigmatic as the Mona Lisa's. "Which thing?"

"I love you." The words weren't easy to say, and he'd never imagined he would ever say them to a woman, not after he came back home. "I do, Belle."

"And I love you, too, Nicholas Reilly."

"I'm a fucked-up mess, though," he said. His tone remained level, and he wasn't upset. He just wanted to make sure she knew the facts. "I never know when I might freak out or get weird. I can't promise I'll ever be totally all right. You have to understand that, and I'm never going to be good-looking...."

Belle reached across the table and touched his hand.

Her eyes sparkled with unshed tears. "Hush. No one is perfect – absolutely no one. Like the song you were singing the other night, I'll take you like you are."

"There's going to be rough times…."

"Everyone has them."

"Not like this."

"No," she said, her voice steady. "Often a lot worse."

He let that digest for a moment, then picked up his fork. After he finished a bite of lemon chicken, he asked her, "How did you know to do that thing, pick good things around you?"

"After my parents died, I had a little bit of therapy. That's one of the things I learned that could help stop a panic attack. Their sudden death, the way they died, and then finding out they never happened to mention I was adopted hit me pretty hard, Nicholas."

"Babe, I'm sorry that happened to you."

"So am I, but hey, good came out of the bad, right? I've found a new family, and you. I really like Ethel – I think I'll probably come to love her once I really get to know her. If it wasn't for being adopted, I would still be in Kansas City, lonely in that little apartment, just going through the motions. When I met you, I woke up again and started living."

He'd never thought about it like that. For him, she'd been the one who arrived in his life without warning and changed everything for the better. The realization it had been mutual surprised and pleased him.

"So, we start now," he said, as he devoured a rangoon.

"What?"

"A new shot at living, at getting this right, the whole shooting shebang."

Belle laughed. "I suppose so. For now, let's eat. This food

is awesome."

Realizing he could love someone pleased him, but it also terrified him. For the moment, though, he decided not to obsess over it but to enjoy the rest of the evening.

"What else did Suzanne say when you talked to her?"

"Marshall, I guess that's her husband, went back out on the road. She invited us to come over to see the tree – Teagan really wants us to come."

He'd dined in public and eaten meals at someone's home more often recently than he had in years. Christmas, like the other major holidays, hadn't been something he participated in or celebrated. The last few years, he had gone over to see the tree to please his niece but nothing more.

"I suppose we should."

"Teagan would like it – if you want to go, call your sister tomorrow and find out when we should come."

"I will – but I'll warn you now, I don't really do Christmas anymore."

"I didn't last year, but I was hoping maybe this year I would," Belle said. "She hasn't said, but I expect Ethel will invite us over, and your cousin asked if you were coming down to Texas, didn't he?"

Nicholas had almost forgotten that but nodded. "Yeah, he did — for that and Grandpa's birthday."

"Will you go?"

Just like that, they were back to the difficult stuff. "Only if you go with me, Belle. Probably not Christmas – but we will for Grandpa's birthday. He'll turn ninety."

"I will go with you for the holidays if you want, and you already said we'd come for his birthday. And you should. He won't be around forever."

He recalled she'd lost her folks and had none of the family she'd grown up with remaining. He had spent the recent years so consumed with self-pity and loathing that he hadn't thought about that. He loved Grandpa Reilly, a crusty old Irishman who'd come to Texas in the 1950s. Growing up, the old man took him fishing, told him stories and taught him songs. During his brief time home after being burned and wounded, he'd spent a little time with his grandfather, who had been among the few who didn't judge him or treat him like a mutant.

Memories surfaced, for once, good times from the past and not bad.

He had to have been five, maybe six, tucked beside Grandpa in his recliner watching television, Cheers, about a bar in Boston. It didn't matter what the program might be, but Nicholas felt safe beside his grandfather and loved. Then he saw them sitting at the Formica-topped kitchen table, eating vanilla ice cream before bed. Granny had fussed, but every night Seamus Reilly had his ice cream on doctor's orders. Once, he'd been a heavy drinker, and when he stopped of his own accord, a doctor told him his body would miss the high amount of sugar, so eat ice cream. Must have been an Irish doctor, Nicholas thought, as he spooned the sweet confection into his mouth. Any time he spent the night with his grandparents, he got ice cream. There had been the Christmas he wanted a bike, and Grandpa got him one, the Halloween Grandpa took him trick or treating because his mother was sick. They'd carved a pumpkin – and a turnip in old Irish tradition. And, when his granny died first, he'd gone over every Saturday morning to help his grandfather, but it had been a toss-up who helped the other the most. When he came back with a scarred face, Grandpa had never seemed to notice, although he'd talked about his own da and grandda, who had been involved in the 1920s fight for Irish freedom. Grandpa always had a buck in his pocket for an ice cream if the truck came around or money to see a movie with a carton of popcorn on the side. He'd taught him to drive, too, in his old vintage truck and how to drive a stick shift. And, he had taken his grandson to Mass when no one else did. Grandpa had been his sponsor for Confirmation and drilled him on the catechism until Nicholas knew it backward and forward.

"Hells bells," he said. His appetite waned. "You're right. I'll have to go sometime. I'd hate it if he passed away before I see him again."

After the trip he'd just made, Nicholas realized going home would be difficult, but maybe with Belle at his side, he could do it.

Maybe, he reflected, he could do a lot more than he had believed possible.

Time and experience would tell.

Chapter Thirteen

Suzanne lived in a small blue house not far from her grandmother Ethel's farm. They'd passed it by more than once, but on Friday night, for the first time, they went inside. It was small but cozy. The kitchen opened from the living room and included a dining area. Another door from the front room led into a short hall with three bedrooms and a bath. The Christmas tree stood before the large picture window overlooking the road and was dazzling.

Teagan rose from a child-sized rocker in front of the television and threw herself into her uncle's arms. "Uncle Nicholas, you're finally here! Look at the tree – isn't it pretty?"

It was hung with unique ornaments, a variety of garlands, and lights, large and small, white and colored. Belle spotted Santas and snowmen, angels, and elves among the classic round glass ornaments. A lovely angel topped the tree.

"It's beautiful," he said, scooping her up into his arms. "But where're the presents?"

"Santa will bring those, silly. And look, we got a new

Nativity this year."

"Nice," he said. He had one somewhere, still packed in a box. Maybe this would be the season when he'd take it out and display it.

"Belle, come watch Rudolph with me," the little girl said, tugging at her hand.

Suzanne emerged from the kitchen and shook her head. "Maybe Belle can come help me, and your uncle can watch the Christmas show with you."

Nicholas rolled his eyes but let his niece lead him over to the sofa. As the familiar songs of the holiday classic rang through the house, Belle followed Suzanne into the kitchen. Several pots and pans were on the stove. A delectable aroma issued from the stove, and Belle guessed at the main dish.

"Ham?"

Suzanne nodded. "Nick loves ham – or at least he used to love it, so I'm fixing ham, scalloped potatoes, wax beans, shoe peg corn, candied sweet potatoes and deviled eggs. I baked bread, and for dessert, I made a Wacky cake, that old-fashioned chocolate cake with a few weird ingredients. I know it's like a holiday meal, but I figured he won't come over on Christmas. If I want to see him, I go over there. He doesn't come here very often. Even though Nick lives so close, he's only come over to eat maybe three times and then once on the Fourth of July. That was a disaster, though.:

Belle could imagine the effect fireworks would have on Nicholas. Explosions would be almost certain to trigger his PTSD. "How long have you lived here? How long has Nicholas?"

"We moved here after we got married, and we waited a few years to have kids. Teagan's six, so almost ten years. Marshall is from the area, and he likes it. Besides, I don't think he was too happy living under my family's microscope in Rusk. Nick came after Teagan was born, five years or so. For a long time, he might as well have been in Texas, no more than we saw him, but my baby girl changed that."

"He's very fond of her, isn't he?"

Suzanne nodded. "They're crazy about each other. I'm still getting used to her calling him Uncle Nicholas, not Uncle Beast."

In Belle's opinion, the child never should have been allowed to call him by the self-imposed nickname, but she didn't say so. "I think he likes that a lot. I've been trying to get him to realize he's not just the scars. He's still a person underneath all of them."

"Good luck," his sister said with a sarcastic laugh. "I mean, he's done some totally amazing things since you're around, and it's good for him. I'm glad to see him like this. But he's never going back to being the same guy he was before. He was hot, like freaking movie star hot. And before he went to the Marines, he was fun – crazy and wild and funny. But he was caring, too. You would have to have known him then, Belle."

"He still has a good heart," she said, sad that even his sister judged him by before, not now. "He can be funny now, and I didn't realize how well he could play the guitar and sing."

Suzanne paused and stared at her. "Nick played the guitar?"

"Yeah, he did and sang."

"That's amazing. I never thought he would again, Belle."

"Maybe you don't give him enough credit." Or support or patience, she thought.

"I worry about him all the time. I love my brother – I guess I'm just used to his limitations."

Understanding much better now why Nicholas was wary

to go home and why he hadn't stayed in Texas, Belle said, "Most of them are self-imposed. I was raised with the idea there's no such word as 'can't' – because you can do anything."

"But there are some things my brother can't," his sister said. "He just can't. And I have to say this – what are you doing with him? He's a hot mess these days, and he's scarred so much no one's going to call him handsome. If you're wondering, he doesn't have any money, not beyond the disability he gets, so he's not a good candidate for a sugar daddy. If you have some agenda, then I want to know – and I want you to pack your shit and leave before you cause Nick any pain. He's all in, I can see that, and that makes me afraid he's being set up for a hard fall."

Anger, as bright red as cherries in season or a fresh apple, kindled, and Belle bristled.

"You don't need to worry – I love Nicholas," she said. "I'm not trying to get anything from him, least of all money. If I wanted a sugar daddy, I'd have stayed in the city. You really have a nerve. How dare you suggest I'm out to damage your brother? Oh, and by the way, he sure as hell can do almost anything. He's a survivor, in case you didn't notice, and he's still got the heart of a Marine. That he overcame being shot three times and suffering such severe burns says a lot about his stubborn endurance. Maybe we should go home – I don't feel welcome here, not at all."

Belle hadn't lost her pride and prepared to flounce out of the kitchen. She planned to grab her purse, coat, and Nicholas, not necessarily in that order. An awkward silence hung in the air between the two women, heavy as a deep snow. Suzanne had the grace to blush a little, then in a softer tone, Belle, reconsidering, said, "Do you think I should make a fresh pot of coffee, or will Nick drink iced tea?"

Suzanne replied. "He can't do a lot of things, Belle.

Wanting him to try things doesn't make it possible. I've been worried you push him too hard. He seemed moody on the phone, not as happy."

Belle blew out air and pushed a stray strand of hair out of her face. "He has shit to deal with, true, but I'm not forcing him to do anything. I'm also not treating him like an invalid."

"Maybe you should," Suzanne replied. "I know he has those bad headaches, and he gets stomachaches. I think some tender loving care might do more to help him than making him go to McDonald's or to Kansas City. I'll guess he probably had an episode or two, didn't he?"

She didn't want to argue with Nicholas' sister, but biting down the hot words that rose to her mouth was difficult. As Belle searched for what she could say without starting a fight, Nicholas spoke from the doorway.

"I did," he said. "But not because of Belle, and it wasn't her idea to do either. It was mine. Suze, I'm a mess. I have issues and probably always will, but I'm tired of hiding out. I'm sick of living like a recluse who's too afraid of what people think. Don't you ever think I might have been lonely over there at my lair? Did you ever count how many days went by when I saw nobody and never left the place? Hell, till Belle came, the phone barely rang."

"Nick!" Suzanne cried. Her face flushed red. "I didn't know you were in the kitchen."

"I'm sure you didn't, sis, and I heard plenty. Don't rag on Belle."

"I wasn't, but…."

"You were." His voice, though quiet, had an undernote of steel. "What you said to her is inexcusable and plain wrong. I love her. I'm not an idiot, and if I thought she had an agenda, some secret plan, I'd hope to shout I'd see it. I know you worry, Suzie-Q, and you mean well, but you know what Granny also said about those good intentions, that the road to hell is paved with them."

Nicholas stepped forward and put his arm around Belle's shoulders. "Don't quit what you're doing with me, baby."

She tilted her face toward him. "I won't."

He kissed her quick and sweet, then let her go. "I came to tell you I'm taking Teagan outside for a few minutes. Her tummy started hurting...."

"She needs to go lie down in her room, then," Suzanne interrupted. "I swear I don't know what's got into the girl."

Nicholas leaned against the counter and picked up a deviled egg, nibbling it as she spoke.

"She gets tummy aches when she's upset or scared or nervous, Suzanne. When she thought the little reindeer and his pals were going to get eaten by the Abominable snow monster, that's when she started holding her belly. She'll be fine if you show her a little sympathy. It began happening when she started school, right? That's because school is different, and she's uptight."

"Oh, Nick, the doctor said it's to get attention...."

"Could be, but the same thing happens to me, Suzanne. Stress triggers my gut, and that's what happens to the kid. Come on, the food smells fantastic, so let's enjoy it and not fight."

Suzanne's cheeks turned pinker, and her expression was sour.

"All right. I'll shut up for now, but if Belle does anything to hurt you, Nick, I won't be responsible."

"It's not yours to fuss over. Where's the kid's coat?"

Suzanne asked no more questions and became a little less

hostile as they worked in tandem to finish the meal.

An hour later, they sat down to dinner, linked hands, and asked a blessing. Both Teagan and Nicholas had returned chilled but in good spirits after their walk. Over the meal, she chattered about the squirrels they saw in the treetops and the deer they glimpsed at the tree line.

Belle settled down and enjoyed the food, which was delicious. She ate a little too much but offered to wash the dishes for Suzanne. After a tiny hesitation, the other woman agreed. Nicholas offered to dry, but Belle sent him into the other room with his family. She didn't mind the chore because it gave her time to think.

They watched a Christmas movie without any lamps, just the light of the Christmas tree, and the evening was pleasant. When Teagan's bedtime came, Nicholas carried her to her room and read her a story, then they departed.

On the way home, he said little, but he seemed laid back, so Belle enjoyed it. Her head and heart were full of thoughts, both pleasant and not as nice. Although she had enjoyed most of the evening at Suzanne's, the rocky moments in the kitchen still rankled. She'd failed to realize that his sister had such major concerns about their relationship or that she dismissed Nicholas as a broken-down handicapped man. That bothered her a lot. When he appeared in the doorway and had heard it all, he'd supported her and that made her heart brim full.

They lingered outside for a few minutes, gazing up at the stars in the clear night sky. He pointed a few of them to her until she shivered. "You're cold. Let's go inside. We can stargaze another time."

He stirred up the fire without any apparent angst, then touched the site where a mirror had been over the mantle until he smashed it. "I probably need to fix this," he told her. "I'm thinking maybe some decorative tile might look good here."

"It would," she said, thinking he wanted to repair, not destroy.

"We'll go look at some soon, see what's available. There's a few other things I can get, too, to fix up the place."

"Sure."

Nicholas reached for his guitar and strummed it. Then he began to sing more old songs, rich with meaning and full of emotion. Belle listened, and sometimes she sang along if she knew the words. Toward the end, when the clock hands crept close to midnight, he sang an old Christmas carol, "What Child Is This?". It was one that Belle knew well, and so she accompanied him, her alto voice rising and blending with his as she sat at his feet.

When he stopped, laid down his pick and put the guitar aside, Nicholas glanced at her.

"You know what?"

"No idea."

"I used to like Christmas," he said. "I really liked it, even in the sandbox."

"What changed?" Belle knew, but she asked anyway.

"My world exploded. I almost died, and for a long time, I wished I did. But now…."

When his voice trailed off, she filled in the silence. "But now what?"

"I'm glad I didn't," he said. "I never expected to ever say that, but I'm glad I'm alive."

Belle leaned against his knees and touched his arm in a gentle caress. "Nicholas, so am I."

He gave her a small smile and then said, "I may want to

do Christmas this year. I don't know. I want to, and I don't. Hell, the idea almost scares me, but that's what I'm thinking."

"We could do it," she said, hoping they would. She'd ignored Christmas last year, but now she longed to celebrate.

Nicholas offered her his hand, and she took it, rising with him. He wrapped his arms around her and cradled her close. His lips nuzzled her throat. "It's cold, and I'm tired. Let's go to bed."

And they did, hearts full and dreams from the past surfacing with hope.

Eventually, they slept.

Chapter Fourteen

He remembered Christmas and all it brought, that delightful aroma of fresh evergreen, the anticipation, the cut-out sugar cookies, Midnight Mass, the songs, the stories, and the secrecy of gathering gifts. Nicholas had loved it, one of the reasons that his cousin, Timothy, nicknamed him 'Saint' for St. Nick. The rest of his family had followed suit, although he'd never thought he was anything like Santa, not the saint or the legend. He'd just happened to be born on the saint's feast day, hence both his name and nickname. As a kid, he started building up the excitement for his birthday and Christmas as soon as Thanksgiving was over.

In his earliest memories, the tree had been real. Later, because his mom was tired of sweeping up dry needles and worrying about fire, they got an artificial tree. Grandpa never cared for it, and in secret, neither did Nicholas. On Christmas Eve, he could remember staring out of a window looking north, watching for Rudolph's red nose. They always kept the Irish custom of a candle in the window, but it was electric, not one with a flame. By the time he was old enough to go to church at midnight, he'd surrendered his belief in Santa.

His last good Christmas had been a year he came home on leave for the holiday. Suzanne got engaged to Marshall Benning that year and no one got into any heated arguments. Dinner at the Reilly house had been a multi-generational event. There was plenty of food – turkey, ham, and goose with all the sides. Nicholas remembered the love, the laughter, and the hugs when he left to return to base.

Christmas in Afghanistan had been surreal, hot, and dry, with scenery that looked more like Tatooine than the North Pole. Despite the heat and the war, there'd been caroling, makeshift trees decked with everything from ammo and foil stars to one made from discarded bottles, a 5K race, and Santa hats were everywhere. Suzanne had sent him a string of lights in a care package, and Nicholas had used it to make his quarters festive. Most of the family had sent him gifts as well as much coveted cookies.

That had been the last decent Christmas. Fast forward a year, and Nicholas had been in the hospital, stateside at Walter Reed Medical Center in Washington. Although his parents, his brother Nathaniel and Suzanne had come to visit the week before Christmas, the holiday was dismal. He'd been recovering from another surgery, been bummed about his permanent scars, and deeply depressed. The worst place to spend any holiday, he thought, was a hospital. Staff efforts to make it merry and bright were a major fail.

Since becoming a civilian, Nicholas had ignored the day. Last year, his brother Jordan had called him, and they talked, but not about the holiday. Then he'd called his grandfather, and they'd had a good conversation. That had been the best part of the season for Nicholas. Suzanne had invited him over for dinner, but he'd declined, although he'd dropped off presents for them on the 23rd.

Beside him, Belle slept, snuggled close, unaware he lay awake, his thoughts turning back to the past. Nicholas leaned down and brushed a kiss against her cheek. God, he loved her more than he ever thought he'd be able to love anyone. He hadn't intended to sing a Christmas carol, but his fingers played the chords, and he was singing it before he thought. When she joined him, he shivered with a delicious anticipation he hadn't known for ages. That was when he decided he might do Christmas this year, that he *wanted* to participate.

In the morning, Belle surveyed her totes and belongings. So did Nicholas, wondering how they would absorb it all into the house. He liked order and things to be neat, so leaving it wasn't an option. Before he told her so, she said, "I have a few ideas, Nicholas."

"About?"

"What to do with all this stuff. I figured you don't want it sitting here in the way very long."

"That's true," he said. He smelled work in his immediate future. "What are you thinking?"

"We should move into the front bedroom. It's much larger, there's a huge closet, and we could use my bed. It's queen-sized, and it would give us more space. Plus, I think it would be warmer. That back bedroom where you sleep is too little for both of us, plus it's cold."

Belle had valid points, but he decided on a whim to do even better.

"I like the idea, and you're right – that bedroom is too small, now. But instead of using your furniture, what if we go buy a king-sized bed? It'd be more comfortable, and we could put your bed in one of the other rooms. If we ever had a guest, it would be nicer than what I have."

Her expression brightened. "Could we? That sounds awesome, Nicholas."

"Then we'll go into town today and shop for a bedroom outfit."

Belle hugged him. "I'll go fix a quick breakfast so we can go."

"We can eat at the diner again if you want." In for a penny, in for a pound, his Granny used to say. If he was going to brave furniture shopping, he might as well take her out to breakfast. It would stress him, but he was trying to get his shit together to learn to deal with life despite his scars and PTSD.

He had pancakes with bacon, and she ordered a waffle with sausage. They sat in a round corner booth, and he fortified for shopping with plenty of coffee. Sunshine streamed through the windows as they finished breakfast, too warm for the stocking hat. He'd settled for a baseball cap and wore his jacket, the one with a hood. Maybe it wouldn't hide his face, but it would make the scars a little less noticeable.

The store offered both major appliances and furniture. They wandered through the aisles that wound around groupings of sofas and loveseats and bedroom sets until Belle stopped.

"I like this one," she said. "What do you think?"

Nicholas cared if it was comfortable and if it made her happy. He looked forward to the extra space, but the appearance didn't matter. Still, he studied it. The four-piece set appeared to be solid, fashioned from a dark chocolate wood. There was a king bed with a high headboard and low footboard, two nightstands and a dresser, all in the same deep shade. A mirror above the dresser made him step back so he wouldn't see his reflection.

"It's good – just no mirror, please."

"We'll need a mattress, too," Belle said. He admired that she was a quick shopper and a practical one. He paid for the furniture and the mattress they selected. To his surprise, the store manager offered delivery that afternoon.

Now they needed bedding, so they headed off to the discount store. Nicholas opted to wait in the truck, and Belle agreed, delivering a quick kiss before she headed inside. He almost wished he could be with her, holding hands, picking out sheets and comforters. It would seem so normal, he thought, but he wasn't ready to face the bargain store crowds at noon on Saturday. Nicholas hoped she wouldn't pick anything pink or feminine, but he promised himself he wouldn't bitch if she did.

She emerged a good hour later, pushing a cart laden with bags. In addition to a bed-in-the bag king size set, she'd picked up a few groceries, some shampoo and other HBA items, and a bag with Christmas ornaments. She'd also bought some lights, garlands, and other decorations.

"I hope you don't mind," she said after stowing the bags in the back. "If we don't decorate, it's fine. And I hope you like the comforter set I picked."

Nicholas had more interest in what she'd picked up for supper. With all the shopping, they'd missed lunch altogether, and breakfast had been hours earlier. He wasn't disappointed, either.

By evening she'd managed to assimilate the bulk of her stuff into his home. There were more homey touches now, a couple of bright throw pillows on the couch and some rugs on the floor. Her books and movies were now beside his, and she'd brought a couple of framed paintings, just discount store reproductions, that hung on the wall. Her little dab of kitchen goods had been put away. The biggest difference was the bedroom. Not only had they changed rooms, but it'd become theirs, no longer his. The comforter had a rustic motif in dark green, brown, and tan with bears, elk, and pine trees. Nicholas liked it, and the matching curtains she'd hung at every window had an appeal. Belle had put down some rugs. She'd put her things away in the dresser and closet, then moved his computer desk from the smallest bedroom to the other side of the larger front bedroom. While she went to cook the meal, he moved his smalls and few garments into the new space.

He had a few moments when the sight of her perfume and other items on the dresser gave him pause, the same for her shampoo, hairbrush, and cosmetics in the bathroom downstairs. As much as he wanted Belle there, he had a sense of invasion, that she'd moved in lock, stock, and barrel. For a few brief moments, he wanted to toss her things, kick her out, and return to his lonely self-imposed exile.

Nicholas drew deep breaths and realized his emotions sprang from PTSD, not his heart. If he had acted on those feelings, he could well have destroyed whatever fragile beginnings they had, which was the last thing he wanted.

At the table, she served up a concoction she called "Mexican lasagna," flour tortillas layered with red beans, rice, seasoned hamburger, and cheese. From the taste, he guessed she'd flavored the meat with some cream soups to give it a rich taste. He thought there were onions, fresh mushrooms, and maybe cilantro in the mix as well. She had a basket of corn tortilla chips and some salsa to serve on the side.

"What do you think?" Belle asked.

"It's tasty, and I like it."

She flashed him a grin. "Good. I was worried maybe a Texas guy wouldn't like my effort. It's definitely not authentic."

Nicholas laughed. "We ate more regular food than anything Mexican, other than chili, so you didn't need to fret about that."

"Well, I was concerned about your stomach, too. I didn't know if spicy food might set it off."

He shook his head. "My belly trouble is more about the PTSD than what I eat, babe. If I get a bellyache, it won't be from this."

"Does it stress you, all these changes?"

God, she could be intuitive, and so he gave her honesty. "A little bit, yeah. I didn't like change much, even before. But I'm happy about it, Belle, so it's good. It just takes a little adjusting."

She nodded. "There's not much left to do – I thought tomorrow we could set up my queen bed in one of the bedrooms as a guest room, then sometime I want to get a few things for our bedroom too."

He cringed a little at that. "My pockets aren't that deep, baby."

"I'll spend some of my savings. Plus, I have that $200 from my old landlord."

That made him laugh, so he nodded. "My old room could be a guest room, too, although I'm not planning on doing a lot of entertaining."

"You never know – Teagan might want to spend the night sometime. One of your brothers might want to come up, or Timothy."

Nicholas had never thought that far ahead, but he nodded. "You have a point, I suppose. It could happen."

Probably wouldn't, but it didn't hurt to be ready, he

reasoned. "By the way, next week is my check-up down at Fayetteville."

"What day?"

"Tuesday."

"How early do we need to leave?"

"Early. My appointment's at nine."

"Then I'll plan for that. Do you want another serving?"

He'd eaten two large pieces, so he shook his head. "I'm good."

"Let me get the dishes washed."

Nicholas put his hand over hers. "Soak 'em," he said. "I'd like us to go break in the new bed if you don't mind."

As delicious as supper had been, he coveted more than food. From the quick smile that flirted with her lips, so did Belle. "I don't."

They barely made it up the stairs, kissing and dropping garments as they went. After years of celibacy, with nothing more than occasionally spanking the monkey, sex had a major appeal. As a young man, as a Marine, he'd enjoyed the act but with no strings attached. He'd lost his virginity on prom night, practically an American rite of passage, and until he got injured, Nicholas had enjoyed dalliances with willing women. Some had been girlfriends, others just a temporary interlude. With Belle, intimacy was nothing like he had ever experienced. He wanted her, body and soul. Every one of his five senses was engaged when they came together. He enjoyed the sight of her, naked and not. Nicholas liked both the sound of her voice and the noises she made when aroused, as well as the joyful shrieks she made with orgasm. Her feminine aroma aroused him, both the natural scent and her perfume. Nicholas delighted in tasting her, from mouth to pussy, and he savored the touch of her hands on his, her body against his.

He had stayed celibate in fear of rejection, and to be honest, on the day of his recovery, he hadn't even considered sex. He'd been too focused on survival. He figured any woman he might desire would be repulsed by his Freddy Krueger resemblance, and he knew he couldn't handle that.

Belle had been different from the first. Not once had she shown any sign of disgust or loathing. She'd come to him willingly and with a tenderness he hadn't expected.

In the upstairs hall, he pulled her close against him and removed her bra. Her blouse lay somewhere on the stairs with his T-shirt. By the time they entered the bedroom, both were nude. He almost took her standing up in his haste, his extreme need but found enough control to push back the new comforter before they lay on the bed. His hands skimmed over her body, pausing to fondle her beautiful breasts. He lowered his mouth onto first one nipple, then the other and suckled. Nicholas buried his face between her breasts and kissed her there, then moved his lips down. He kissed her belly, paused at her belly button, then went lower.

As he stroked her, Belle's hands were on him, sometimes clinging, often caressing his body. When he put his head down between her legs, she made a soft noise, and he used his tongue to lave her there, to taste her most personal parts. Her hands became claws as she raked his back with her short nails, too short to damage but long enough to deliver exquisite sensations that radiated through him. With her flavor on his lips, he kissed her, then entered her with his proud cock.

Her flesh gave way to his, the heat radiating from her box, heating his dick like a fever. He went deep, and she received him, squeezing the walls of her box tight against him so that he had to concentrate not to come yet. Nicholas drove until he knew he'd penetrated the very center of her womanhood, then he rocked his cock, raising it up and down while her moans increased.

They traveled together toward that peak, and he gloried in each moment, every stroke. His breath caught and came short as he sought release, and she became just as breathless. Any moment he would go, explode, but he wanted to bring her with him and did.

Belle cried out, a wordless shriek of delight that made him empty into her faster. They shuddered together, bodies shimmying and shaking as if caught in an earthquake. He yelled, too, a triumphant shout as they came together, light and heat in triumph over every darkness. Sensation spiraled through him, sweet and necessary, until they convulsed as one, then he lay, still joined, gasping but smiling.

For him, it was beyond physical. When he made love to Belle, their souls touched. Even after he pulled out, handing her a towel to catch the wet between her legs, he craved to be close.

The sheer delight of not wearing a condom pleased him, and he remembered she said she got birth control shots. *Need to remind her to find somewhere to get those here,* he thought as they lay together, *or I'll have to buy a box of Trojans.*

For now, they needed the birth control, but he realized for the first time in his life that having a child with Belle could be a very good thing. He loved his little niece and cared for the other nieces and nephews in Texas, but a child of his own would be monumental. Until now, it wasn't something he thought he'd ever consider, but this woman changed everything. She turned his world every which way but loose, and for the love of God, Nicholas liked it.

Chapter Fifteen

She dressed up, not down, on the day of his appointment with the Veterans Administration. Belle chose a tailored black pantsuit, jacket, and trousers, with a bright red blouse beneath. As a reporter, it had been her go-to outfit for important events, something classic and timeless that presented a professional appearance. She put on a pair of pumps with it and added a necklace, a silver Celtic knot design. Nicholas, who wore jeans and t-shirts daily, had put on a polo shirt at her urging, but that was as far as he would dress up for the occasion.

"It's just two doctor's appointments," he said, when she had suggested a nice button-down dress shirt. "They don't expect me to look fancy."

"I just wanted to look good," she told him.

"You do, babe. You look very pretty, so sophisticated."

His compliment made her blush. "Thank you. So, it's two appointments, not one?"

"The first one is a check-up with an MD," he replied. "The

other is with a shrink. You know, for the PTSD and all."

Belle hadn't, but she nodded. "Absolutely. And afterward, we're going to eat at What-A-Burger?"

Nicholas held back for a few seconds, then said, "Yes, we are."

On the ride down, he seemed quiet, but in good spirits, so she gave him the space he appeared to need. Belle rode beside him, her hand on his thigh. From time to time, he shifted his hand from the wheel to touch her. Although she'd done some traveling, visiting Arkansas was a first.

"I'd stop for breakfast if I could," he told her as they rolled through Rogers, Arkansas. "But I imagine they'll take blood samples since they always do, and they prefer I fast from midnight. But if you're hungry, I can get you something. We've got time."

His consideration pleased her. "No, thanks, but I can wait too."

"Trust me, What-A-Burger is worth waiting for," he said with a smile.

"Are you nervous?"

He gave a quick nod. "Hell, yeah, always am. I just never know what they might say or find, that's all."

"Do you expect them to find something?" The possibility concerned her.

"No, I don't. It's just me being anxious, that's all."

At the VA Medical Center, a massive four-story brick building with white columns flanked by much newer construction, Belle felt lost, but Nicholas knew his way. He stopped at a lab area where he pissed in a sample cup – without her help – and was stuck to get some blood samples. After that, they sat in a waiting room for what seemed like a long time, and Nicholas was called back. He stretched out his hand to her, and she took it.

"Come with me."

"Will they allow that?" she asked, although she had hoped she could accompany him.

He shrugged. "If I say I want you, why not?"

First, the nurse who weighed him and led them into an exam room questioned her presence, then the doctor did.

"Nicholas, who is this?" he asked, staring at her over the top of his glasses.

"Maribel Barbier," he replied. "She's my lady."

She liked the fact that he gave her full name and liked it even more than he claimed her with pride. If he'd said "girlfriend," she would have accepted it, but the term seemed juvenile for adults.

"Is this a recent thing?" the doctor asked. "You've never mentioned a significant other before."

"You didn't ask," Nicholas replied. "And yeah, I want her here."

The doctor – whose badge said he was Dr. Samuel Carter – waved his hand. "Very well. Climb up onto the exam table, and we'll get started. Are you experiencing any problems?"

Belle took a seat in the lone chair against the wall and reached in her purse for a reporter's notebook and pen. She prepared to jot down anything important that was said.

Nicholas talked about his ongoing issues, his occasional insomnia, the digestive trouble, the headaches, and the anxiety. None of these were new, and the doctor discussed them with casual indifference. "Unless you tell me otherwise, I'm going to assume that all those symptoms are associated with PTSD," he said. "And Dr. Bonner will talk more about that with you at your next appointment. Any issues with your scar tissue? Any pain?"

"Sometimes," Nicholas said, his voice low. That surprised

Belle. "Nothing I can't manage."

Dr. Carter raised Nicholas' shirt to probe the scars on his chest and back. He ran his hand over them. "I don't see any major inflammation, although if it's a problem, we can always talk about new grafts, although that would involve surgery."

"No."

Then the doctor turned on a bright light to illuminate Nicholas' face and neck, "I can send you for a consult with a plastic surgeon if you want to free that right eye up more and the same for your lip."

"No."

From the sound of his voice, Belle knew he had become tense and that he could be heading for an episode. Although she had no doubt that the VA doc could handle it, she figured Nicholas wouldn't want it. He'd regret it later, and so she said, "If he's okay with the scarring and there's no problems, then why not leave it as it is."

The medico scrutinized her with a piercing gaze. "That's really for Nicholas here to answer, but if he can see some minor improvements, I'd recommend them. Obviously, he's going to remain scarred, but...."

"It's just a face," Nicholas said. "And it's mine. There aren't going to be any more surgeries, Dr. Carter. I don't like it – probably never will – but I'm learning to live with it. Can we stick to the check-up if you don't mind?"

He used my line, Belle thought with triumphant joy. *Those are my words. I guess he took them to heart more than I thought.*

After a long silence, the doctor nodded. "We can. I see your weight has increased by about ten pounds. That's good – you've been underweight for a long time, so this is excellent, as long as there's no medical reason."

"It's from good cooking," Nicholas said with a faint hint of a smile. "That and some TLC."

"Then that's all good," the doctor said. "I don't see any evident problems. The blood test results will be back in a day or two. You can look them up online, and if there's any issue, of course, we'll contact you."

"Remind me what all you test for," Nicholas said.

"Blood sugar, in case of diabetes, cholesterol, thyroid, cell counts, any STDs, anemia," Dr. Carter said. "I also meant to mention to you that now that there's a VA clinic in Joplin, you could go there. It's much closer."

"I'd heard that," Nicholas said. "I'll think about it."

"Very well. Barring any unexpected results from your blood and urine tests, you're doing quite well. I didn't expect to see you with a significant other, but I'm pleased. Make an appointment to come back in six months. If you do decide to transfer to Joplin, that's easily done. You can take care of it online."

"Thank you," Nicholas said as he jumped down from the exam table. "C'mon, Belle, it's onward to the next."

In another building in the vast complex, Nicholas was ushered into his next appointment. Dr. Bonner proved to be Dr. Berniece Bonner, an attractive blonde, probably around fifty. She greeted him with familiar warmth but balked when she saw Belle.

"Nicholas, you know how personal and sensitive our sessions are," she said. "I'd rather not have your – aide, assistant...."

"My lady," he said. "She's been more helpful to me with my PTSD than anyone ever has been. She's seen me in bad times and good times. I want her to stay."

They debated her presence for a few more minutes, and

although Belle wanted to stay, she considered bowing out just to keep the peace. She didn't, though, not when Nicholas had her hand in a tight grip.

In the session, he talked openly about his recent episodes, breaking the mirror, his response to Kansas City, and his health issues. He also detailed how he'd taken Belle, his sister and niece to McDonald's to dine inside and how he'd stood firm with the landlord at her place. He mentioned going to Thanksgiving at her grandmother's home with many guests, spoke of the chance he'd observe Christmas, then dropped the biggest bombshell of all.

"I'm going home to Texas for my grandfather's birthday, his 90th," Nicholas said. Belle observed how the physiatrist's professional mask vanished when he told her that. Apparently, he'd talked about his issues with his family and his hometown. "Belle will be with me. I probably wouldn't go if she wasn't."

"Are you becoming co-dependent?" Dr. Bonner (call me 'Berniece' please) said.

Although his hand tightened his grip on hers, Nicholas never hesitated. "No, not in the least. Her support is invaluable. She understands me."

"Does she? If so, that's admirable. I assume this is a platonic relationship?"

Belle's cheeks heated, and she knew they had turned pink. Nicholas laughed out loud.

"You know what they say about the word assume," he said in his best Texas drawl. "That is, it makes an ass out of you and me, right? Well, let's just say it's not me. No, it's not platonic in the least."

"I'm amazed," Dr. Bonner said when she recovered her voice. "And pleased, of course, but after what we've talked about in the past, I never expected you to move past the barriers of a relationship. You were fearful of rejection, if I recall, and very hesitant about performance. What changed?"

"I met the right woman," he said.

The session lasted another thirty minutes. Nicholas resisted the doctor's offer to write new prescriptions for either Paxil or Zoloft. He seemed to listen when she talked about some coping techniques he might try, and Belle jotted them down. Later, she'd research them further online.

"I've quit the whole beast thing," Nicholas volunteered. "I don't call my place the beast's lair anymore, and even my little niece dropped the whole 'Uncle Beast' thing."

"That's progress, certainly."

Belle, who he had once again introduced as Maribel, held her breath, hoping he wouldn't mention her name so the doctor wouldn't make the whole Belle/Beast connection from the old fairy tale. It might be too much to explain, she thought, not that it bothered her in the least.

At the end of the session, the doctor removed her glasses and gazed at Nicholas.

"You're doing well, Nicholas, the best I've ever seen you. I'm pleased, of course. But you still have the issues with bellyaches, headaches, and insomnia, correct?"

"I do," he said. "And on occasion, a nightmare or flashback."

He'd mentioned it all earlier, so Belle wondered why the doctor brought it back up now.

"I don't expect that to change anytime soon, if ever. I can treat any of those conditions with drugs, but I know you'd rather not. If, however, any of them become unbearable, you need to make an appointment with me as soon as possible. You just must remember PTSD isn't going away. It's a lifelong condition. It can be volatile and tricky at best. You can live with it, of course, but there's no cure. And you, Miss Barbier, you're fully aware of this, as well?"

"I am."

"Very well, then. I'll see you in six months unless you need to see me sooner. Best of luck, Nicholas. If any of my patients could use an upbeat change, you do."

He said little as they wound their way through the facility and back to where he'd parked the truck. Although temperatures were cool, the sun was shining. At the truck, he stopped and opened his arms. Belle walked into them, wrapping her arms around his neck as he cuddled her close. He kissed her long, slow, and sweet.

"Thank God that's over," he said, with feeling. "If I wasn't starving, I'd say let's go find a motel, but I want to eat, then go home. What do you say?"

"Take me to What-A-Burger!"

Belle found the iconic burger chain delightful and the food delicious. "You're right," she said as she blotted her lips as she munched through her double burger. "It's one of the best I've ever had."

"Told you," he said. "It's good stuff."

Traffic was terrible on the way home, but once they exited Arkansas, it began to lighten. For once, Belle, accustomed to driving in Kansas City's worst, was glad she wasn't driving, and she worried if the stress would affect Nicholas. He seemed to be fine, though, as he wound through multi-lanes of speeding vehicles. On the home stretch, the last miles from the state line home, he admitted he was tired.

"Me too," she replied. "There's plenty left from last night

for an easy supper. We can chill out, watch a movie, and go to bed early if you want."

From his answering grin, he approved.

Then, because he told Belle he had restless energy to expend, he went for a tromp through the hills and woods for an hour. Nicholas returned, more than a little windburned and chilled, but he came back calm. He settled down into the recliner, and before Belle could say much, he fell asleep.

Belle curled up on the sofa and watched. A book lay open in her lap, but she couldn't keep her mind on the story. His maimed face was as relaxed as she'd ever seen it, giving him a younger look. He'd never said how old he was, not exactly. At thirty, she figured he had to be older, maybe even ten years her senior. Age didn't matter to her, and neither did his disfigurement. The first time she'd seen his face, there had been a moment of shock and surprise but no horror. Now, she loved every curve and line of his face because it was his. Nicholas wasn't ugly, just scarred.

Looking at him, she didn't notice the scars anymore.

"I love you," she whispered. "I love you so much."

He didn't stir, but soon she would tell him when she thought the moment was right.

Nicholas was still asleep when the wall phone in the kitchen rang. She hurried to answer, hoping it wouldn't wake him.

"Hey, is Saint around?" It was his cousin, Timothy.

"I'll get him," Belle said.

He entered the kitchen before she could, sleepy-eyed but wide awake. She handed him the phone. "It's Timothy."

"Good to hear your voice," Nicholas said as he stretched the phone cord out to take a seat at the table.

His cousin must have asked where they'd been. Maybe

he'd called earlier.

"We were in Arkansas, had my six-month checkups at the VA," he replied. "Good reports for both. What's shaking?"

Although Belle could hear Nicholas' side of the conversation and not the rest, she could gather most of what was said.

"I'm always ready to see you, Timothy. Come on up. We'll be glad to have you. Even got a guest bedroom set up. Yeah, it'll be like living in style, my man. What? Yeah, Belle's still here – she's living here now. Oh, did she? I'm not surprised."

He's talking about Suzanne, I guarantee it, Belle thought and sighed.

While Nicholas was on the phone, she heated them each a portion of the Mexican lasagna and poured them both a tall glass of sweet tea. Once the call ended, he dug in.

"So, I guess maybe you heard – Timothy is coming up to visit."

"I did – when will he be here?"

"Friday. He can be the first to sleep in the new guest room."

"I'll get the bed made up and the room ready," Belle told him. "What did Suzanne tell him about me?"

He flushed. "Her same old thing, that she's not sure what you're after, she's worried you're going to leave me and devastate me, all that."

"I'm not."

Nicholas grabbed her hand across the table. "Babe, I know that, and so will Timothy once he's here. Just be glad she didn't call my parents."

Belle digested that and swallowed a lump of food, her appetite gone.

"Well, we have a lot to do," she said. "We'll start in the

morning."

On Wednesday, they bought tile to replace the mirror over the fireplace, and after a quick lunch, Nicholas started on that project. Belle dipped into her savings to buy a few more things for both the guest bedroom and the house, then stocked up on groceries. An insurance check arrived in the mail, forwarded from Kansas City, so she resolved to start a bank account. Then she could buy a car to replace her Toyota and be mobile, as well as a little more self-reliant.

Belle could see how much Nicholas looked forward to his cousin's visit, so she did too. She hoped, however, that Suzanne was satisfied with the turmoil she'd added to their lives, delivering far more stress than Belle ever had.

Chapter Sixteen

He'd found the tree on his trek through the woods after his trip to the VA, a well-shaped cedar that would fit into the corner of the dining room or in the entrance way. Nicholas woke Belle earlier than usual on Thursday and announced they were going to bring the Christmas tree home.

"Dress warm," he told her. "And wear boots."

"All right," she'd replied. "But we won't be outside long, will we? Is there a tree lot in town?"

"No, city girl, we're going up on the hill and cutting down the tree like old times. Then you can decorate it."

He saw the momentary hesitation on her face and laughed. To him, it felt wonderful just to be pumped up about trekking after a tree. After she glanced at him, her expression changed.

"I'm in," she said. "This is a new experience for me."

The cedar sat almost at the top of the highest hill on his property, sheltered enough it hadn't been damaged by the wind or weather. It was almost as tall as Nicholas, so a good six foot, he figured. He'd carried the chainsaw with him and felled it quickly while Belle stood back, pretty with her cheeks pinked by the chilly breeze. Once down, he hauled it back to the house over a good half mile of rugged terrain. Halfway there, he started singing Christmas carols, and she joined in.

He parked it outside until he could be sure it was free of any critters while she went to dig out the tree stand that she'd bought. After a light lunch of soup and sandwiches, Nicholas brought the tree inside and, at her suggestion, placed it in the corner of the dining room beside the door leading into the living room.

"I don't think we have enough decorations," she told him after he'd wound the multi-colored mini lights through the branches. "I bought some things, but I wasn't expecting this tall of a tree."

"We'll improvise," he told her, recalling some of the makeshift trees he'd seen in the country.

"With what?"

Inspiration struck. "We'll go old-fashioned. Start popping some corn, and I'll show you how to make popcorn garlands. And if there's foil, I'll make a star for the top."

While beef and gravy simmered on the stove, they strung popcorn, a tedious process, nibbling a little as they worked. She'd also bought cranberries, so Nicholas fashioned those into garlands as well. The whimsical little ornaments she'd bought were added to the branches, one at a time, with a meticulous eye. Belle wrapped each of the garlands around the tree with care. Two were tinsel, one red, one silver, but the others were made to resemble old-time hard candies. To finish it out, he found some late Queen Anne's lace still on the stalks and brought them in, spraying them with her hair spray to preserve them. Nicholas placed these on the tree and inspired Belle to add some silk roses she culled from a door decoration she'd brought. After digging into a drawer, he located some construction paper and put together a couple of paper chains. He topped it with his handmade foil star.

"It looks good," he said, surveying it.

"It's pretty," Belle told him. "It reminds me of something out of the Little House on the Prairie books."

Nicholas liked the way the aromatic cedar scent filled the house, bringing the fresh aroma of the outside within. When Belle produced several Christmas stockings, then wrote names on them with a glitter pen, he grinned.

"You bought stockings!"

"Of course, just for me, you and Teagan."

Once hung, they were festive, especially with the new neutral tiles he had put in to replace the broken mirror.

"Too bad there isn't any mistletoe," he commented.

Belle pointed to a bunch she'd hung over the doorway, and he grinned. Then he kissed her, savoring the sweet taste of her, reigning in his desire so he wouldn't take her before they had time to eat.

"I'm celebrating Christmas," he said, with something like awe.

"You are – and you should call and see if your sister will bring Teagan over. School's out by now, and she'll love it."

Her grandmother stopped by with a wreath she'd bought in town, and Nicholas invited Ethel to stay for supper. Suzanne and Teagan arrived a short time later, and when the little girl saw the wreath on the door, she squealed. "You're having Christmas, Uncle Nick!"

"I am," he said. "Come see our tree."

Suzanne forced a smile, and he could tell for some reason she wasn't thrilled with the holiday décor.

"Come, I'll show you," Belle said, holding out her hand to Teagan. "Ethel, you come see it too."

Nicholas faced his sister and folded his arms across his chest. "What?"

"I didn't say anything."

"You didn't have to – I thought you'd be delighted I wanted to do something for Christmas."

"I am – if it's your own idea, if she's not forcing you."

"You mean like sending Timothy up to spy on me? To get a handle on what's happening here, right? And to send Belle packing if he agrees with you?"

Suzanne's face went brick red, and her eyes glittered. "Guilty, but it's for your own good, Nick. I just don't trust her...."

"I do. And it's over, Sis, this insane suspicion, this paranoid bullshit. Belle's done more for me than anyone. I went to Arkansas the other day, to the VA."

"What did they say? Is everything all right?"

Her genuine concern eased his temper a bit. "Better than it's ever been since I came home," he replied in a dry tone. "And that's due to Belle's help. She went with me."

"Why? What was in it for her, Nick?"

He'd been irritated, but anger flared now. "Suz, I'm fucking done. You either let this go or stop coming around, you hear me? I don't want Teagan to suffer from your pig-headed attitude, so chill. Are you going to quit?"

She stared at him, then nodded. "I will because I don't want anything to come between us, Nick. You're my brother, and I love you. And I worry."

"Then let me live a little," he told her. "You surely didn't think I should stay holed up like a wounded animal for the rest of my life, did you?"

Suzanne shook her head.

"Come see the tree and the rest of the house. If you're nice, you can come upstairs and see the guest rooms."

"I didn't know you had guest rooms," she said, her tone both mollified and muted.

He slung one arm around her shoulders in a hug. "There's a lot you don't know."

For the first time since he'd lived in the old farmhouse, supper was served in the dining room because Suzanne, Teagan and Ethel all accepted his invitation. The beef and gravy served over rice was delicious, and eaten in the shadow of the first Christmas tree he'd ever put up in the house, Nicholas enjoyed it. His sister managed to behave and said nothing more about Belle.

On Friday, Belle went on a final cleaning frenzy in advance of his cousin's visit. Timothy called when he hit the Missouri state line, and she took time to change clothes, exchanging her faded jeans for a pair of slacks and a sweater. On impulse, Nicholas put on a dress shirt and almost had the courage to glance in the mirror.

Timothy rolled up in the vintage Mustang he'd restored, a cherry red 1965 model with a white hardtop. He parked, and Nicholas dashed down the porch steps to greet him. Timothy grabbed him in a bear hug and yelled, "Oorah, gunny!"

"You're looking good, pard," he said as they headed inside.

"Yeah, right," Nicholas said. "Like a nightmare on Elm Street, sure."

Timothy paused in the entryway. "Stop already. I mean it. You look happier than I've seen you in years."

"I am. Come meet Belle and forget everything Suze told you about her."

His cousin didn't advance. "You're sure about her, right? Your sister made her sound like the worst gold digger or something more. She had me more than a little worried."

If he hadn't been so glad to see Timothy, he would have been angry.

"No need, cuz. Belle's the best thing that's happened to me in years."

As if summoned by speaking her name, Belle came out of the living room, and Nicholas tried to see her through his cousin's eyes. She was petite with a good shape and generous breasts. Her light brown hair touched her shoulders, although she had it pulled up into a ponytail. Her oval face had a light dusting of freckles over the bridge of her button nose. She gazed at Nicholas with warmth in her blue eyes and came to him. He put his arm around her and introduced her.

"Timothy, this is Belle," he said. "This is my cousin."

"I made fresh coffee," she said. "And I baked cookies if you're hungry."

"Not cake?" Nicholas asked her, and she smiled at the personal joke.

"Not today. Have you seen our Christmas tree?"

Nicholas waved his cousin to go first, pausing beneath the mistletoe to kiss Belle. Although she'd put on some light makeup when she dressed up to welcome Timothy, she didn't balk but kissed him back. In the past, he'd had women who didn't want their lip color compromised by a kiss, but it didn't bother Belle. The kiss meant more, and he loved that.

The strip steaks were perfect, rare enough to preserve both flavor and tenderness but not bleeding onto the plate. Belle served them with twice-baked potatoes and a salad she'd tossed. Although she and Nicholas drank sweet tea, Timothy enjoyed the Lone Star beers they'd stocked in the fridge.

For the first time in ages, Nicholas craved one. He had limited his drinking since he got out of the hospital, originally, so the booze wouldn't interact with any meds but later, just to prevent any loss of control. A few times, in loneliness and despair, he'd gotten drunk but regretted it the next day. Since Belle came into his life, he hadn't drunk anything except adding one shot of whiskey to his coffee the day she announced she planned to stay. That had been no more than a little boost of liquid courage, something it had turned out he hadn't needed.

He wanted a beer, not just because he craved the taste but wanted to share the camaraderie with his cousin. Once the talk had shifted from the polite yet meaningless into catching up, Nicholas wanted a brew.

He'd asked Timothy how Thanksgiving had gone, and the answer set his nerves on edge.

"It was about what you'd expect," Timothy had replied. "We had it at Grandpa Reilley's house since it's bigger, but my mom and yours did all the cooking. Most of the family brought a covered dish, too, so there was more food than we could eat in a week. They had both turkey and ham, but you know Grandpa, he groused because there wasn't goose. I ate too much, of course, and was glad when it was over. I hear you went to Belle's grandmother's house."

"We did, Suzanne and the kid, too," Nicholas replied. "First time I've been anywhere for a holiday in years."

"So come home for Christmas. Everyone asked about you. Your mom said she wished you would – she hasn't seen you in a long time."

"Did you tell them I'm coming for Grandpa's birthday?"

Timothy opened another beer and took a long swig. "I did. Gramps liked that – your mom said she'd believe it when she saw you walk through the door. And Uncle Billy Henry said he didn't think you have the stones to show up, that you'd left your balls behind in Afghanistan."

He didn't expect his cousin to sugarcoat, but the stark reality hit him hard.

"Nice," he said. That was when he got up and grabbed his own beer from the fridge.

"Grandpa tore him a new ass over it," Timothy said. "Told him you had bigger balls and more courage than Uncle Billy ever had and to shut up or get out of his house."

"Did he go?"

"No, but he shut the fuck up and didn't say anything more the rest of the day."

The beer tasted wonderful, rich and full flavored in his mouth. Maybe he'd have another or two or six. "So, nothing's fucking changed?"

"Did you think it would? Uncle Billy Henry's also been an asshat, and you know it. Oh, and I've got cards for you. Your mom didn't mail them because she figured they would be late anyway. Don't let me forget to give them to you."

Belle had been unusually quiet, but now she spoke. "Cards?"

Nicholas cringed as Timothy filled her in. "Yeah, for his birthday."

"His birthday?" she repeated and turned to him with a confused look.

Timothy, fueled by multiple beers, guffawed. "Didn't he tell you why we call him 'Saint'? He was born on December 6, St.

Nicholas Day."

He watched her face, saw the realization that his natal day had come and gone without notice and that he'd never mentioned it. Her expression shifted from confusion to surprise and then hurt.

"No, he didn't," Belle spoke in a level voice but then she pushed back her chair, leaving almost half her steak uneaten and vanished from the room.

Nicholas wanted to bolt after her but didn't. Timothy followed the exchange with great interest, laughing until he realized he'd pissed off his cousin.

"I'm sorry, man," he said, spreading both hands wide in apology. "I didn't realize she didn't know. Why didn't you tell her?"

Nicholas shrugged. First, it hadn't really occurred to him to mention it, and when he thought about it, he said nothing. He'd figured she'd make a fuss, and he'd half expected Suzanne would tell her. His sister hadn't, and with everything, his VA appointments, his decision to decorate for the season, and his cousin's visit, he'd never thought about it again. Now he realized he should have.

"She looked pissed," Timothy offered.

"No, she's hurt," Nicholas said. "I hurt her feelings, and she's upset. That's the last thing I wanted to do."

"Are you going to go talk to her?"

He was, once he found the words to explain what he didn't understand. "I will," he replied. "But first, I'll have another beer."

Despite the delicious steak dinner, his gut felt like someone had slammed an iron fist into it. His belly twisted into a painful knot, and he knew the beer would make it worse, not better. Still, he downed another in a few gulps before he followed Belle's trail out of the kitchen, wondering where she'd gone.

He found her in their bedroom, one of her suitcases lying on the bed. Belle stood in front of the closet, arms across her chest, and when he came in, she didn't even look up.

"Belle."

She gazed at him now, her eyes bright with anger and wet with tears. "Happy belated birthday, Nicholas."

"Belle, I should have mentioned it."

"Yeah, you should have, but you didn't, so hey, I get the message."

"What message? I just didn't tell you because…."

"Because you can't totally open up to me," she said in a voice as brittle as thin glass. "I thought – well, never mind what I thought – but I think I'll go stay with Ethel for a few days. She's invited me more than once, and I think now I could use the distance. I really need to think, to reevaluate this."

If she left, she probably wouldn't come back and that knowledge increased his bellyache from a pain level of four to eight. He almost moaned aloud and fought against bending double over his twisting, hurting gut. "Belle, please don't."

She whirled to face him. "Give me a good reason not to go."

Nicholas took two steps closer to her and told her what he'd meant to say for days but hadn't. "I love you."

Her face changed, and tears poured down her cheeks. "I wish I could believe that. You have a damn weird way to show it."

"You can believe it, Belle. I love you more than, than anything. Just don't go."

He touched her face, his hand light against her cheek. Belle brushed it with her fingers, still crying. "Nicholas, I love you. But now I don't know...."

A sharp cramp doubled him over, and he groaned.

"What's wrong?"

"Gut hurts," he gasped. "Fucking PTSD."

Belle steered him to the bed, and once there, she kneaded his shoulders with her hands. She talked to him, too, her voice calm and low as she talked him through the episode. As his taut muscles relaxed, she rubbed his back, shoving his shirt up so she could touch his bare skin. She helped him to ground, to lay down his emotions and to ease. As his abdomen calmed, he focused on her and knew she promised she would stay.

The three words that mattered were 'I love you,' and she repeated them until he forgot about his aching belly and his cousin downstairs. All he knew was that she was staying and that she loved him.

And how much he loved her.

Chapter Seventeen

A gracious hostess would never abandon her guest during dinner, but Belle bailed, manners forgotten the moment she realized Nicholas had never shared his birthday with her. The day, one that she would have delighted in making special, had come and gone, lost without any recognition. The omission loomed huge to her, even more so because apparently his nickname, Saint, wasn't just because he shared a name with Santa Claus but because he'd been born on the saint's feast day. He could have told her – and should have. There might be a reason, but she couldn't imagine one, so she ran.

Belle didn't think about where to go. She ended up in their bedroom, the one she'd just decorated with such love and hope. She fought the desire to throw herself on the bed like a teenager and cry. Instead, she put one of her suitcases on the bed, unopened and contemplated packing. Since she'd given up her home, the only place she could go would be her grandmother's house, and Ethel had offered. Originally, she'd planned to stay there for a couple of nights before heading back to KC. This might be the time to accept the woman's invitation, she thought. She needed space to think.

She'd thought Nicholas cared, maybe even loved her too. Now she wondered if she were just a convenience for him, that he needed her out of loneliness, not love. For all she knew, maybe he'd brought other women home to stay with him and remembered an old expression her adopted great-grandmother had often used, 'at night, all cats are gray.'

At first, she thought he'd bolt after her and planned to offer him a frosty shoulder. When Nicholas didn't follow her, she waited, still ready to offer him nothing but a chill. Once she realized he hadn't immediately come after her, the tears knotted in her chest broke loose, and she cried, furiously scrubbing her cheeks as she stared into her closet. If she opened that suitcase, once she pulled things from the hangers and put them inside, it would be over, and she knew it. Her leaving would make him angry, and if he couldn't be bothered to share his birthday with her, he would let her go.

"Belle." He said her name like a prayer, and she resisted the urge to turn to him, to bury her face against his chest to find comfort. Instead, she responded with anger and hurt. She had been about to remove a blouse from the closet and walk it to the suitcase when he said the one thing that had the power to change her direction.

"I love you."

The sweet words fell on her ears, as welcome as rain in a drought. Then he added, 'more than anything,' and she knew she wouldn't go, not unless he drove her away. He stroked her cheek, and she lifted her fingers to touch him when he hunched forward, bowed over his stomach, and moaned.

"What's wrong?" she asked, although she knew. His PTSD often manifested in the form of bodily ills. Sometimes he had bad headaches, and sometimes his stomach reacted to stress with pain.

Once he laid down on his side, Belle massaged his shoulders. His muscles were taught. When she slipped a hand beneath his shirt to touch his abdomen, it was rigid and hard. It must be cramping because beneath her hand, his belly spasmed, and he groaned.

"I'm not leaving," she told him. "I promise. I love you, Nicholas."

He mumbled something, and she kept talking, doing her best to ground him and to lighten his stress. She lost track of time, but as his shoulders relaxed, she shifted her hands to his back, rubbing it beneath his shirt.

After a long time, his posture straightened. "Loving me can't be easy."

Belle laughed. "No, it's not, but you're worth it."

"Even if I didn't tell you when it was my birthday?"

"Yes."

"I'm sorry." He twisted around to look at her. "I haven't really celebrated it either, not since before. I didn't mention it because I didn't want you to feel like you had to do anything for it and...."

She understood now, at least a little. "I'm surprised Suzanne didn't tell me. But then, she's trying to make you think I'm after something, so I can see why she wouldn't. Feel better?"

"Yeah. I shouldn't have drunk the beer. It probably made it worse. I'm a fucking mess, huh?"

Belle lay down and put her arms around him from behind. "I'll take you like you are."

He hummed a few bars of the Horton song and nodded. "Good. Belle, I'm tired."

"Then get some sleep. I'll say something to your cousin."

"Okay, then come back."

Downstairs, she was surprised to see that Timothy had cleared the table, put away the food and washed the dishes. He sprawled in one of the recliners, watching an old John Wayne movie, not a Western, but a war movie. Belle thought it was called 'Back To Bataan.' She thought he might be asleep, but he stood up. "Hey, is Saint okay?"

"Yeah, but he's gone to bed."

"He looked sick."

Belle sat down, noting the concern in his cousin's voice. "I'm sure you know he suffers from PTSD. He gets terrible headaches, sometimes, and stomachaches too. It's not just anxiety and flashbacks. But he's all right now, and we're good."

"He really loves you, and you apparently love him. That's good. He needs it."

She nodded.

"And hey, I'm sorry – didn't mean to mess you two up."

"In the long run, you didn't. Is his dad really that uncaring?" Belle wanted to know.

"Sometimes, but he's a complicated man," Timothy said after a pause. "A lot of it comes from the hurt that he doesn't come home, and part from no one knows how to treat him. Nick gets mad if they baby him and madder if they act like nothing has changed. Are you coming home with him in March?"

"I am." Nothing, even family discord, would prevent it.

"Good. He'll need you, and I think they'll realize you're a force to be reckoned with. Suzanne needs to get that. If she hasn't, she will – I'll make damn sure of that."

"Thanks."

She pointed him to the guest room and returned to Nicholas, who was still sleeping.

In the morning, the two cousins headed out to fish on a fair but cool day. Both invited Belle to tag along, but she shook her head and said 'no.' Someday she wanted to see this Grand Lake o'the Cherokees that Nicholas liked so well, but she didn't want to intrude on their reunion. Besides, she had promised her grandmother she would come over to talk. Ethel had photo albums she wanted to show Belle, and Belle craved more details about her adoption.

Tonight, after the guys returned, they were eating at Suzanne's again. This time, her husband, Marshall, would be there to grill burgers and dogs. If Nicholas and Timothy caught enough fish, they would have a fish fry on Sunday.

Before heading to the farm, Belle opened a bank account at the same place Nicholas banked, using her insurance check. Then she did a little early recon around a few car lots, noting a few likely prospects. Next week, she planned for Nicholas to go with her to buy a car. Today, she borrowed his old truck, and they'd gone in Timothy's Mustang.

Ethel served lunch, homemade potato soup and biscuits. Both were delicious, and Belle wondered if she'd inherited some cooking skills. Her adopted mother couldn't boil water and preferred take-out or quick prep meals. As they ate, Belle asked the question she'd brought with her but hadn't ever had the chance to ask.

"What happened that I was adopted?" she asked Ethel. "I didn't even know I was until my parents died. All I know is that I was four months old and that it happened after my birth mother died."

"That's about all we know, too," her grandmother replied, buttering a biscuit. "Your mom was Sheree Johnson, and she was sixteen when you were born and sixteen when she died. Peter – your dad – started dating her when they were in the eighth grade. They were together all the time, dating before he could drive, and he planned to marry her. But when she turned up pregnant, her family wouldn't let him see her anymore. Peter offered to get married, but they said no. The Johnsons were a trashy bunch, though. Sheree's older brothers both did time in juvie for burglary and later got picked up for drug possession. They moved from here over to Springfield, and I always thought it was to keep your dad away from you."

She listened, digesting the information, although it would take a long time to fully accept it. "Why? Didn't they like him?"

Ethel shook her head. "No, they never did. He was an honor roll student – all the Johnsons barely passed their classes. He knew he would go to college, but most of that family dropped out as soon as they could. You come from good stock on our side. Your dad was just sick when he didn't know where Sheree was or when you were born. After we found out, we worked with a lawyer to find you and to get some visitations set up. Your grandpa was willing to pay child support if need be just so we could have you in our lives."

Belle sat stunned. She'd been wanted, at least by her birth father's family. Her life – which had been good, she had no complaints – could have been very different.

"That didn't happen, though," she said. "Why?"

Ethel finished her soup and pushed the bowl away. "Oh, honey, there were so many reasons. First, they didn't tell us when you were born, so we didn't know for a couple of months. Then, Baxter – that was your grandpa, my husband, got cancer, and he was very sick. I was focused on that. Your dad was still in high school, in speech and debate, so he went almost every weekend to tournaments. That year, he qualified for state and then went on to nationals. Penny and Paula – your aunts – were in junior high, and Philip, your uncle, was still in grade school. By the time we found out Sheree was dead, you'd already been adopted. We thought about trying to get you, but the people that took you sounded like good people, so we made the hard choice to leave you with them. They were teachers, if I recall, and we thought that would be good for you."

"Wow," Belle said. It sounded like a cheap soap opera plot, she thought.

"We don't even know your birthday, honey. When is it?"

Here she'd thrown a fit because Nicholas hadn't shared his date of birth, and her family didn't know the date of hers. Neither did he.

"April 30," she said. "Mom always said they almost named me April. I wonder if they even chose my name."

"Probably – Sheree was big on fancy names, and Maribel sounds like something she would choose. Besides, the high school art teacher at the time, her name was Maribel, so we always thought that's where poor Sheree got it. Peter planned to ask her, but he found out she'd died."

"What happened to her?" Belle figured to hear it'd been a car wreck or something else common to teens.

Ethel heaved a sigh. "She overdosed on drugs with you in the room," she said. "She had rented some tiny little apartment, and when the authorities found her, DFS took you. They put you in foster care, then after the family gave up all rights, offered you for adoption. Those Barbiers must have either had an inside track or were lucky because they were able to adopt you right away."

"I wonder if there were any pictures. I always wondered why my parents, my birth parents, didn't have any newborn photos."

Her grandmother rose from the table. "If you'll stack the dishes in the sink, I'll get the photo albums. There's one, the only one any of us ever had, but there's a few of your mom and lots of the family."

The tiny infant face in the small pose had no resemblance. "You look more like the Simpkins, or my family, the Allisons," Ethel said. "You didn't take after the Johnsons at all."

She took a photo out of a page and handed it to Belle. In it, a very young girl in a short blue satin formal dress stood with her arm through that of a teenager. The guy wore a white tux, and Belle recognized him from Thanksgiving. "That's my dad. That's Peter."

Ethel nodded. "It is, about thirty some years younger and skinnier. And that's Sheree."

Belle scrutinized the photo but felt nothing, no connection or rush of emotion for the teenager. She had a waifish look about her and something restless in the way she posed. Nothing about her resembled Belle, and she was glad.

There were two more with her teen parents, a photo taken beside a creek where both were wet and laughing. The other one was of her mother alone in another formal, wearing both a smile and crown. "She was homecoming queen," Ethel said.

For the next hour, they browsed through several albums. Her dad's life was chronicled from birth until marriage, along with his siblings. Her grandfather, who apparently had died the same year Belle had been born, had been a handsome man, a farmer in overalls with a quirky grin.

"Who's this?" Belle asked, pointing at a baby picture.

"That's your sister, Dominique," Ethel said. "You met her at Thanksgiving. She's Peter's daughter too, with his wife, Pam. And you do favor each other some."

She could see it but wasn't sure how she felt about that yet.

"Thank you, Ethel," she told her grandmother when they put away the old pictures. "I have a better sense of how I came to exist now."

The older woman nodded. "That's good, and I'm glad we finally found you. You're as much a part of the family as anyone. I'm glad you got in touch, and I'm happy you've moved here. Do you think you'll stay?"

Belle had no idea. "I'm here as long Nicholas and I are together."

"He's a good man," Ethel said. "Troubled but with a good heart."

She ached to confide in someone, so she said, "I love him."

Her grandmother smiled. "I figured."

She might have said more, but the phone on the wall rang, so Ethel rose to answer it.

"No, he's not here, but Belle is," she said and handed her the receiver.

"It's Suzanne."

"Hello," Belle said, trying to sound friendly. She liked Nicholas' sister, but the fact the woman had been launching a one-woman anti-Belle campaign rankled.

"Where's Nick?" Suzanne sounded both breathless and agitated.

"He went fishing in Oklahoma with Timothy. They'll be back in time for supper at your house."

"Well, that's part of the problem. Marshall won't be here to grill. The trucking company called him to pick up a load because another driver got sick, so he's gone."

"I can grill if necessary," Belle said.

"Well, that's not all."

"What's wrong?" In the background, she could hear Teagan wailing.

"I really need my brother," Suzanne said. "I don't know what to do – Teagan's been suspended from school. I tried to call Tim's cell phone, but no one answered."

Belle imagined the dark-haired, diminutive kindergarten student and asked, "What could she have possibly done?"

"She got into a fight," Suzanne said. "She slapped another girl, and then she bit her on the arm. I had to go pick her up from school early, and she's suspended until after the winter break. She's really upset because they had a police officer come talk to her, and she thought he was going to take her to jail. The principal was talking about counseling and anger management, and I don't know what all, but it's out of control."

"It sounds like it."

"She wants her uncle," Suzanne said. "She's back to calling him 'Uncle Beast,' and he's why she got into a fight."

"I don't understand."

Suzanne blew air into the phone. "I'm leaving part of it out – here's what happened. This other child in her class, Winter Cox, started telling kids on the playground that she saw Teagan with either Krampus or Satan at McDonald's. Some of them didn't know who Krampus is, but they all knew Satan. Teagan got into a fight defending her uncle, and now she's suspended, her stomach hurts, and she's crying for Nick. I can't do anything with her. She's almost hysterical."

"They won't be back until dark, at least."

The other woman started crying. "I wish Marsh hadn't gone. I don't think I can do this. She won't stop crying, and she's holding her tummy. What if she's really sick this time, or what if the other girl hit her and hurt her? I don't know what to do."

Belle didn't either, but something had to happen. "I'm at Ethel's, just down the road. I'll be there in five minutes, okay? I don't know what to do either, but I'm coming."

At Suzanne's, she found the little girl curled up into a ball on the couch, rocking back and forth, clutching her abdomen. She couldn't stop crying, and her face was brick red from the effort. Belle sat beside her and tried to coax her into her arms so she could talk to her the way Nicholas did. Maybe that would calm her down and ease her pain. At first, the little girl ignored Belle, but after about half an hour, she sniffed hard and said, "I want my uncle, Belle."

"He'll be here as soon as he's back from Oklahoma," Belle told her.

"Will he be mad?"

He would be furious, but not at the kid. "No, honey, he won't be. How do you feel?"

"My tummy hurts."

"Is it like it usually does?"

"Yeah, right here."

"Do you want to sit on my lap for a few minutes, like you do with Uncle Nicholas?"

The little girl crawled into place, and Belle held her. The sobs slowed, and by the time Nicholas walked through the door with Timothy, Teagan had fallen asleep. Suzanne still mopped at her eyes with a tissue, and Belle wished she could sleep for about twelve hours without any emotional storm to handle.

She recalled an old saying Nicholas had shared, something

his grandfather often said about wishes and sighed. For now, it seemed like the shit would always win.

Chapter Eighteen

The day beside the water had been good for his soul, and when he returned, Nicholas was in high spirits. Their catch hadn't been the best, but he had enjoyed the day, and so had his cousin. Fishing had brought many memories from their shared childhood, pleasant times from long before either man went into the Marines or saw action. Grandpa Reilly took them fishing as often as he could, imparting age-old wisdom about catching fish from across the sea in Ireland. If it hadn't been for him, Nicholas might have never realized that fishing was popular there too.

It had been too long since he wet a line, Nicholas thought or shared such fellowship with his brother of the heart. They smoked a couple of cigars, a vice he seldom indulged in, and ate lukewarm sandwiches on the lakeshore. Now, wind-blown, probably more than a little smelly, they headed to his sister's house and his lady.

Nicholas had thought of Belle throughout the day. The fact she loved him made him feel taller and stronger. He thought less about his scars and his issues because of her. He wanted his grandfather to meet her and anticipated the big birthday bash in less than two months. As they shared memories, he realized how much he missed the old man.

His contentment faded as soon as he walked into his sister's house. Suzanne sat curled up in a swivel rocker, blotting her streaming eyes with a crumpled tissue. On the couch, Belle sat holding Teagan. Although the child slept, her face bore the marks of tear tracks. Her clothing was all awry, and from Belle's expression, he realized everything wasn't well at all.

He halted so fast that Timothy ran into him, then sidestepped around him.

"What happened?" he asked, glancing from one woman to the other. His brother-in-law's absence made him concerned something had happened to him. "Something's wrong – what?"

Suzanne started telling him, but her account was garbled, and she kept pausing to cry. Nicholas couldn't make heads or tails from it and looked at Belle for an explanation.

"Teagan got into a fight at school, so she's suspended until after Christmas," she said. "She's upset, and so is your sister, but she's all right, I think. She had a bad tummyache for a while, but she's okay now."

"Shit," he said. He sat down beside Belle on the couch while Timothy took the remaining seat in Marshall's recliner. "What in the hell does a kindergartener fight over?"

He imagined a squabble over a doll or other toy, maybe a confrontation over who got the best swing or someone taking Teagan's lunchbox. Nothing serious, he figured, until his niece opened her eyes.

"Uncle Beast," she wailed and shifted from Belle into his lap. "I got in trouble."

"That's what I'm hearing. Are you okay?"

She nodded. "They said you were the devil or Krampus, that I hung around with bad people, and that made me wicked, maybe even a demon."

Nicholas cuddled her close, angry and upset that anyone, even another child, could suggest this precious little girl was evil. "Who said such a stupid thing?"

"Winter," Teagan whined. "She's in my class, and she said she saw us at McDonald's, that I was with the devil or maybe Krampus."

"Who the fu...who is this Krampus?" He moderated his language at the last moment.

"The opposite of Santa Claus," Belle said. "It's an old European legend. He comes to punish kids instead of giving them gifts."

Half-forgotten German from a high school class he'd taken surfaced. "And the name means "claw."

"I think so," she said. She appeared almost as frazzled as his sister and the kid. Belle's hair had come loose from her ponytail and trailed down her shoulders. Her eyes drooped with fatigue, but she offered him a half-smile. "Not a nice guy, that's for sure."

"Half man, half goat," Timothy added from across the room. "Big dude with gnarly horns."

Nicholas shot him a look that should have killed him. "What?" his cousin said. "I saw the movie – it sucked, by the way."

Visions of every red-faced, fanged, horned, ugly and frightening images of Satan he'd ever had already popped into his mind. All were ugly as well as terrifying. Now he could imagine this Krampus as well and repressed a shudder. Nicholas mouthed a silent 'fuck you' to Timothy.

"That kid must need glasses," he said, the first thing he could come up to explain. "I may be ugly as homemade sin, but I don't look that bad, do I?"

Teagan shook her head against his chest. "Uh-uh, Uncle Beast."

He did, though, and he knew it damn well. It took a tiny kindergarten student who couldn't be older than six to remind him and all but destroy his niece's Christmas with a few careless words. "Then you don't have anything to worry about, do you?"

She began sobbing again. "I do, Uncle Beast. Now everything thinks I'm with the devil or Krampus, and they'll hate me. And I'm scared."

If she said she was afraid of him, he'd probably head for the woods and take up the life of a hermit. Or worse. "What are you afraid of, honey?"

"That the devil will come for me or that Krampus will come instead of Santa."

His emotions and guts were in an uproar, but Nicholas kept his voice calm. "It won't happen, baby girl."

"Will you protect me?"

Nicholas wanted to cry. Tears caught in his throat and burned like an untended fire. "With my life, but you have the angels too. Have you learned this prayer? Angel of God, my guardian dear to whom God's love commits me here, ever this day be at my side to light and guard to rule and guide, amen."

"Yes."

"First prayer I remember learning," Nicholas said. "Your guardian angel will keep you safe, Teagan."

"Even against the devil?"

"Especially against him," Nicholas said. "I'll let you wear

my St. Michael medal, too. You know who St. Michael is, right? An archangel and a warrior. He carries a sword, and he put Satan in chains. He's the patron saint of all warriors...."

"Even Marines?"

"Most of all Marines."

Nicholas touched his neck where he'd worn a St. Michael medal for many years. It wasn't there because he stopped wearing it after he was injured, thinking the saint hadn't saved him. Now he reflected that he probably had, or he would be dead.

"Don't you wear it?" his sister asked.

"It's at home." He wasn't explaining why not to her, not now. "I'll bring it for Teagan to wear if it makes her feel better."

They could say the St. Michael prayer, too, he thought. Everyone present would know it, and in a little bit, he'd ask them to say it. Right now, Nicholas was seized by a volatile stew of emotions. There was anger at the base, rage that anyone, even another child, would plant such a terrible seed in his niece's mind. He had to wonder what kind of parents the kid must have. Added to the anger was a deep sadness, but the main ingredient was despair. He glanced down at Teagan's tear-stained face and decided it was his fault. If he didn't resemble a monster or creature like Frankenstein, the kid wouldn't have been harassed. Maybe the outing to Mickey D's hadn't been a good idea after all, he thought, beating himself up with regret.

Nicholas noticed the absence of his brother-in-law. "Where's Marsh?"

"He left early this morning," Suzanne replied. "They called him in to take a load to Los Angeles."

"Does he know what happened?"

"Not yet – I'll tell him when he calls home."

That would be days, Nicholas thought. "No cookout?"

"Belle said she could do the grilling."

Nicholas shook his head. "No, she'll be coming home with me when I go. I don't think anyone's in the mood for it anyway."

He wasn't, and from the glum expressions in the room, neither was anyone else. Teagan, sprawled on his lap and sucking her thumb, an old habit he thought she'd shed, raised her head, and said, "I want some pizza, Uncle Nicholas."

Until she spoke, he would have vowed she was asleep. To put a smile on her cranky little face, he'd do almost anything she wanted. "We can get pizza."

"Nick..." Suzanne said. "They won't deliver out here in the country."

"I'll go get it," he said, although right now, he'd rather hide out and never show his face in public again.

Timothy and Belle spoke at the same time, both saying they would. Belle called in the order, and his cousin headed to pick up three take-and-bake pizzas after receiving precise directions from Suzanne. His niece seemed to recover from her experience, and by the time the pizzas were in the oven, she was skipping around the room, talking about the Christmas tree. She ate three pieces of her favorite hamburger pizza before Suzanne whisked her off for a bath, then bed.

Everyone else followed Teagan's lead, chattering and laughing as the level of stress diminished. Nicholas didn't, though. He felt detached, numb inside as he struggled to adjust to the idea that he'd been compared to both Satan and Krampus. Over the years, he'd almost gotten used to looking like movie monsters like Frankenstein or Krueger and made bitter references himself about resembling Quasimodo and the Elephant Man, but a resemblance to the devil reached a new low.

Belle had restored a little of his self-confidence, and

although he wouldn't look at his own reflection willingly, he sometimes forgot about his scarred looks. He'd dined out, gone to several large box stores with her, and walked in the skin of the man he'd once been. That illusion had vanished as he realized it was just smoke and mirrors. Her pronouncement that "it's just a face – it's not you" turned out to be wrong. In his sour mind, he changed it, remembering the old chant from school, 'you are what you are,' and silently chanted, "I am what I look."

For a while, no one noticed his distress. Belle became aware when he barely finished a slice of pizza. Sitting beside him on the couch, she put her hand over his stomach. "Does it hurt?" she asked, voice quiet.

Nicholas shook his head. She frowned and touched his forehead. "Headache?"

"No," he told her. Physically, he had no pain, but emotionally, he was in agony. He doubted he could find the words to explain, and if he did, it wouldn't be with an audience.

"What's the matter?"

"Nothing." He drew the word up from the well of his soul and spit it out. Even to his ears, it sounded harsh and combative.

The frown that divided her forehead deepened, and her lips tightened into a thin line.

"Let's go home," she suggested, and he nodded. When she offered her hand, he accepted it and stood up. Belle handed him his coat and shrugged into hers.

"We're taking off," she announced. "Good night."

Nicholas had already told his niece bye and hugged his sister. He said something jovial to his cousin and then trailed out with Belle. When she started to climb behind the wheel, he held out his hand for the keys, and after a slight hesitation, she dropped them into his palm. He needed to be in control, so he drove the short distance home and parked the truck. Then, he rested his forehead on the steering wheel, silent until she stroked his back.

"Tell me what's going on," Belle said.

He wanted to spew, to unburden all his negative thoughts, tell her how being compared to Satan and Krampus wrecked him, and to explain why he'd realized his scars were indeed him. He was as ugly as his disfigurement and always would be. No one was going to judge the man inside, not when the exterior came straight out of hell. Nicholas didn't, though. He couldn't, so instead, he shrugged and said, "Nothing's going on, Belle."

"I'm worried."

"Don't be," he said and lifted his head. "I'm not worth it."

Nicholas leapt out of the truck and stomped into the house, It wasn't late, but he longed to go to bed, to curl up and hibernate for the rest of his life. He started for the stairs, then remembered he shared both a room and bed with Belle. If he went, she would follow. He went into the living room, where the fire had gone low. Temperatures were predicted to be cold, and he should stir it, add some wood, and bring it back. Maybe he would, but right now, he didn't. He stared at the tile he'd put up in place of the mirror and considered smashing it. He might not be able to shatter it, but he could hit it hard enough to crack the surface and ruin it. Then it would be just like his face.

He wasn't far gone enough not to realize he was thinking crazy, so Nicholas stepped away. In the dining room, he resisted an urge to topple the tree and smash the pretties that hung on the branches. Better yet, he could stuff the tree into the fireplace and watch it burn. He paused, considering it, but Belle entered the room. Her eyes were dark with trouble, and she wore a frown.

"Would you like me to make coffee?" she asked, her tone

the kind he'd heard from many a patient nurse, so he hated it. He opened his mouth to refuse, but he craved caffeine, so he nodded.

In the kitchen, he glared at every cup, plate, and glass, judging its potential to shatter. Nicholas sat down at the table and splayed his hands flat to ground himself. He felt like the Incredible Hulk, about to transform into a raging beast and fought it. He might be trying to shut out the world, but he still had a few limits. He loved Belle too much to go totally berserk, at least not yet.

Nicholas drank the first cup slowly, then added some Jack Daniels to the second and tossed it down fast. Belle's expression sent a pang of guilt through him, but he said nothing. When he rose, he caught sight of his reflection in the window over the sink. Outside, the night loomed black, so he saw his wavering image and pulled back the cup to throw it through it. He almost did when a flashback hit hard.

Someone decided it was time he should see his healing burns. Several grafts had taken place, and he'd been bandaged for weeks. His skin itched beneath them, and Nicholas was eager to get them removed. They had explained there would still be scarring and that right now, they would appear redder and more prominent than they would later. He'd seen a few Marines after serious injuries, and he figured his couldn't be much different.

It had been spring, he remembered, at the burn unit in San Antonio, where military personnel from all branches were sent for treatment. He'd been in the unit for several months, interacting with others who had also been damaged. It was always hot because a lot of burn patients had trouble regulating body temperatures, and Nicholas looked forward to moving into a room elsewhere. He'd been promised one that overlooked a green space as soon as the bandages were off.

His parents had come from Rusk for the day, and so had his brother Jordan, the youngest. In a private space, away from any eyes, the medical team parked him in a chair and cut away the bandages. Before he could raise the hand mirror to see the results for himself, he'd heard his mother's gasp. His dad had mumbled a few cuss words, and Jordan had made a slight retching sound, then rushed out of the room.

Aware that it would be worse than maybe he'd imagined, Nicholas raised the mirror and gazed into it. For the first moments, he couldn't make the connection to the mangled features, the skin still red in places, shiny in others. There were ridges of scar tissue, and one eye drooped. His lips were not right. He could see that, and his right ear was no more than a nub attached to his head. His first thought was, wow, poor guy and then it sunk in this was him. The Marine with the face that appeared to have been made from melted wax was his, that of Nicholas Reilly.

His stomach threatened to erupt, and somewhere he could hear his brother puking. No wonder, he thought. His mother wept softly, and his dad still cursed. Nicholas took one more look at his ravaged face and thought I'm a freak, I'm a fucking freak, a monster.

"So, what do you think?" the nurse asked. "It's healing nicely and...."

Nicholas threw the mirror and heard it break when it hit the floor. Then he howled like an animal, a wounded beast or a werewolf, the sound eerie and loud. When he stopped howling, he screamed, and they had to sedate him to stop.

He was screaming now, he realized a harsh and terrible shrill sound that echoed through the kitchen as he stood on his feet, unable to move, transfixed by his own image. The cup remained in his hand, and he gripped it hard.

"Nicholas, Nicholas," someone said, and he realized it was Belle. She pried the cup from his grasp and set it down. "Honey, come sit down."

She wrapped an arm around his waist and maneuvered him into a chair at the table. His scream had downgraded to a loud moan, and he shook, his hands trembling and his body quivering. The sound of her voice was like a lifeline to a drowning man, and he clung to it, listening until the words made sense.

"What happened?" she asked, voice shrill with concern. "Tell me what's going on."

"Flashback," he managed to say, his voice hoarse and harsh. "Remembering when they took the bandages off this ugly mug."

"Breathe," she told him. "Take slow, deep breaths, Nicholas. It's in the past, and you're here."

At the same time, she rubbed his shoulders, kneading them. He didn't realize that he still made sounds until Timothy, who had stayed later at Suzanne's, burst into the kitchen, his face wild with alarm, and skidded to a stop. "What the hell's going on?"

"Flashback," Belle said, and he was glad she replied because he couldn't, not right now.

"What can I do to help?"

"When we can, help me get him upstairs to bed," she said.

That would work, Nicholas thought. The only better thing they could do for him would be to put him out of his misery, but he knew neither would.

Chapter Nineteen

One child with a thoughtless mouth spoke, and the result hit Nicholas hard and sent him spiraling backward, erasing the recent progress he'd made and terrifying Belle. Just when he'd become confident enough to show his face in public and to leave the ski mask and hoods at home, some little girl taunted his niece into a fight because she'd said she saw Teagan with either the devil or with Krampus. Both were ugly and evil. Nicholas was neither, but he changed since the night Teagan told him about the incident.

He'd come close to smashing the kitchen window because he saw his reflection, which had triggered a flashback. He'd slept late the next morning. When he woke and came downstairs, he had kept his distance from Belle both physically and emotionally. Nicholas answered when she spoke to him, but he didn't start any conversations. If she tried to cuddle up beside him on the couch, he shifted to the recliner. In bed, he might as well have been elsewhere, his position as close to the edge as possible without falling onto the floor.

Before his cousin headed home to Texas, Nicholas rebuffed him too, having little to say and refusing any outings Timothy suggested. He wouldn't go with Belle to buy a car, so Timothy did, and when she returned home with an older Toyota, Nicholas had scant interest.

"Do you like it?" she asked after she'd prodded him outside to see the vehicle.

He shrugged. "You need wheels so you can escape when you're ready," he'd said, then retreated inside.

Nicholas wouldn't talk to his sister on the phone or anyone else who called. When Suzanne invited them to come when they headed to Carthage to see the amazing Christmas lights at the Vietnamese Catholic community there, Nicholas agreed but sat in the back, face turned away at both there and at Precious Moments. He didn't sing along to any of the music, and when they stopped to grab a quick bite to eat, he insisted on eating his burger in the car, so they all did.

Only Teagan could coax a fleeting smile from her uncle. He listened to her and was patient in a kind way. She could still crawl into his lap, and he would hug her, but he let no one else that close, not even Belle. He had given the child the promised St. Michael medal with a Marine Corps emblem, and she wore it around her neck, refusing to remove it even for baths.

He ate little at meals, leaving them half-finished most of the time. Sometimes he complained that the food was too cold or too hot, too seasoned or too bland. If he suffered stomach pain or headaches, he never said, but Belle thought he did. She caught him sitting hunched over his belly at times or rubbing his forehead.

Nicholas returned to the snark and sarcasm he'd displayed

when she first knew him, although Belle knew it was a shield, a weapon he used to keep others away. His mother called, and he wouldn't talk. Grandpa Reilly began phoning daily, and although Nicholas wouldn't speak to him either, Belle did. She got to know the old man and soon loved him. He became the rock she could lean against, and he, along with everyone else, gave her hope.

There were chinks in his façade, though. Sometimes in his sleep, he would move closer and hold her tight. If she touched him as he slept, he often grasped her hand. They hadn't made love since that night, but once they came close. Belle caught him at the foot of the stairs, and before he could retreat, she put her arms around him and kissed him, her lips locked on his with want and heat.

Nicholas responded. He kissed her back with hunger and need. He cradled her against his chest, and as her nipples perked up, she felt his erect cock come to life. The kisses continued until he wrenched himself away.

"No," he gasped. "I won't. You deserve better than Satan himself."

"You're not Satan," she had said, struggling not to weep. "I want you, Nicholas and I love you."

He mumbled, and she caught the words 'I love you too' before he said, "You shouldn't. I'll just cause you grief the way I have everyone else."

Then he'd stormed out the front door outside where a cold rain fell, and he didn't return until he'd been thoroughly drenched. That had been two days before Christmas, and he'd shivered by the fire until he went to bed, only then removing his sodden clothes.

Christmas Day dawned bright and sunny, with temperatures near fifty degrees. As they had planned before everything changed, Suzanne, Teagan, and Marshall, back from his run, joined them for gifts and dinner. So did Ethel. She tried to coax Belle to come over to visit the next day, but she declined, afraid to leave Nicholas in his present state.

She hadn't met Marshall previously and wasn't impressed. Belle picked up on the fact that Nicholas wasn't too fond of his brother-in-law, and she understood why. He was a pudgy man, short as well as heavy, with an attitude that sat on his shoulder like Humpty Dumpty on a wall. His sense of humor was crude, he made more than one fart joke, and he paid little attention to either his wife or child. He sneered at the gift card Belle handed him, a joint gift from her and Nicholas and remarked, "Yep, another card for Wally World. I suppose I can use it to buy a sandwich or some cookies or something."

Belle roasted a large turkey and made a big dinner, although her heart wasn't in it. To her surprise, Nicholas provided two gifts she hadn't known about – one was a four-foot-high wooden doll house for Teagan, one patterned after the castle from her favorite fairy tale. The rooms included miniature furniture as well as some of the familiar characters, including Lumiere. There was even an enchanted rose. It came with 12-inch dolls of both Beauty and the Beast. Teagan adored it.

"That won't fit in my car," Suzanne said.

"I'll bring it over," Nicholas promised. If he did, that would be the first time he'd left the house since the night of his niece's fight.

Both the gift and that gave Belle a flicker of hope, but his gift to her provided even more.

He'd given it to her that morning before anyone else arrived, and she cried when she unwrapped it. It was a silver heart locket with the Marine Corps emblem on the front. Inside, he'd placed two photos of himself – one from before he was injured, handsome and young in his dress blues, the other scars and all. The card with it said in his distinctive scrawl, "For my Belle, my heart, my love, who I am and who I wish I still was, Love Nicholas."

At her request, he put it around her neck, his fingers fumbling and submitted to a kiss that lingered.

"I hope you like your gift," she said, tears still brimming in her eyes. "I thought it would keep you safe."

To replace the medal he'd long worn, then giving it to Teagan, Belle had found a 5-way St. Michael medal. It boasted the Marine emblem in the center, flanked by St. George, St. Joan of Arc, and St. Michael.

For a few brief seconds, she caught a glimpse of his unguarded face. He liked it, she thought, and it moved him. He dropped the endless chain over his head and nodded. Then he kissed her again, this time like he meant it with powerful urgency. If he'd wanted, he could have taken her there on the floor, and she wouldn't have complained. He broke free when his sister arrived, but he did meet her gaze, then say, "I do love you, Belle. I do, but I'm sorry I'm not enough."

The words shattered her heart. "You're everything to me, Nicholas," she cried. "Don't say that."

But he had, and he moved away from her. It wasn't the Christmas she'd dreamed about, but it came anyway, then it went.

If she had hoped Christmas would make a positive difference, it didn't.

Nicholas developed a cough she first noticed on Christmas night. He'd been nursing a cold since the night he dashed coatless out into the rain, but the cough was new. It sounded deep and painful.

Two days later, croaking like a frog in a beer commercial, he admitted he was sick.

"Belle," he said, rousing her from a fitful sleep. "Belle, I don't feel good."

"What's wrong?" She went on high alert.

"I'm sick," he said and coughed hard.

"Where does it hurt?"

Nicholas put a hand on his chest. "Hurts when I cough," he wheezed. "I'm cold. I just don't feel good, babe."

He took her hand, and it burned against her palm. Alarmed, Belle put her hand across his forehead. "You're burning up, Nicholas. Get comfortable, and I'll go get you something for the fever, aspirin or ibuprofen."

"I'll go downstairs," he said.

She tried, but he argued the point.

"After fifteen surgeries and almost two years in the hospital, I'm not staying in bed," he told her.

Downstairs, he settled into the recliner, tucked in place with pillows and a blanket Belle provided. She dosed him for fever, then brought him the cup of coffee that he requested. He drank it without a fuss but didn't eat much of the toast she provided.

"Jello," he said when she asked what he might like. "Strawberry jello and chicken soup with rice, maybe. I'm not hungry, Belle, and I feel like shit on a shingle."

"I'll make a quick run to get some," she said. "Or I'll see if Suzanne will go."

Nicholas had shut his eyes after the last coughing bout but opening them. "Don't you tell her I'm sick, or she'll be over here," he said, voice hoarse. "If you want to go, I'll be fine while you're gone. I'm sick, not dying and trust me, I've been a helluva lot worse."

Belle kissed his forehead and winced at the heat. "I know you have. Do you feel like making a trip to the doctor?"

He frowned. "No way. It's probably bronchitis but no. Just don't take long if you go. I like having you close."

Funny way to show it, she thought but didn't say so aloud. Apparently, being under the weather lowered the barriers he'd erected. Although his illness concerned her, Belle was delighted he was talking. He'd said more to her this morning than in the past two weeks.

"Then I'll go now and come straight back. What else would you like?"

"I don't care," he said. "Belle?"

Halfway into her coat, she paused. "Be careful, okay?"

On the way into town, she did exactly what he didn't want and called his sister. Suzanne had been almost as worried as Belle about Nicholas' recent behavior.

"He's sick," she said when Suzanne picked up the phone.

"What's wrong with Nick?"

"He thinks it's bronchitis, but I don't know. He's running a temperature, and he's coughing a lot. I wanted him to see a doctor, but he said no way."

"That's no surprise, but he probably should go. Do you want me to help you drag him?"

Belle considered it, then said, "No, it would be a fight and maybe make him worse. I just wish I knew a doctor who'd make house calls or a nurse."

"Call Ethel."

Belle slowed as she reached the highway. "Why? Does she know someone?"

Suzanne laughed. "She's a retired nurse – you didn't know that?"

She hadn't. "I'll call her."

The trip to the discount store and back took almost an hour, frustrating Belle, but she returned with bags that included ready-made strawberry gelatin, boxes of several flavors of jello, fresh fruit, canned soup, the making for homemade soup, an array of over-the-counter medications, boxes of tea, a digital thermometer, clear soda, orange juice, tissues, and a contour neck pillow. Better still, her grandmother would meet her at the house.

Belle heard him hacking as soon as she entered.

"Hey, that sounds awful," she said as she came over to kiss his forehead.

Nicholas wheezed, then shot her a faint grin. "I'll do. What took so long?"

"I hurried. Did you miss me?"

The question was more than a little facetious since he'd done his best to ignore her, but he nodded. "Yeah. I feel like the fever's up. I'm hot."

Belle took his temperature and found he was right. "It's 101.5," she told him. "I'll give you more ibuprofen, and hopefully, that will bring it down. Ethel's coming over…."

"What for?" he sounded cranky.

"She used to be a nurse, so she's going take a look at you," Belle told him. "I'm worried – you might have bronchitis or something else. It's Ethel or a trip to the doctor."

Ethel arrived wearing a mask and with a small medical bag. She checked Nicholas' temperature, took his blood pressure, and listened to both his chest and heart with a stethoscope. Then she quizzed him about his symptoms and, when she finished, said, "I'm not a physician, but I'd say you definitely have bronchitis. There's not a lot a doctor can do unless you get worse. You need to stay hydrated, so drink plenty of liquids, get a lot of rest, don't exert yourself, eat even when you don't want to eat and stay warm. Take acetaminophen to keep the fever down, and if a cough suppressant helps, take one. You'll be better if you get the crud out, though. If you don't improve or if you take a turn for the worse, you do need to see a doctor, okay?"

Nicholas nodded. "All right."

"And eat, damn it. You've lost weight – I can see it. And talk to Belle. I don't know what exactly put you in a tailspin, but you're hurting her when you shut her out. She loves you. If that's nonsense about Satan, forget it. You're giving power to the words of a five-year-old child, Nick."

A coughing fit seized him, and Belle watched as Ethel patted him on the back. When it stopped, he sighed and said, "It's hard not to, Ethel."

"Try harder and be nice to my granddaughter, Nick. I'll check in with Belle to see how you're doing."

Belle walked her grandmother to the door and hugged her. "Thank you for coming."

"No big deal. I'm glad you called me. If you weren't here, that big dumb lug would lay there till he ended up with pneumonia or died. He's behaving badly, you know. Don't make any excuses for him. And try not to get sick too."

The possibility had never entered her mind, but she nodded. "I will."

It was obvious that Nicholas pretended to be asleep when Belle returned, so she headed for the kitchen and made soup, a rich chicken and rice concoction with plenty of onion, celery, garlic and more. She seasoned it with a bit of sage, some thyme, and some parsley. She used brown rice, not white and made a huge pot.

Once it was simmering, she checked on Nicholas. She put the new pillow beneath his neck and tucked the blanket in place. Belle poked up the fire so it wouldn't get chilly in the room and then, because he appeared to be asleep, sank down on the floor at his feet. She leaned against his knees, savoring his proximity. She'd missed him and had no idea how to move forward, how to debunk his notion that his appearance truly was as bad as Satan. An old REO Speedwagon song flitted through her mind, and she whispered an echo of the refrain, "I'll keep on loving you."

Belle put her head down on his knees, and he put his hand on the back of it, then stroked her hair. His touch soothed her and filled a need she'd had for days.

"I'm glad you are," he said, his voice little more than a murmur. "Belle, I know I don't deserve it. You should have so much more than I can give you, but I love you, and your love means everything. I know I've been an asshole, and I'm sorry. I know I've been remote and shut you out. Right now, I feel too damn shitty to keep a distance. I'm surprised you didn't leave me standing and take off, but I'm happy you didn't. Whatever I do, don't leave, please."

He said everything she'd missed hearing, what she needed and more. "I won't, Nicholas," she said, close to crying. "Just don't shut me out like that ever again."

He rested his hand on her head. "I'm a broken man, a real piece of shit," he told her. "I'm flawed, and I don't know if I can be fixed, but baby, I'll try. That's the best I've got."

It wasn't enough, she thought, but it would do for now, so she nodded. Then she scooted from her knees to sitting, then stood. "I'll take it."

For the present, they were in harmony. She fed him homemade soup, dosed him with medicine, put a cool cloth on his brow when the fever rose, and loved him. She had no fear of catching bronchitis. If she did, she did, but Nicholas needed her, so she would take the risk.

If it took being sick to heal his broken spirit, then so be it.

Either way, Belle was in for the long haul.

Chapter Twenty

He hated being sick. Being sick was worse in some ways than being hurt, and Nicholas had been hurt severely. Other than his long recovery from his war injuries and wounds, he seldom became ill, but when he did, it usually was acute. He'd been in low spirits since the day Teagan got into a fight at school after another student claimed they had seen her with either Satan or Krampus. Teagan knew they were talking about him, and so did he. His niece had been upset and lashed out, earning suspension from school until the new year. That seemed a harsh punishment, but he had no stake in it. The comparison, though, slammed Nicholas far more than his niece and brought him down.

Every lurid, grotesque depiction he'd ever seen of the devil haunted him, and so did visions of Krampus. His self-esteem turned out to be a thin shell, easily broken. Nicholas suffered a flashback that same night and then endured the remainder of the holiday season. His mood pissed on Christmas, so he might as well be Krampus, he thought, bringing those around him from joy to despair. The tree he'd wanted and decorated with Belle now mocked him, and he wanted no presents. Earlier, he'd ordered a castle doll house fashioned after the Beast's enchanted castle in the fairytale, and Teagan adored it. After a lot of soul searching, Nicholas gave Belle the locket he had found and was touched by the five-way medal she gave him. He wore it around his neck daily, the one constant connection he kept with her.

It would be better if she left, and he knew it. Someday, at some point, she would realize she was intimate with the devil incarnate, a man as ugly as Lucifer himself and one who had done many things he would answer for at judgement. He'd been a Marine, proud of his service, but he'd killed, and that was a sin. Belle would be better off without him. He would drag her down into his darkness and ruin her life. Teagan would thrive without his influence, and he should wean off her love for him before it hurt her again.

Nicholas ached for Belle. He longed to kiss her, to share the ultimate act of love skin to skin as they so often had, but he restrained. Abstaining was a way he could punish himself and to make her think there was no reason to stay. He stonewalled her and knew it, hated it.

The one day he yielded to her kisses had been sweet until he realized what he was doing. He'd broken free and dashed out in the rain on a chilly day without bothering to grab his coat. He'd already been incubating a cold, so it had been foolish. Nicholas had been wet when he returned, soaked enough to shiver. A nagging cough was the first sign he would be sick, but he ignored it. Denial kept him from doing anything to prevent getting worse.

But, when he woke coughing so hard his chest ached, shivering with a chill, he knew it meant he probably ran a fever. He wanted Belle. Nicholas felt too ill to pretend indifference, so he woke her, and she responded with her usual tender loving care, exactly what he needed. He lacked the strength to keep the wall he'd erected in place, and when he heard her whisper the words from an REO song he had long loved, it broke his resolve to remain aloof. He apologized and asked her not to leave. Being Belle, she promised she wouldn't.

As soon as I'm well, I'll go back to being a beast, he thought. *If I'm terrible enough, she'll figure out she's better to let me go. I can't let her go – I need her too much, but if she makes the choice, then I'll live with it.*

"*Carpe diem*," Nicholas told her as he ate what he could of the soup she'd made from scratch. Maybe she wouldn't understand the Latin, but that would be his motto while he was sick.

"Seize the day," Belle said. "Good motto, Nicholas."

"I had a drill instructor who often said it. You know it?"

She nodded. "I love the song from *Newsies*. Have you ever seen it?"

He'd heard of it, but Broadway musicals hadn't been a priority for a Marine. He'd never been a fan. "No. I guess you have, though."

"I saw it on Broadway," Belle said, invoking a world unfamiliar to him. He'd traveled around the world in the Corps, but he'd never been to New York City and certainly not to Broadway. "It's a good show – the songs are fantastic, but "Seize The Day" is my favorite. I'll play it for you after a while if you feel up to listening."

"Okay," he said. He handed her back the soup bowl, overwhelmed with a deep fatigue and coughed. "Later, okay?"

For now, he reveled in her care, enjoying the way she tucked the blanket around him and put the pillow under his head. He felt like shit on toast, but he liked her cool hand on his hot forehead and the way she stroked back his hair. Her concern brought him a sense of contentment. For a few moments, eyes closed, he speculated on what it might have been like if Belle had been around during his long ordeal and recovery. It would have made a difference, he thought, but then let go of the idea. It hadn't been and wouldn't ever be. All he could do was savor this while it lasted.

Nicholas had lost track of time while being ill, but when he woke, it was after dark. Belle had tucked herself into a corner of the couch, and he thought she was asleep, but she roused when he spoke her name. Then he had a coughing attack, and she brought him some cough suppression tablets. He downed them, although it hurt to swallow. If anything, he felt worse but managed to sip some of the lemon tea she brought him, laced with honey.

"Want to listen to music?" Belle asked.

"Sure," he said. He'd rather listen to Johnny Horton or Cash or even The Judds, but he knew she'd play the song from *Newsies.* As hateful as he'd been lately, this time, Nicholas vowed he would be polite and listen.

Belle popped a CD into the stereo and hit play. The song began slow, almost sweet, and he inwardly cringed. This was everything he found wrong with musicals, he thought. In high school, he'd had a drama teacher enamored of the 1968 musical *Oliver!* The class watched it, and he liked some of the action, the plucky little orphans, the wicked but good-hearted Fagin, Nancy, the classic whore with a heart of gold and young Oliver but not the music. Every time the cast broke into song, he'd tuned out, waiting for action. He'd felt the same way about other musicals he'd caught on television, *My Fair Lady, Oklahoma* and *Guys And*

Dolls.

He was only half-listening when the tempo picked up, and he began to hear the words. Some stood out to him, battalion, courage, brothers. Nicholas paid more attention, and when it had played, he said, "Play it again, would you please?"

After he'd heard it, Nicholas said, "What's the story? What's it about?"

He caught her smile. "It's based on a true story. In 1899, a bunch of newsboys – some were girls, too – called newsies in New York City went on strike for fair wages. It's a real David and Goliath story because the kids went against the biggest newspaper publishers of the time, Joseph Pulitzer and William Randolph Hearst. And they won."

Impressed, Nicholas said. "That's freaking awesome. So, these rag-tag newsies won?"

Belle laughed. "Yes, they did. The musical paints a prettier picture of what happened, I'm sure, but the strike led to better working conditions for kids, not just ones who sold papers. If you want to watch it, I'll rent it later from Amazon. They have a stage version, filmed at a theater in California, but it's the same as the Broadway production. There's a Disney one, too. I have it if I dig through my stuff."

"We'll watch the Broadway one," he said. "This evening, maybe."

She planted a kiss on his forehead. "Honey, it *is* evening."

They didn't watch it till the next day, but that worked. By then, they'd finished the soup, so Belle had made a hearty beef stew with chunks of meat, potatoes, carrots, and onions that was very good. Although he still felt terrible, they watched the musical, and maybe it was because he was so low it brought tears to his eyes in a few places. The pluck and sheer courage of the young newsies reminded him of Marines back in the day, although theirs was a different struggle. It didn't change his perception of his horrific looks, but it raised his spirits a small fraction. A tiny seed was planted that if the newsboys could succeed, maybe he had a chance.

"What did you think?" Belle asked as she switched his stew bowl for a serving of jello. "Did you like it?"

Nicholas nodded. "I did, and I'm not normally into musicals, but it's good."

He shivered with a sudden chill and handed her his dish. Belle fussed with his blanket and tucked it tighter, wearing a worried frown. "How do you feel?"

"Awful," he said, pulling the cover closer. He hacked hard enough to bring up some disgusting yellow and green mucous he caught with a tissue.

"Would you feel better upstairs in bed? It might be more comfortable."

"No," he said with a wheeze. His chest was sore, and he doubted he had the extra breath to climb the steps.

Belle stuck the digital thermometer in his mouth. Thank God she wasn't ramming it somewhere else, he thought. She grimaced when she read the results.

"Your fever's up a little."

He could feel it. The heat across his skin and the ache went deep into his bones. The chills came when the fever rose, and he knew it.

"I'll be all right," he told her and hoped it was so. He'd been half out of it when her grandmother came over, but he thought Ethel had said bronchitis might last a week to ten days. Unless he'd lost count, this was day three or four. "How long have I been sick anyway?"

"Four days today. Have you changed your mind about going to the doctor?"

Nicholas shook his head. He didn't feel well enough to go upstairs, let alone trek into town to the clinic. "Just give me some more pills, and I'll try to sleep."

The acetaminophen and cough suppressant went down hard, but he swallowed both and drank as much water as he could. He did sleep, and when he woke up, Nicholas had a coughing spell but decided he didn't feel quite as rough.

"Hey, Belle?" he said, wondering where she might be.

"I'm here," she replied, walking into the room with a cordless phone at her right ear. "I just made coffee if you'd like some."

"I would," he said. "What's with the phone?"

He had an old-fashioned wired to the wall phone, not a cordless model.

"I bought it when I went to town," Belle said. "That way, I can use the phone from anywhere, and if you want to talk to anyone, I can bring it to you."

Nicholas had little desire to use the phone, but he nodded. "Who would want to talk to me?"

Belle shot him a hard glance. "Your sister, your cousin, your grandfather, and even your mom," she said. "They've all been calling for the last couple of weeks. Teagan, too. You wouldn't talk to any of them, but I figured in case you changed your mind, you could."

The notion of talking to any of his relatives made him weary. If he hadn't talked to them since his mood bottomed out, Nicholas didn't really want to talk to them now. He did realize, though, that each one of them cared and that maybe he should.

"Do they know I'm sick?"

"Of course," she replied. "They're worried, too. Suzanne wants to come to see you, but so far, I've said no because I figured you didn't feel up to visitors."

He didn't, but he sighed. "I don't, but I guess she can come over. I'm surprised she hasn't broken down the front door. I suppose I should call her."

Nicholas dialed the number and, as soon as his sister answered, said, "Hey, it's me."

"Nicholas, thank God," she said. He could hear the relief in her voice. "How do you feel?"

"Pretty gnarly, but I'll live," he told her, then paused to cough.

"That sounds awful."

"Sounds worse than it is." That was bravado on his part. "If you want to come over, you can, Suze."

"I do. I won't relax until I can see for myself you're basically all right," she said. "It's late now, and I'd have to bring Teagan."

He'd like to see the kid. "Bring her. She's not back in school yet, is she?"

"No, not until after New Year's Day."

"Is Marsh still home?"

Suzanne didn't answer for a moment, then sighed. "No, he's not, but it's a long story. I'll see you tomorrow, Nick, and I'll bring Teagan if you think you're up to it."

"Sure," he said. "What's going on with you and Marshall?"

He'd never liked his brother-in-law much. Marshall Benning had always spent more time on the road than at home with his family. Although Nicholas was aware that that was necessary for a trucker, he still thought Marsh's priorities were backward. When he was home, he tended to hang out with his friends, go on long weekend fishing or hunting trips, and he gambled. One of the reasons that his niece loved him so much was that Nicholas gave her the attention that her daddy didn't.

"Same old, same old," Suzanne said. "Don't, Nick. I'd rather not rehash it. Take care, and we'll see you tomorrow."

In the morning, he took a shower, and afterward, he felt a little better. Being clean and wearing fresh clothes made a difference. Belle traded the blankets he'd been using for ones she'd just washed, and he made an effort to sit up when his company came.

Teagan approached with a slow tread, face sober, clutching a piece of paper with crayon work. Nicholas watched as she came up to within a few feet of the recliner and stopped.

"Hey, baby girl," he said.

"Hi, Uncle Nicholas," she said, voice softer and more muted than usual. "Mommy says you're really sick."

She's scared, he thought, *and concerned.* He tried to sit up straighter and to look less ill. "I'm a little under the weather," he said. "That's all."

"Is it your tummy?" she asked.

"No, Teagan, it's not."

Tears welled up in her eyes as she said, "Are you gonna die?"

Nicholas wanted to weep. "Of course not, honey. I'm just a little sick, but I'll be better in a few days. I'm not dying or going anywhere."

"Do you promise?" she said. "Cross your heart? Pinky swear?"

He traced a cross on his chest and held out his crooked little finger. She attached hers to his and smiled.

"I made you a get well soon card," she told him and thrust the paper at him.

She had spelled out his name in large, straggling letters written in crayon. "Get well" was scribbled at the top, and when he opened the homemade card, a piece of plain paper folded in two, he smiled at the drawing of a man. "Is that me?"

Teagan moved closer. "It is. See, there's your blue uniform from when you were a Marine and that jacket with a hood you like to wear."

He studied it more closely. "And what's this on my back?"

It looked to him like a backpack, but her answer stunned him.

"That's your angel wings," the little girl said. "'Cause everybody but stupid Winter knows you're not a devil."

Nicholas put a hand to his chest, which already ached. He thought his heart had just cracked, but when Teagan continued, he knew it had shattered.

"Besides, the devil isn't always ugly. Sometimes he's pretty," Teagan chattered. "In our class at church, the teacher said so. And Santa's real – he's St. Nicholas – but Krampus isn't. He's fake. And you're real. You're my really real uncle. You're a hero *and* an angel. Is it okay to hug you?"

He nodded. He couldn't have spoken if he had to, not with a sob caught deep in his throat and tears ready to blind him. Instead, he opened his arms to the child, and she climbed into the recliner. Her small arms went around his neck, and he held her the way he had when she was a baby, the same position he did when he'd soothed her.

She lay her head against his chest, happy, and because he knew she couldn't see his face, Nicholas wept.

Chapter Twenty-One

The harsh insults of one little girl had all but destroyed Nicholas. Now Belle observed as Teagan's words brought down his defenses and restored something in his soul. She exchanged looks with Suzanne, who wiped a few stray tears from her face. If she had the leisure, Belle thought she would put down her head and howl like a wounded toddler, but instead, she figured it might be best to distract Teagan before the child realized she'd brought her uncle to tears. As a kindergartener, she doubted the girl would understand why he wept.

"Teagan, do you want to come help make some cookies for Nicholas?" she asked. "I think he's gone to sleep."

He hadn't, but as she watched, he gave her a thumbs-up sign.

"Sure. Is it chocolate chip?"

"We'll make chocolate chip and peanut butter cookies," Belle said. She extended a hand, and the little girl crawled off Nicholas and took it. If he needed an ear to listen, Suzanne would be there.

As she sifted flour and measured sugar, as she blended butter and added other ingredients, Belle's mind was on Nicholas. She longed to be with him. The expression on his face when Teagan called him an angel had demolished her emotions. The raw reaction he had rocked her, and she prayed it might repair the damage that the opposite comparison had caused.

Love, she reflected, was like a recipe. You took various things, some sweet, some savory, some even sour and blended them together. Alone, they made nothing but together, they created something worth making, something of substance.

Teagan gabbed as she helped, although she pouted when Belle wouldn't let her eat raw cookie dough. While the first two trays of cookies baked, Belle washed up the dishes and utensils they'd used so far and let the little girl taste the first cookie when it came off the tray. The rest she spread on waxed paper to cool. After she'd baked six dozen chocolate chip, they switched to peanut butter, and she let Teagan use a fork to make the indentions on each cookie.

Nicholas wasn't asleep, and she knew it. Belle heard the rumble of his voice and his sisters as she worked. No matter how hard she tried, she couldn't make out any of the conversation, but at times, his voice rose either with anger or dismay. If Teagan heard, the girl gave no indication, but once they had the cookies made, Belle selected a couple of each and asked her to take them to Nicholas.

Figuring he'd prefer coffee to milk, Belle followed with a fresh cup.

He looked relaxed, his expression calm, and he met her eyes when she handed him the drink. "Thanks, babe."

"I see you already have the cookies," she remarked.

Teagen hovered on the edge of the couch, nibbling on a cookie. "I gave them to him."

Nicholas took a bite and nodded. "Delicious. Thank you, ladies."

Belle sank down beside his recliner, needing to be close. "How do you feel?"

He flopped his hand back and forth. "No worse."

She cupped his face with one hand. His skin remained feverish, but it wasn't burning hot. "Do you need anything else?"

Nicholas shook his head. "I'm okay for now. I thought maybe Teagan and I might watch some cartoons so you and Suzanne could have some cookies in the kitchen."

Something more was up, she thought, although his tone was casual. "Sure," she said. "Sounds like a plan. Holler at me or send Teagan if you want something."

"Will do," he said. "Just hand me the remote, please."

Before she reached the kitchen, the upbeat sound of some vintage cartoon echoed through the house, and she couldn't help but smile. She poured two mugs of coffee and placed the cookies in the center of the table as Suzanne sat down.

"So, what's the deal?" Belle asked. "Obviously, Nicholas sent us in here to talk."

Suzanne let out a long breath. "We're getting divorced. Marshall told me – over the phone – that he wants out. He has a new girlfriend tucked away somewhere in Las Vegas. He said if I don't go file, then he will next time he's home."

Belle had no idea what to say. "Should I offer condolences or congratulations?"

Suzanne hooted a single dry laugh. "That's a good question. I don't know. I'm sure you have seen we don't have much of a marriage. He's never home, and he doesn't help parent at all. He does provide a living. I don't think I'll really miss him. It's funny, but I got used to him not being around, so it's been weird when he's home. I haven't told Teagan yet, though."

"Is she close to her dad?"

"She barely knows him. He never paid much attention to her. I think that's one reason she adores her uncle so much. He's always been here for her, and he loves her. Marshall didn't even want kids. That's why there's just Teagan. I wanted more, but it's for the best now. I'll probably need to get a job, maybe even move. I don't know."

"If I can do anything to help, just say the word," Belle said. "I'd be happy to pick her up from school, babysit if you need it, whatever."

Suzanne picked up a peanut butter cookie and ate half of it. "Thanks. Nick said you would, and he'll be there. I don't even have to ask. How is he, anyway?"

Belle pretended his sister meant his current illness. "He's doing okay. The bronchitis is kicking his butt, but he should be better in a few more days."

"No bullshit, Belle. I know all that talk about Krampus and the devil brought him down. He barely said anything when we were here at Christmas, and I know how easily he backslides."

She downed the rest of her coffee and, for a moment, considered adding a splash of whiskey to it.

"He took it really hard," Belle replied. "He's been distant ever since, withdrawn and sad. He hasn't been talking to me much, not until he got sick. From what little he did say, I got the idea he thought I deserved better, and I think he was trying to run me away. He wouldn't kiss me, and we hadn't made love."

"Too much information," his sister said, with a spark of her old sass. "But I thought so, on all the rest. But you didn't give up on him, did you?"

"Never," Belle said. "I didn't, and I won't. I could see he still loves me, and so I was here. When he got sick, he needed me, and we started talking. I hate that he's not well, but it's wonderful to have him back."

"Is he going to get past this?"

It was a fair question, but it rankled. "Yes, he will. I think what your daughter told him earlier, that he's her angel and hero, made a huge difference."

For the first time, Suzanne grasped her hand. "You're the one who's brought him back from where he was, Belle. Before you came, I worried myself sick over Nick."

"I've been plenty worried these last few weeks."

She couldn't begin to explain how much. Before she could try, Teagan danced into the room.

"Uncle Nicholas says we can take down the Christmas tree," she cried. "He said, 'get that thing outta here.'"

Unsure if that was a good or bad development, Belle went to find out.

"So, you want the tree gone?" she asked.

He smiled, and she knew everything was cool. "I figured we might as well. It's dried out and could be a fire hazard. It's almost a new year, so I thought we'd get going on a fresh start. When is New Year's Eve, anyway?"

She grinned, liking the idea of new beginnings. "Tomorrow."

"What are we doing to ring in the new year?"

"You're going to get better," Belle said. "We can celebrate later."

"Are we having ham for dinner?"

"If you want, we are."

"I want."

"So go buy a ham," he told her. "You probably need a break from nursing. Suzanne and Teagan will be here."

Free as a high school kid skipping school on a spring day, Belle headed for town. The sun was shining, and the day was warmer, with temperatures near fifty degrees. Her bright mood reflected the change she saw in Nicholas, and her spirits were high. She sang along to the car stereo, tuned to classic tunes. She accompanied Suzie Quatro and Chris Norman in their hit, 'Stumblin' In," and REO Speedwagon's 'Keep On Loving You.' The songs were all the sweeter because now she identified them with Nicholas.

She picked out a brown sugar spiral-cut ham, some sweet potatoes, and a few other items for the holiday dinner. Nicholas had been right that she could use a break. She lingered, looking at more items that she planned to buy, then indulged in a bottle of her favorite fragrance and a long-sleeved Henley for Nicholas. It was made from the heavy thermal material used for long underwear so it would be warm, and besides, Belle wanted to get something for him.

Encouraged by the weather, she dawdled on the way home, taking the long way along roads she didn't know and pausing to gawk like a tourist at a few sites. Belle pulled into a public access along the river near her grandmother's and marveled at how the bare trees reflected in the still water.

It was past noon when she returned to find the tree gone and all the decorations packed away. Nicholas wallowed into a sitting position when she entered, laden with multiple bags. "What took so long?"

"I didn't get in a hurry," she told him.

"He was concerned," Suzanne said. "He had us wait lunch

for you."

Belle kissed his forehead. "What is for lunch?

"She made chicken tortilla soup," Nicholas said.

He insisted on making his slow way to the table to eat, saying soup was difficult to enjoy in a recliner. It was the first time he'd come to the kitchen since falling ill, so Belle relished the sight of him, eating the hearty fare by careful spoonful after spoonful. She'd planned to come home to either warm up leftovers or open a can of soup, but this was a major improvement.

"This is delicious," she told Suzanne. "Thanks for making it."

"It's one of his favorites," the other woman answered. "Our mom used to make this all the time and probably still does. I made a double batch so you can have it for supper, too."

A few minutes later, after Nicholas had trekked back to the living room and Suzanne had gone home, the phone rang. Belle still had the cordless in her pocket, so she answered, "Hello."

"Hi, you don't know me, but I'm Linda Reilly," a voice with a soft Texas accent said. "I'm Nicholas' mom, and you must be Maribel?"

"I'm Belle," she replied. "Everyone calls me Belle."

"I called because I'm worried about my son. My nephew, Timothy, came home telling tales of how Nicholas had a bad flashback, and then Suzie-Q called to tell me he's down sick. I haven't talked to him in months or seen him in more than a year. Would he feel up to talking to me for just a minute? Billy Henry's concerned too - that's my husband - but he figures Nicholas won't talk to him, but I thought he might to me."

Her first reaction was to wish she hadn't answered the phone. If she had just let it ring, Belle wouldn't have to deal with the call. She didn't know what to say - Nicholas might or might not speak with his mother. "I'll go ask, Mrs. Reilly."

"Thank you. Is he very sick?"

"He has bronchitis and doesn't feel very well, but he's all right," Belle said.

"And the flashback?"

She drew a hard breath before she dared reply. "Ma'am, he has PTSD – post traumatic stress disorder, so he sometimes has flashbacks or some rocky moments."

"I know." His mom sounded like she might be crying. "It's just that he's so scarred and…."

"Yes, he's got scars, hard-earned scars that mean he's alive," Belle said, heedless of what his mother might think. "Like I keep telling him, it's just a face, and it's his face. The scars don't define him – they don't make him a lesser man. He's still Nicholas Reilly, and if people would quit treating him like he's a freak show or a monster, he'd be better for it. Don't judge him by his scars, and don't act like he's an invalid. Treat him the way you always did. Take him at face value, as he is, for who and what he is. That would do more for him than all the coddling in the world."

"But…."

Belle had launched a tirade and couldn't stop. "He doesn't need tears or pity or someone puking at the sight of him. He doesn't need to be ignored because someone doesn't know what to do or say. He needs to be loved, not treated like he's on hospice. Hang on, and I'll see if he's up to talking to you, please."

"Is it my mother?" Nicholas stood in the kitchen doorway, frowning.

She nodded. "She wants to talk to you."

"I figured," he said. "But she's still on the 'poor Nicholas' kick, isn't she?"

Belle hesitated as he held out his hand. "I heard you talking to her, and what you said, she needs to hear it. Let me have the phone."

She surrendered it, and he sat down at the table. He paused with a round of coughing, then said, "Mom? It's me."

Belle wished she could hear both ends of the conversation, and as if he had read her mind, Nicholas put the call on speaker.

"Nicholas, oh, son, how are you?"

"Sick as a dog."

"Your sister said you have bronchitis. I wish you were home so I could take care of you, son."

"Belle's got my six, Mama. She's taking care of me just fine."

As he spoke, he reached out his hand and took hers. Belle lifted it to her lips and kissed it, his words a sweet balm for her heart.

"I'd rather you were here…."

"And I'm sure you'd prefer I wasn't scarred," Nicholas said. Belle felt a rush of pride as he confronted the elephant in the room. "Wish in one hand, shit in the other, right? The shit always wins. I'll get over bronchitis, but the scars are always gonna be there. They're part of me. Listen to my lady, Mom. She gets me in a way no one else has since that roadside bomb blew my life apart."

"I wish you'd come home."

"Mama, I'll come to visit when y'all can treat me like part of the family, home to see the folks and not a poor, pitiful wretch that needs constant care. I'll come when no one will walk on eggshells around me."

"Don't be hateful, son. I raised you better."

Nicholas laughed despite the anguish in his mom's voice.

"I'm not," he said. "But Mama, that's the first time you've talked to me like your son in years. I like it. And don't cry. I'm not mad."

"Will you come to see me sometime?"

Belle held her breath, waiting for the answer.

"Maybe," Nicholas said. "I told Granpa I'll be there for his birthday in March. I won't promise anything else except when I do, if I do, Belle will be with me. I love you, Mama. I need to go lay down, but I'll talk to you soon."

He handed Belle the phone, his mother still speaking.

"Ma'am?"

"Belle, call me Linda," she said. "And, please, take care of him."

"You can count on it," Belle replied and ended the call.

As new beginnings went, it was a rocky start, she thought, but it was a place to commence.

Chapter Twenty-Two

By the time the fever had gone and the cough went away, Nicholas was thoroughly sick of being sick. The new year was underway, and things had improved. After a few dark and terrible weeks that had overshadowed the only Christmas he'd anticipated in a decade, he'd fallen ill. Although he'd felt awful, being sick brought him up out of the depths of his own despair. He'd spiraled after hearing that another child compared his appearance to the devil or Krampus. Belle never gave up on him, loving him no matter how badly he acted, and Teagan erased the negative comparison when she said he was her hero, her angel.

"It's almost time for Teagan," Belle told him as he came through the kitchen. He'd been up the hill, savoring the view of his acres. "The bus will be here soon."

Nicholas nodded. Since his sister filed for divorce, she'd started working in town at a local call center. Since the same bus route looped past both Suzanne's small house and his driveway, Teagan was picked up each morning at home, then dropped off after school at her uncle's. He drove down to meet her at the road since the driveway was long, and he didn't want her to walk it alone. Nicholas enjoyed her chatter and appreciated the way she looked at him with total acceptance. Sometimes he had to remind himself she'd never known him any other way, but the fact she saw him without judgement meant much. He liked the way Belle saw him, too.

"Uncle Nick," Teagen cried as she raced toward where he waited by his truck. "Guess what we had for lunch today?"

"Snips and snails and puppy dog tails," he guessed, reciting part of an old rhyme he remembered.

"No," she giggled. "We had pigs in blankets, and they were *good*."

"Pigs, huh? Weren't they big for the lunch tray?"

"No, silly. It's hot dogs wrapped up in a roll," she said. "I like them. And we learned a new song at circle time, and we got to be outside for recess...."

Nicholas listened as he drove back to the house, but he wasn't paying full attention until he heard the child say, "So I told them you'd be my show and tell, Uncle Nicholas, so, will you? Will you come to school for show and tell time?"

"What's that?"

Teagan sighed. "It's show and tell. Kids bring something special, like their favorite doll or teddy bear or a book or something that belongs to their grandma, an an-t-q...."

"Antique," he corrected. "I get the idea. Why me, though, kid?"

"'Cause I told them you were a Marine and that you're not the devil. I want them to see that, especially dumb old Winter."

He winced. He'd prefer not to revisit that incident when the girl named for a season had taunted Teagan that she'd seen her at McDonald's with the devil or Krampus. The fight that followed got Teagan suspended from school and sent him into a tailspin. Facing down a classroom of kids, including this Winter, sounded like a trial by fire he'd rather not endure.

"I don't know," he began.

"Please, oh, please," she cried. "Pretty please with sugar on top! I already told my teacher you would."

Not quite six years old, stubborn as a mule wearing a suit and tie, she backed him into a corner. If he said no, it would hurt her feelings, but if he said yes, he'd regret it as sure as the sun would set in the West. She offered him a sweet smile, and he caved. After all, how long could it take, and how many kids could be in one kindergarten class? He'd make Belle go with him.

"All right, Teagan, I will."

He told Belle about it while the little girl colored at the kitchen table, and Belle made supper. She paused as she rolled out biscuit dough. "Are you up to it?" she asked.

"Hell, I don't know. Maybe," he replied. "The kid really wants me to, and it won't last long, will it?"

"I don't have a clue. Do you want me to go with you when it happens?"

"Yeah, you know it."

When Suzanne came to pick up Teagan, Nicholas asked her if she knew the date for show and tell. His sister got a furtive look but nodded.

"It's on Valentine's Day, I think. They sent home a note about it. I'll check and make sure, Nick. Afterward, they're having their parties, and I'm a room parent, so there'll be cupcakes and punch and some candy. You can stay if you want."

"Probably not."

Nicholas had made tentative plans with Belle that day, but

she assured him they would have plenty of time. "February 14 is on a weekday," she told him. "We'll get done with school and do whatever we want."

After January faded into history for another year and February arrived, he began to dread the event. When he found out Teagan wanted him to wear his dress blues, he fussed and cussed, but Belle convinced him to do it.

"She'll never forget this," Belle told him.

"Neither will I," he grumbled, but on the day he donned the uniform, and they made the trip to Teagan's school. His niece had tried to talk him into joining her for lunch, too, but Nicholas balked. It was just after one p.m. when they entered the school and signed in as guests. Although it was a modern building, nothing like the elementary school he'd attended back in Texas, the place smelled the same. It was a blend of kid smell and lingering lunch aromas and cleaner, he thought. He clutched Belle's hand tight as they walked up the hall.

"Where's Miss Goodright's classroom?" he asked, pleased he recalled the name of Teagan's teacher.

"Are you here for the Heroes Show And Tell?" the building secretary asked. "It's across the hall in the multi-purpose room? It starts at 1:30."

He inquired further and learned it was an event for all four kindergarten classes, part of a unit they were finishing up on heroes. His stomach gave a flip, and his head began to ache as they took a seat in the hall to wait for Teagan.

"I don't know if I can do this shit," he whispered to Belle.

"Nicholas, you can."

Something hidden note in her tone made him suspicious. "Did you already know about this?"

Belle stared at her lap. "Suzanne mentioned something."

"And you didn't tell me?"

"I thought if I did, you might not come."

He wouldn't have. Torn between trepidation and anger, he considered bolting now, but if he did, it would upset Teagan. "What if I freak out and have an episode?"

She met his eyes this time. "If I thought you might, we wouldn't be here," she told him. "You've got this. You can do it."

Teagan broke out of line to hug him and got called back to her place by her teacher. They followed the kids in and sat in the first row of chairs while the kids lined up on the floor, sitting with their legs crossed. Behind them, more chairs began to fill up with other parents and family members. Belle turned around, craning her neck to see, but he faced forward. His palms were damp with sweat, and he wanted this to be over. Suzanne swept into the row and sat beside him, smiling.

"You should've told me this was a big deal," he said, voice low.

"Nick, trust me, it's all going to be fine."

The program got underway when the kids burst into song, a tune he vaguely recognized as being from some Disney film about Hercules with a refrain that said something about 'zero to hero.' Once the music ended, a man came forward and introduced himself as the principal.

"I'd like to welcome all of you here today, to our school, to honor a few real-life heroes," he said. "The kindergarteners just finished a month-long study about heroes. Too many times, our young people get their heroes from stories, books, and movies. And that's ok, but I think they need to be aware that heroes walk among us every day. So, today, on Valentine's Day, we're showing some love to a few local heroes. We have a police officer, a deputy sheriff, a firefighter, a retired Army captain and a decorated Marine. Let's give them a round of applause and get started."

Nicholas marked the exits in case he decided to bolt. Teagan turned around to shoot him a smile, and he returned it. Each child introduced their homegrown hero. The police officer talked about the time she saved a man's life by pulling him out of a car that had gone into the creek. The deputy shared a story about the time he'd used the Heimlich maneuver to save an elderly man's life in a local restaurant, and the firefighter talked about rescuing a family from a burning house.

He paid more attention to the Captain, grandfather to one of the kids, a man who'd served in Vietnam and received both a Purple Heart and a Medal of Honor. He was also in uniform, and too soon, he'd finished. Teagan stepped forward, and her teacher handed her the microphone. His niece stretched out her hand to him.

He froze until Belle poked his arm. "Go on, she's waiting."

The hardwood flooring seemed to stretch forever beneath the bright lighting as he walked up to join Teagan. Once there, she introduced him, but he heard little of what she said. His heart pounded, and he wondered what in hell he could tell these children. After a long and awkward moment, he decided he'd speak from his heart. He couldn't think of anything else to do.

"I'm Gunnery Sergeant Nicholas Reilly, United States Marine Corps," he said, into the mic. He couldn't look out at the seated crowd, only at Belle. That kept him focused and not freaked out. "I served in Afghanistan with the 3rd Battalion, 5th Regiment. We were called the Dark Horse Battalion and saw some of the highest Marine casualties there. I would still be an active duty Marine, except I was injured in a roadside bombing in the Sangin District, Helmand Province, in southern Afghanistan. I was shot, and I was burned. I spent a year and a half, almost two years in the hospital and had fifteen surgeries in the first year. A lot of Marines died over there in the sandbox, some who were with me. Some lost limbs, an arm, a leg, or an eye. I can walk, and I can see even though my eye is messed up. I'm scarred, but I'm alive."

His throat was dry, and for a moment, he could swear he tasted the harshness of sand in his mouth. Someone handed him a bottle of water, so he uncapped it and took a long slug.

"I'm always going to look like this," he said. "That's been hard to accept. I used to be good-looking, if you can believe that. And I have a lot of problems you don't see on the outside. I have PTSD – that stands for post-traumatic stress syndrome. Those are big words, but they mean sometimes I remember things that happened in the sandbox. Sometimes I get upset or scared, and sometimes it makes me sick."

Nicholas chanced a glance at the kids. They stared up at him, eyes huge. He had their attention, and he hoped he wasn't saying anything too heavy for kindergarteners. He'd said more about his service at one time than he thought he had to anyone, ever, including Belle.

"My niece, Teagan, asked me to come today. She said it was for show and tell. I guess it is. No one told me anything about heroes. I don't really think of myself as a hero. I'm just a guy, a Marine, who served his country. I love this country, kids, and it was worth what I've suffered to see kids like you safe and whole and happy. A while ago, right before Christmas, some other kid told Teagan she'd seen her at McDonald's with the devil. That girl made a big deal out of it, saying she was with Satan or maybe that Krampus dude. Those were fighting words, as we call them down home in Texas, for my niece. For me, it caused me a lot of pain."

Belle's eyes were on his face. He saw a few tears trailing down her cheeks and figured he might be crying too. His sister had her hands clasped together so tightly that he could see that her knuckles were white. Teagan still stood at his side, and she reached her small hand up to take his. That small gesture of love gave him the courage to continue, to finish what he had started.

"I've learned some things, though, along the way. We have a motto in the Marines, *Semper Fidelis*. It means always faithful, but I found out people who love you are always faithful too, if they really love you. They'll take you the way you are and accept you, scars and all. That motto, *Semper Fi*, is in Latin. There's another old saying in the same language, *Carpe Diem*. It means seize the day, take the day, and make it yours. A very wise lady told me that my face is just a face. It's not me. That's good to know because the scars go farther than my face. She said the scars don't make me who I am – that's all inside. It gives new meaning to taking something at face value. I've been living one day at a time, seizing the day, and being faithful to those who love me the most."

"If that makes me a hero, then I guess I'm one, but really I'm a man, a regular guy under the scars and this uniform. I'm an old jarhead just getting through life. Oorah!"

He had no more words, just the Marine battle cry. If he said more, he might bawl like a baby, which wouldn't impress the adults and might scare the kids. Nicholas turned to take his seat when someone in the back shouted back, "Oorah!". Another Marine, he figured, except the voice sounded familiar. As he tried to pinpoint who said it, the audience came to their feet and began clapping. The roar echoed in his ears, and he picked Teagan up to ground his emotions.

She hugged him around the neck and said, audible over

all the other noise, "I love you, Uncle Nicholas, and you're my hero."

Then she kissed him on the cheek and scrambled down. He thought she was going back to her class, but instead, she dashed toward the back of the room. Nicholas caught sight of another Marine, also in dress uniform. Shock rocked him.

"Timothy," he cried and moved in that direction. Halfway there, he stopped, and the tears he'd done his best to control broke loose. His cousin wasn't the only family member who'd come.

Eighty-nine-year-old Seamus Reilly stood beside his grandson. Next to him, Billy Henry Reilly and his wife Linda waited. Behind them, his brothers Jordan and Nathaniel were present. Suzanne joined her brothers, and Teagan flew into her grandmother's arms.

When Nicholas reached him, they surrounded him, hugging from all sides and talking so fast he couldn't make it all out. Belle stood at his side, her hand linked tight in his.

"You came," he said to his folks. "You came from Texas."

"I'd have come farther still," Seamus Reilly said, his brogue undiminished by decades in the Lone Star State. "Since ye wouldn't come to us, you stubborn *amadon*, we came to you. *Ní neart go cur le chéile.*"

Although he couldn't have spoken more than a few phrases in Irish, Nicholas recognized the phrase. "There's no strength without unity," he said.

"Aye, lad, and ye've had little enough from the lot of them."

"We meant well, son," his dad said. "It's just no one knew what to do or say to you."

"His woman knew right well," the old man said. "'Twas her that schooled your ma on the phone."

Teagan had gone back to Suzanne, and his mother reached for Nicholas.

"She made me realize some things," Linda said. "We always loved you, son, and never understood why you didn't come home."

"I was. I am coming for Grandpa's birthday," he said. "We're coming."

"They gave me to think ye were broken," Seamus said. "I knew better."

"I was for a long time," Nicholas said. "But now...."

"Now ye're a man to be proud of," his grandfather said and hugged Nicholas tight. He smelled the same as he had for as long as Nicholas could remember, of tobacco smoke and soap and the peppermints he loved. As each of his family hugged him in turn, his heart ached less. His father came to his last.

"When you come home, let's wet our lines for white bass over at the Neches River," he said.

"Sure."

Nicholas didn't say so, but home wasn't Texas anymore. Rusk would always be his hometown, a special place where his family lived, but home was here, with Belle. Home was anywhere where he could live comfortably in his own scarred skin.

He invited them all to stay and take advantage of the guest rooms. His parents, grandfather and Timothy did. His brothers bunked at Suzanne's house, but they all ate together in his kitchen. Belle, who'd known they were coming, had baked a ham, one he enjoyed more than on New Year's Day when he had still been sick. Suzanne brought several bags of fried chicken and a cake. They feasted and caught up, both of which salved his soul.

After they'd gone south to Texas, he cuddled Belle on the

couch.

"I thought I'd burst with pride at school," she told him. They'd had little private time until now.

"I don't know how I found all those words," he admitted. "I just spoke from my heart."

"You were amazing. Your honesty and openness made the difference. So did what you said about face value."

Nicholas laughed. "If I'd known my family was there, I probably would have flubbed it up. They think I'm healed. I'm not. I won't ever be, not completely."

"But you're not broken, either."

"The therapy helps," he told her. Although he still refused any meds, he'd started an online program with a therapist, also a Marine who'd served in combat. Having someone to talk to that understood made a world of difference. So did his folks, Teagan, most of all, but it was Belle who brought him out of his darkness.

With Belle as his companion, he thrived. She made him laugh. On occasion, she caused him to cry. She lifted him up, but she could also bring him down with no more than a few words or a sharp look. But in all things, she supported him with love, unconditional and powerful. He wanted that and needed it.

Ni neart go cur le chéile, his grandfather had said. It was true. He was only strong because of his family — and because of Belle.

Nicholas stroked her bare finger on her left hand. "You need a ring there."

He loved the way her eyes glowed and her lips raised in a smile. "Do I?"

"A pair of them," he said. "Belle, will you marry me?"

She sat up, and her deep blue eyes stared into his. "Yes, Nicholas, yes."

"And have our babies?"

Her smile would outshine the sun. "Yes, I want kids, several kids."

"So do I."

"Then tomorrow, we'll go pick out rings."

"And tomorrow, we'll set a date."

Tomorrow. Nicholas savored the word. Tomorrow meant the future, and now he had one. There was no curse or magic spell, no rose dropping petals beneath a glass, and he wasn't a beast, although he'd acted like one for too long. This wasn't a story, but his life, but the one common factor was love. Love had redeemed his scarred face and troubled soul. No, it wasn't a fairy tale, but there was one thing Teagan had known.

Even the worst beast could find a happily ever after, and he'd found his in Belle, his love who took him at face value.

Lee Ann Sontheimer Murphy is a former newspaper editor and reporter who makes her home in the Ozarks. As a widow with three grown children, her focus is on writing romance novels that range from sweet to heat, from contemporary to historical. She has written more than twenty-five novels and novellas, along with a variety of non-fiction and freelance works. A native of St. Joseph, Missouri, where the Pony Express began and outlaw Jesse James met his end, she is a graduate of Crowder College and Missouri Southern State University. She lives in what passes for the suburbs in far southwestern Missouri, a little north of Arkansas and just east of Oklahoma.

www.ingramcontent.com/pod-product-compliance
Lightning Source LLC
Chambersburg PA
CBHW050732180626
46814CB00002B/713